Enrollment Form

☐ **Yes!** I WANT TO BE A **Privileged Woman.**

Enclosed is one *PAGES & PRIVILEGES™* Proof of Purchase from any Harlequin or Silhouette book currently for sale in stores (Proofs of Purchase are found on the back pages of books) and the store cash register receipt. Please enroll me in *PAGES & PRIVILEGES™*. Send my Welcome Kit and FREE Gifts -- and activate my FREE benefits -- immediately.

More great gifts and benefits to come like these luxurious Truly Lace and L'Effleur gift baskets.

NAME (please print)

ADDRESS   APT. NO

CITY   STATE   ZIP/POSTAL CODE

 PROOF OF PURCHASE

Please allow 6-8 weeks for delivery. Quantities are limited. We reserve the right to substitute items. Enroll before October 31, 1995 and receive one full year of benefits.

**NO CLUB!
NO COMMITMENT!**
*Just one purchase brings you great **Free Gifts** and **Benefits!***
(More details in back of this book.)

Name of store where this book was purchased_____

Date of purchase_____

Type of store:

☐ Bookstore   ☐ Supermarket   ☐ Drugstore

☐ Dept. or discount store (e.g. K-Mart or Walmart)

☐ Other (specify)_____

Which Harlequin or Silhouette series do you usually read?

Pages & Privileges ™

_____

Complete and mail with one Proof of Purchase and store receipt to:

U.S.: *PAGES & PRIVILEGES™*, P.O. Box 1960, Danbury, CT 06813-1960

Canada: *PAGES & PRIVILEGES™*, 49-6A The Donway West, P.O. 813, North York, ON M3C 2E8   **PRINTED IN U.S.A**

Remember the job, Reed told himself angrily. Remember the job.

Instead of taking advantage of his chance meeting with Celia Carson to find out more about her, he found himself fantasizing about her.

Not smart, Hollander. Damned stupid, in fact.

He was confident Celia had no reason to think he was anything other than what he'd told her he was—an ordinary tax accountant. She seemed to trust him.

But she still hadn't given him any clue as to what she was doing here.

The thought made Reed strengthen his resolve to keep his distance from Celia Carson. No matter how attractive he found her, no matter how invitingly she smiled at him, no matter how seductively she walked, he still had no intention of making a play for her.

That could only lead to disaster. Professionally—and personally—if he wasn't careful.

Dear Reader,

Special Edition's lineup for the month of July is sure to set off some fireworks in your heart! Romance always seems that much more wonderful and exciting in the hot days of summer, and our six books for July are sure to prove that! We begin with bestselling author Gina Ferris Wilkins and *A Match for Celia.* July's THAT SPECIAL WOMAN! goes looking for summertime romance and gets more than she bargained for in book two of Gina's series, THE FAMILY WAY.

Continuing the new trilogy MAN, WOMAN AND CHILD this month is Robin Elliott's *Mother at Heart.* Raising her sister's son as her own had been a joy for this single mother, but her little family seems threatened when the boy's real father surfaces... until she finds herself undeniably drawn to the man. Be sure to look for the third book in the series next month, *Nobody's Child,* by Pat Warren.

Father in Training by Susan Mallery brings you another irresistible hunk who can only be one of those HOMETOWN HEARTBREAKERS. Also continuing in July is Victoria Pade's A RANCHING FAMILY series. Meet Jackson Heller, of the ranching Heller clan, in *Cowboy's Kiss.* A man who's lost his memory needs tenderness and love to find his way in Kate Freiman's *Here To Stay.* And rounding out the month is a sexy and lighthearted story by Jane Gentry. In *No Kids or Dogs Allowed,* falling in love is easy for a single mom and divorced dad—until they find out their feuding daughters may just put a snag in their upcoming wedding plans!

A whole summer of love and romance has just begun from **Special Edition!** I hope you enjoy each and every story to come!

Sincerely,

Tara Gavin
Senior Editor

Please address questions and book requests to:
Silhouette Reader Service
U.S.: 3010 Walden Ave., P.O. Box 1325, Buffalo, NY 14269
Canadian: P.O. Box 609, Fort Erie, Ont. L2A 5X3

Gina Ferris Wilkins

A MATCH FOR CELIA

Silhouette®

SPECIAL✦EDITION®

Published by Silhouette Books
America's Publisher of Contemporary Romance

For my husband's aunts, who have made me part of their
special family: Nadine Jaggers, Marene Austine,
Edith Rose, Marcelle Wood and June Wilkins.
With love.

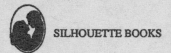 SILHOUETTE BOOKS

ISBN 0-373-09967-3

A MATCH FOR CELIA

Copyright © 1995 by Gina Wilkins

This edition published by arrangement with Harlequin Enterprises B.V.

® and TM are trademarks of Harlequin Enterprises B.V., used under
license. Trademarks indicated with ® are registered in the United States
Patent and Trademark Office, the Canadian Trade Marks Office and in
other countries.

Printed in U.S.A.

Books by Gina Ferris Wilkins

Silhouette Special Edition
*A Man for Mom #955
*A Match for Celia #967

*The Family Way

Books by Gina Ferris

Silhouette Special Edition
Healing Sympathy #496
Lady Beware #549
In From the Rain #677
Prodigal Father #711
†Full of Grace #793
†Hardworking Man #806
†Fair and Wise #819
†Far to Go #862
†Loving and Giving #879
Babies on Board #913

†Family Found

GINA FERRIS WILKINS

This award-winning author published her first Silhouette Special Edition novel in 1988, using the pseudonym Gina Ferris. Since then, she's won many awards, including the Reviewer's Choice Award for Best All Around Series Author from *Romantic Times* magazine. Her books have been translated into twenty languages and are sold in more than one hundred countries.

THE CARSON FAMILY

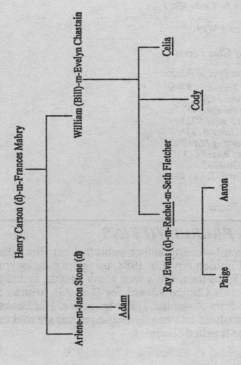

Henry Carson (d)–m–Frances Mabry

Arlene–m–Jason Stone (d)

Adam

William (Bill)–m–Evelyn Chastain

Ray Evans (d)–m–Rachel–m–Seth Fletcher

Paige

Aaron

Cody

Celia

Prologue

Frances Carson and her longtime friend, Lila Twining, were spending an exciting Friday evening together. Ignoring the boring diets their physicians had recommended, they had ordered a large pizza—with everything, of course—and were eating it from paper plates in Frances's living room. They'd rented a video. It starred Mel Gibson, and for a good portion of the film, he appeared without a shirt. Though they were in their seventies, neither Frances nor Lila had lost appreciation for a fine male chest.

The telephone interrupted their avid viewing. Frances sighed and pushed the pause button on the remote control. "I'll be right back," she promised her friend.

Lila shrugged and helped herself to another slice of pizza. "Take your time. I'm in no hurry."

The voice on the other end of the telephone line was young and slightly husky, instantly recognizable to Frances.

The caller identified herself, anyway. "Granny Fran? It's Celia."

Delighted as always to hear from her youngest grandchild, Frances glanced at one of the photographs lining the top of her old upright piano, a picture of a beautiful woman in her early twenties, dark-haired, blue-eyed, dimpled. "Hello, sweetheart. How are you?"

"I'm fine. And you?"

"Never better," Frances answered cheerily. "Lila and I were just scarfing pizza and drooling over Mel Gibson's bare chest."

Celia laughed. "Granny Fran, what are we going to do with you?"

"Arrange a weekend with Mel?" Frances suggested hopefully.

Celia laughed again. "You're incorrigible. And I love you for it."

"I love you, too, darling. So what's wrong?"

"What makes you think anything is wrong?" Celia countered, the laughter leaving her voice.

"I know you too well. Would you like to talk about it?"

"I don't want to interrupt your evening with Lila. I'll call again later."

"Nonsense. Lila doesn't mind if you and I talk for a few minutes. Tell me what's bothering you, Celia."

"I, uh, I guess you could say I'm having a moral dilemma."

Frances waited patiently for her granddaughter to elaborate. She could hear Celia draw a deep breath on the other end of the line, as though working up the courage to continue.

"Damien Alexander has asked me to be his guest for a couple of weeks at one of his exclusive resorts," Celia finally blurted out. "He'll pay my airfare, provide a suite, all my meals—anything I want."

"How very generous of him," Frances said noncommittally.

"He, uh, he promises to be a perfect gentleman if I want him to be, but I can tell he's hoping I won't want him to be. I'm sure he hopes that he and I will . . . you know."

"Become lovers," Frances supplied.

"Yes. Rachel is very much against this, of course. She doesn't want me to go. She's never trusted Damien. She tends to believe everything she reads about him in those sleazy tabloids. I've told her she's just being an overprotective older sister, but she's still opposed to it. Of course, she's been busy with her wedding plans and everything, so we haven't had time to really talk about it, but I know she won't change her mind."

"You're twenty-four years old, Celia. You don't need Rachel's permission to go on a vacation."

"I know," Celia admitted with a faint sigh. "But I wish she wouldn't be so adamant about her disapproval."

"Have you spoken to your mother?"

"No. To be honest, I haven't quite had the nerve the last few times she and I spoke on the phone. I have a feeling that she'll feel the same way Rachel does about it. Cody's staying out of it, but I can tell he doesn't like it much more than Rachel does. I thought maybe you could give me a more objective opinion."

"What do *you* want to do, Celia?"

"I'm not sure I know."

Celia sounded so confused that Frances's heart twisted in sympathy with her granddaughter.

"I've just been so...so bored, lately," Celia added. "My life has become so dull, so predictable. The men here in

Percy are nice, but so unexciting. Damien's different. There's nothing dull or predictable about him.''

"Are you in love with him?''

This time Celia's hesitation was more pronounced. "I don't know,'' she said finally. "I like him a lot. He's charming and fun, but I really don't know him all that well. We only go out when he's in the area, and with his other businesses all over the world, that hasn't been often. He said we could use this time together to get to know each other better.''

"I have to ask again—what do *you* want to do, Celia?''

"I think . . . I think I want to go.''

Frances moistened her lips, tasting pizza and deep concern. It was difficult for her to be objective, but there was only one thing she could say. "You should follow your heart, dear. No one else can make a decision like this for you, not even those who love you and want only the best for you.''

"You think I should go?''

"I didn't say that,'' Frances answered quickly. "I said you should make your own decision. But, Celia—be careful.''

"I will, Granny Fran. Thank you.''

"I love you, Celia.''

"I love you, too. Tell Lila I said hello, will you? I'll let you get back to your dirty movie now.''

"It's not a dirty movie. It's only rated R,'' Frances countered lightly, though her levity was forced.

She hung up the phone a few moments later and rejoined her friend. Lila looked up from a magazine she'd been leafing through. "Everything okay?''

"I hope so,'' Frances answered slowly, a bit worried about what she had just done. "I sincerely hope so.''

Chapter One

A pleasantly warm breeze caressed Reed Hollander's face as he sipped his coffee. He sat at a poolside resort table, beneath the shade of a gaily striped umbrella.

The morning couldn't have been more beautiful, or the colors more vivid. Bright, clear blue sky. Crimson, yellow, orange and white flowers against dark, scrupulously tended greenery. Sparkling turquoise water in the pool, and in the Gulf of Mexico that stretched to the horizon. Brilliant, mostly primary colors, ones a child might have chosen to paint the scene.

Reed felt a bit out of place in his dark gray shirt and lighter gray slacks. No child would have picked such somber shades. The woman swimming laps in the pool, however, fit in beautifully with her surroundings.

Her slender, peach-toned body was encased in a sleek scarlet maillot. Reed knew that her eyes were a bright, crystal blue and that her thick shoulder-length hair, when dry, was a glossy dark brown shot through with red highlights. A potent combination with her delicately oval face and enticing dimples.

He should know. He'd been watching her for three days.

He pulled his attention away from her for a moment to glance around. They were still the only ones out this morning. It was off-season—the first week of November—so the exclusive, South Padre Island, Texas, resort wasn't full, and the other guests generally preferred to sleep late. Reed and the pretty swimmer seemed to be the only early risers on this particular morning.

She reclaimed his attention by flipping into a turn and beginning another lap. She was obviously in very good shape. Not that he'd needed to watch her swim to know that.

He had just finished his first cup of coffee when she called it quits. He knew she was unaware that he'd been watching as she emerged from the pool by way of the steps closest to his table. Water streamed from her slender limbs, dripped from her hair. She looked young, pretty and sweetly appealing. Innocent.

Reed had reason to believe she wasn't quite what she appeared.

He slipped on the horn-rimmed glasses that had been lying at his elbow and stood, reaching her just in time to place a towel into her outstretched hand. "Here you are."

"Thank you," she said, and buried her face in the luxuriously soft towel for a moment. When she looked up, her face dry and vision cleared, she saw him and her eyes widened. "Oh," she said. "I thought you were a resort employee."

"No. I was just sitting here having coffee and enjoying the morning. Will you join me for a cup?" He motioned to the carafe in the center of the table, and the extra cup sitting beside it.

During the past three days, he had made sure she'd seen him a time or two. He had made a point of smiling and nodding, letting her get used to seeing him as just another resort guest, but this was the first time he'd actually spoken to her. He wondered if he'd misjudged the timing.

Glancing at the table, the woman hesitated for a moment, then shrugged lightly. "Sure. Why not?"

She snatched a short, white terry-cloth kimono from the back of a chair and belted herself into it. Reed was aware of a faint sense of regret. The maillot fit her so nicely. Oddly enough, she was just as intriguing when wrapped in terry cloth, her wet hair plastered to her head, her face free of makeup and glowing from her exercise.

"I'm Reed Hollander," he said, courteously holding a chair for her. "From Cleveland."

"Celia Carson," she replied, settling comfortably onto the colorful cushion of the wrought-iron chair. "From Percy. Arkansas," she added with a smile.

"Percy, Arkansas?" he repeated, as though he hadn't already known where she was from. "Is that anywhere near Little Rock?"

"An hour's drive north. Have you been to Little Rock?"

"No," he lied, thinking briefly of the two investigative trips he'd made to Arkansas in the past three months. "But I've heard it's a nice place to visit."

He was very good at that. Lying. He didn't even have to think about it much, anymore.

"I've never been to Cleveland, either. I haven't traveled much," she said, and he wondered if she was as skilled at deception as he was.

"Are you enjoying the resort?"

"It's a beautiful place. The staff is very nice."

He didn't bother to point out that she hadn't exactly answered his question. "Quiet this morning, isn't it?"

She glanced around them at the otherwise deserted pool area. "Very quiet. We seem to be the only ones who aren't sleeping the morning away."

"I don't know about you, but I'm having a hard time breaking that up-early-for-the-office routine."

She smiled. "Yes. So am I. This is my third day here and I still feel as though I should be doing something constructive with my time."

"I know the feeling. It must take awhile to get used to the life of the idle rich."

Celia tossed her dark, wet hair back over her shoulder and gave him a raised-eyebrow look. "So you're a working stiff, too?"

"Tax accountant," he replied with a faint sigh, as though aware that it wasn't the most interesting career in the world.

"I work in a bank. Assistant loan officer."

"Do you like your work?" he asked. He knew what she did for a living. Knew exactly how long she'd worked there. He wished he knew a few more details about her—like, just how involved was she with Damien Alexander?

Celia shrugged. "I like my work okay. It's a job, and it pays well enough, compared to the average salary in my hometown."

Reed poured them both a cup of coffee, handed hers to her, then lifted his own in a mock toast. "To all the working stiffs who had to punch a time clock this morning."

She smiled, and lifted her own cup. "Bless their little hearts," she added and took an appreciative sip of the steaming brew.

Satisfied that they'd gotten off to a good start, Reed set his cup down and leaned back in his chair. "This resort isn't my normal style of vacation," he admitted. "The trip was a birthday gift from my parents. They said they're trying to get me out of my usual boring routines."

"And what do you usually do on vacation?" Celia asked, probably just to be making casual conversation.

"I'm not sure," he confessed, a bit sheepishly. "I haven't had a vacation in so long I've sort of forgotten how." That part, at least, was the truth. "What about you?"

"I usually spend my vacations visiting my parents in St. Louis." She motioned around her. "This isn't my usual style, either. I'm here as a, umm, as a guest of the owner."

Reed lifted an eyebrow, feigning surprise. "Damien Alexander? You're a friend of his?"

"Yes. Do you know him?"

Reed shook his head and gave her a wry smile. "I'm a working stiff, remember? I don't usually mingle with the rich and famous. I've read about him, though, in the business and society pages."

He could have sworn Celia's cheeks pinkened, though she looked away too quickly for him to be quite sure. "He and I met through business," she explained. "We've become friends. I haven't even seen him since I arrived. He was called away for an emergency at one of his other resorts the same day I flew in."

There was a bit of a stammer in her explanation. A touch of self-consciousness, as if she were worried about what he might be thinking.

She was either a very talented actress, or nothing more than the quiet-living, small-town woman his background checks had indicated her to be. In which case, Reed rather pitied her. Alexander had a reputation for being attracted to innocent, unsophisticated young women. By the time he lost interest and moved on, they were neither innocent nor naive, though they were often considerably better off financially. Alexander had never been accused of not being generous with his . . . friends.

Reed wondered how far Alexander had already taken Celia Carson in her introduction to the fast-lane life-style. And then he reminded himself that it made no difference to him. All he wanted to know was how deeply involved Celia Carson was with Damien Alexander's less publicized financial dealings.

Celia didn't linger after finishing her coffee. She thanked him politely for the invitation, told him it had been very nice meeting him, and said she had a few calls to make. And then she turned and walked away.

Reed knew where she was going. To the luxurious suite she'd been provided, located directly across the hall from Alexander's own private rooms. Confident that she had never noticed him, Reed had watched her enter and leave that suite half-a-dozen times or more during the past three days. Always alone.

And the more he'd watched her, the more she'd fascinated him, despite his best efforts to view her as nothing more than another routine assignment. A handy tool for bringing down another dangerous, unconscionable crime organization, an organization Damien Alexander was suspected of masterminding.

He ran a hand through his short, dark hair in self-annoyance. Maybe it *was* time for a vacation, he found himself thinking. A real one.

Celia took a leisurely shower, blow-dried her shoulder-length hair, then dressed in a brightly colored, short-sleeved cotton jumpsuit with a heavy macramé belt. It felt odd to be wearing summer-weight clothing in November; back home, she'd be more comfortable in a sweater and wool slacks.

She slid her feet into leather sandals, slipped a chunky gold-link bracelet over her wrist, donned a pair of dangly gold earrings and touched her eyelids with taupe eye shadow and her lips with a deep rose gloss. And then she sat on the edge of her bed and wondered what she was supposed to do for the rest of the day.

It was just after 10 a.m. Between the softly billowing curtains at her Gulf-view window, she could see that the other resort guests had begun to stir. There were a few in the pool, four or five on the beach, a couple going into the restaurant for a late breakfast. Everyone seemed to be with someone else. Couples, families, friends. No one appeared to be vacationing alone. No one except her, of course, she thought with a wry sigh.

And Reed Hollander.

She thought of the man she'd met by the pool that morning. She'd seen him around the resort a couple of times during the past few days. He'd looked exactly like the accountant he'd claimed to be. His neatly pressed shirts and slacks and sober horn-rimmed glasses had looked odd in contrast to the usual resort uniform of T-shirts and baggy shorts.

He'd been attractive, in a rather ordinary way. Neat dark hair, intelligent-looking hazel eyes, a nice—if somewhat bland—smile. She'd thought at first that he was making a clumsy attempt at a pickup when he asked her to join him for coffee this morning, but he'd been nothing more than politely friendly. Just another self-proclaimed working stiff looking for a little companionship over coffee.

Another misfit among the idle rich.

The unbidden thought annoyed her. Okay, so this wasn't her usual style, she thought, looking around the exquisitely appointed suite in which she'd been staying for the past three days. Three lonely days.

She wasn't accustomed to bathtubs that seemed as big as a small swimming pool, or beds the size of the kitchen in her efficiency apartment. The suite Damien had provided for her consisted of the bedroom, with its huge bed, antique fainting couch, enormous old armoire converted to hold a TV, VCR and stereo, complete with a selection of popular videos and CDs; a huge, shamelessly decadent bathroom; a walk-in closet she could have parked her little red sports car in; and a sitting room furnished with antiques that looked so valuable she was almost afraid to touch them.

She certainly wasn't accustomed to having solicitous staff hovering at her elbow to cater to her every whim, as she was sure Damien had instructed them to do. She wasn't used to sleeping late, or waking with nothing more to do than to pamper herself. She couldn't quite grow comfortable with ordering anything she wanted from the restaurant's extensive menu—without even glancing at the price! Expensive little chocolates left on her pillow, fresh flowers delivered daily to her room, exotic fruits in fancy little baskets flanked by small bottles of champagne with names she couldn't even pronounce.

Just because she'd never lived this way before didn't mean she couldn't learn to like it. Eventually.

If only she had something to do to occupy her time. If only Damien hadn't been called away. Damien made quite an art of being charming and entertaining.

She was fully aware that Damien also made quite an art of seduction.

Which brought her right back to the "moral dilemma" she'd been battling ever since Damien had extended the invitation for her to be his guest at this resort.

If Damien hadn't been called away, would she have given in by now to his enticing smiles and skillful kisses? Would she have finally decided, once and for all, whether she wanted to become intimately involved with a man who'd kept the tabloid writers in a gleeful feeding frenzy for more than a decade now?

Celia liked Damien. She really did. Despite her older sister's reservations—based entirely on overblown tabloid gossip, since Rachel had never actually met Damien—Celia suspected that much of Damien's reputation had been exaggerated. Not all of it, of course. One had only to look into his wicked blue eyes to know that he had more experience with women than most men dreamed of.

And Celia was well aware that he hadn't gotten where he was by always being a "nice guy." Damien could be ruthless in business, thoughtless and sometimes arrogant in his personal life. But he wasn't the shameless heartbreaker or relentless debaucher he'd so often been labeled. He'd been a perfect gentleman with her from the first time he'd taken her to dinner.

Rachel might not trust Damien, but Celia did, for the most part. She never would have accepted his invitation if she hadn't trusted him to not force her into anything she didn't want.

She had been so bored lately, so restless, so hungry for change and adventure in her depressingly routine existence. Still, it had taken her several weeks to decide whether to accept Damien's generous offer of a free vacation at this resort. He'd made it clear from the first that he expected to be here with her, as a companion, a guide—and a lover, if she'd agree. He hadn't been pushy about it, but he'd let her know that was what he hoped would happen. Celia had finally accepted, on the condition that he give her time after her arrival to decide if she wanted him as anything more than a good friend.

Of course, neither of them could have known that the question would turn out to be academic, at least for the first few days of her visit. Damien could hardly seduce her from a faraway island in the Caribbean.

She remembered the discomfort she'd felt when she'd told Reed Hollander that she was Damien's guest. She knew what he must have thought. What anyone would have thought.

She'd been foolish to immediately try to convince him that she and Damien were nothing more than friends. For one thing, it was none of the accountant's business. For another, why should it bother her so badly for someone to think she and Damien were lovers when she'd been seriously considering making that suspicion a reality?

Really, she thought with a rueful shake of her head. Her small-town upbringing had a nasty habit of cropping up at the most inconvenient times!

Celia left her room later that morning determined to do something interesting. Here she was in a tropical paradise and she'd been sitting alone moping! How depressing.

She'd come to this resort in search of adventure. A break from a life that had become so safe and predictable that there were times she had thought she'd scream in frustration. After the weeks she'd spent working up her shaky courage to come, it was ridiculous to spend the whole time hiding in her room, just because she didn't know how to have a good time on her own.

The first person she saw when she stepped out of her suite was a tall, well-dressed man coming out of Damien's rooms. He smiled when he saw her. "Miss Carson," he greeted her. "Good morning. Is there anything you need?"

"No, thank you, Evan. I was just on my way out to find something to do. I'm rather tired of sitting in my room." And wasn't *that* an understatement?

Damien's personal secretary's dark face creased with a worried frown. "Aren't you having a nice time, Miss Carson? Mr. Alexander told everyone to make sure you enjoyed yourself in his absence. Is there anything I can do to make your stay with us more pleasant?"

Celia shook her head and gave him a reassuring smile. "Thanks, but I think I'll just wing it for a few hours. I'm sure I'll have a lovely day."

"If you need anything—anything at all—just ask one of the resort staff," Evan reminded her. "The social director has a full list of activities arranged for today. The schedule is posted in the main lobby. If you don't find anything on the list that you'd like to do, perhaps we can arrange something special for you."

Celia nodded and thanked him again, biting the inside of her lip against a rueful smile. Damien must have left stern orders concerning her welfare while he was gone. His entire staff had all but turned handsprings to please her. Unfortunately, their attention made her rather uncomfortable.

She simply wasn't used to this.

She slid a pair of sunglasses onto her nose as she stepped out of the relatively small side building that housed her suite, Damien's rooms and the resort offices. She spotted a few white-jacketed resort employees among the milling guests, but made no move to attract attention. She certainly didn't want anyone else hovering over her to make sure she was having fun!

She turned and slipped quietly down the path that led to the beach.

Chapter Two

A wide strip of sand stretched from the resort complex to the Gulf beach. The beach was markedly uncrowded in contrast to the plethora of buildings on either side behind her. Farther north, the island was untamed and undeveloped, an eighty-four-mile stretch of federally maintained sand dunes and sea oats, popular with bird-watchers and beachcombers. Yet this part of the not-quite-three-mile-wide island at the southernmost tip of Texas was completely covered with resorts, condominiums, hotels and restaurants.

Damien's resort—the Alexander—was one of the largest on the island, a huge complex built in a horseshoe shape around fountains, pools, tennis courts, volleyball nets, a lushly landscaped common. A health club, sauna, game room, restaurant, snack bar, and a lounge were part of the amenities provided for the guests; not to mention a variety of activities including horseback riding, parasailing, sailboarding, golf, fishing... Name it, and Damien made sure it was available.

So why was Celia so darned bored?

Standing at the edge of the sandy beach, she looked wistfully at the few couples lying cozily beneath colorful umbrellas, or strolling along the water's edge, looking for seashells. One romantic-looking duo in the distance were arm in arm as they wandered slowly out of sight.

Celia sighed and kept walking.

Then she stopped again when a familiar figure caught her eye.

She smiled.

The "attractive in an average sort of way" accountant she'd met that morning was standing at the edge of the beach, brushing sand from the hem of his neatly creased gray slacks. His once shiny accountant's shoes were coated with sand and there was a piece of broken shell stuck in the one-inch cuff of his right pant leg. His only concession to the casual atmosphere had been to turn up the sleeves of his dark gray shirt into neat, precisely matched cuffs.

His crisp, short hair was a bit wind-tossed, so that it ruffled over the tops of his horn-rimmed glasses. She watched as he ran a hand through the recalcitrant lock and efficiently restored it to its rightful place.

"Mr. Hollander," she said, hoping her amusement at his out-of-place attire wasn't evident in her voice. "We meet again."

She appeared to have caught him by surprise. He blinked at her through his glasses, then smiled. "Miss Carson?"

"Celia," she corrected him, because it seemed ridiculous to be so formal on a beach.

"And I'm Reed," he reminded her. "Nice day, isn't it?"

"Yes. Are you having a good time?" she asked with a perfectly straight face.

He exhaled deeply and glanced around him. "I'm trying to. My parents would be terribly disappointed if I didn't."

She certainly knew how hard it was to have fun just to keep from disappointing someone. "I hear the social director has a full schedule of activities lined up for this afternoon," she suggested helpfully.

Reed made a face. "Yes. Parasailing and volleyball. Or for the more sedate guests—a bridge tournament."

"None of those appeal to you, I take it?"

He smiled sheepishly. "I'm afraid not. I'll probably just sit by the pool this afternoon. I brought an intriguing-looking book with me—a newly published account of the invasion of Normandy. This seems like a good time to start it."

Celia couldn't think of anything less appealing than sitting by the pool reading a World War II history book. Honestly, this guy was worse than *she* was when it came to vacations! She forced a smile. "Sounds...relaxing," she said.

"Yes, though I'm sure you have much more exciting plans."

Oh, yeah, she had great plans. Walking down the beach envying everyone who wasn't alone. Counting her yawns. Maybe she'd strike up a fascinating conversation with a hermit crab.

"There's so much to do here, it's hard to decide where to start," she said, wondering if her bright smile looked as fake and plastic as it felt.

Reed looked wistful. "I suppose it must seem that way to most people," he murmured.

Celia glumly agreed. So much to do...yet, she and this poor schmuck were feeling as out of place as two nuns at an orgy.

Funny, she hadn't realized how truly unadventurous her life had become in the past couple of years. So much so, she seemed to have almost forgotten how to play altogether.

Her older sister would understand. After being widowed at a young age, left with two small children to raise and her late husband's business to run, Rachel had had little time for fun and relaxation. But recently she'd met Seth Fletcher, a laid-back lawyer a few years her junior, and Seth had brought fun back into Rachel's life. Now they were making wedding plans.

Celia heartily approved. She had already grown very fond of her almost-brother-in-law. She'd seen the new happiness glowing in her sister's dark eyes... and she couldn't quite ignore a touch of envy. Rachel had found love twice, while Celia was still waiting for romance to find her.

Their brother, Cody, the middle Carson sibling, didn't need anyone to teach him about having fun. He would have hooted in derision at Celia's inability to enjoy herself in this hedonistic paradise. Though Cody had settled down some since his party-hearty college days, which had ended when he'd quit during his sophomore year, he was still the most spontaneous and energetic member of the family. He was always the joker, always the life of the party, though he was no longer the heavy drinker he'd been before a near-tragic car accident had turned him into a teetotaler. Cody now owned half interest in a moderately profitable country-western restaurant and dance club in which nothing stronger than beer was served to the loyal patrons, but the responsibilities of his job hadn't dimmed his sense of fun.

Celia couldn't help wondering what had happened to her own.

She'd almost forgotten that Reed Hollander was still standing nearby until he suddenly cleared his throat and brought her out of her somber introspection. "Be careful of that sun," he warned. "It's getting close to the dangerous stage, and you don't want to burn that fair skin of yours."

He was studying her face as he spoke. His scrutiny seemed more analytical than personal, an almost scientific assessment of the affects of ultraviolet light on her complexion. Celia thought in wry amusement that the brief time she'd spent with this man certainly hadn't done anything to boost her ego. So far, he'd behaved rather like an indulgent uncle.

Which, of course, was exactly the way she wanted him to behave, she assured herself hastily. Damien Alexander—her conspicuously absent host—was the only man she should be concentrating on for now, even if she *should* find herself suddenly, unexpectedly attracted to someone else.

Not that she was, of course.

Feeling her cheeks going suddenly warm, she took a hasty step away from Reed Hollander. "Enjoy your book," she said, her tone politely dismissive.

"Thanks. Have a nice day," he answered cheerily.

Blinking a bit, Celia watched him walk away.

Have a nice day? The man was a walking cliché, for heaven's sake. He even talked like a tax accountant. He was exactly like the men she knew back in Percy—genial, dependable, hard-working, predictable. Ordinary.

The type of men who made Damien Alexander look so dashing, exciting and fascinating in contrast.

Turning back to her walk, Celia told herself that the only reason she was spending any time at all thinking about Reed Hollander was because Damien wasn't around. What other reason could there possibly be?

Celia saw Reed again when she returned from her long walk down the beach. He was sitting by the pool, seemingly absorbed in his thick hardcover book. Celia didn't think he even noticed when she passed within a few feet of his chair on her way to her suite.

Not that she'd particularly wanted him to notice, of course.

She had just stepped through the doors of her building when someone called her name. "Miss Carson! I'm glad I've found you."

She looked around with a curious, lifted eyebrow. She saw Damien's secretary again, rushing toward her from the hallway that led to the resort offices. "Is something wrong, Evan?"

He shook his dark head and smiled reassuringly. "No, not at all. Actually, Mr. Alexander is on the phone. He asked me to try to locate you. He wants to talk to you. I'll transfer the call to your suite, if you like."

Celia agreed and hurried toward her rooms. Maybe Damien was calling to tell her that he'd be rejoining her this evening, she thought hopefully. She envisioned an evening of dinner and dancing, strolling on the beach—all the things she'd looked forward to when she'd accepted his invitation.

"Celia?" Damien's whiskey-smooth voice flowed through the lines between them. "I hope I haven't called at a bad time."

"No," she assured him. Since she didn't want him to ask for details about what she'd been doing to entertain herself in his absence, she asked, "Are you still in the islands?"

"I'm afraid so. And it looks like I'm going to be held up here for another forty-eight hours. The storm has all but devastated the resort, and I have to make sure all the repairs are underway before I can leave. I can't tell you how sorry I am about this, darling. If there was anything at all

I could do to be there with you now, I would certainly do it.''

Though she was disappointed, Celia tried hard to be gracious about it. "I understand, Damien. You certainly had no control over the weather. I'm only sorry so much damage was done to your resort. Was anyone hurt?''

"My manager was trapped beneath a fallen tree and suffered multiple fractures of his right leg. His injuries were the most serious anyone suffered, but he's expected to make a full recovery. Fortunately, there was enough warning to evacuate the resort before the storm hit. Only a few staff members remained behind—by their own choice.''

"And the buildings?''

"Major damage,'' Damien answered with a sigh. "It will be at least a couple of months before we're able to re-open.''

"This sounds like a terrible time for you to be away from your business, Damien. Maybe it would be better if I go back to Percy. We can try this another time.''

"Celia, you've already taken two weeks vacation from your job. I'll be there Monday morning, at the very latest. That will still give us a week to spend together. You have full run of the resort in the meantime. Please, take advantage of it. Enjoy yourself. Unless you aren't pleased with the facilities?''

Celia hastily assured him that the resort was beautiful. Everything anyone could want. She couldn't possibly tell him that she'd been bored out of her mind. He would never understand. She wasn't sure *she* understood.

"Then you'll stay?'' He sounded very anxious for her to agree.

She swallowed a sigh, and tried again to sound gracious. "I'll stay.''

"You won't be sorry. I'm going to show you a great time, I promise."

Though she knew he couldn't see her, she forced a smile. "I'm looking forward to it."

The problem was, she wasn't at all sure she *was* looking forward to it. The more time she spent alone here, with Damien so far away, the more she was beginning to doubt the wisdom of accepting his invitation in the first place. Though she wouldn't go so far as to say that the tropical storm had been an omen directed solely at her, it still felt oddly like a sign. She didn't fit in here, wasn't comfortable in Damien's world.

Of course, she hadn't been particularly comfortable in her own world lately, either.

She hung up the phone with a dejected sigh.

This vacation definitely wasn't turning out the way she'd hoped it would.

Reed turned another page of what surely had to be the most boring history ever written of any battle ever fought. He glanced over the top of the book toward the building into which Celia had disappeared over half an hour earlier. She spent a lot of time in there by herself. On the phone, perhaps? Taking care of Alexander's illicit side business while Alexander dealt with the crisis at his island resort? She certainly didn't act like a young woman on a vacation.

He was confident that she hadn't seen him following her during her leisurely stroll down the beach. Nor could she have known that he'd settled into this chair behind his book less than ten minutes before she'd returned.

Celia hadn't talked to anyone during her stroll, hadn't done anything except walk and look pensively out over the Gulf. She hadn't looked particularly happy. Trouble in paradise? And, if so, was it business or personal? Was she pining for Alexander?

Reed scowled, wondering why he hated the idea so much. If Celia Carson was involved in what he suspected, she certainly didn't deserve his sympathy. And if she wasn't—if her only involvement with Alexander was a personal one—then she was still off-limits, as far as he was concerned. Reed had no interest in picking up the pieces of one of Alexander's shattered conquests. No matter how beautiful that conquest might be. No matter how appealing her sweetly dimpled smile.

His scowl deepened and he turned his attention doggedly back to the book. He would do well to keep his distance from Celia Carson during the rest of this assignment. He'd never gotten personally involved in a case during his entire federal law enforcement career. He had no intention of doing so this time.

The paperback hit the wall of Celia's sitting room with a resounding splat. She shoved herself off the dainty little sofa and pushed a hand through her hair. "This," she said aloud to the empty room, "is ridiculous."

It was just before noon. She'd been sitting alone for over half an hour, trying to concentrate on a glitzy saga that was just too overblown and pretentious to stomach.

She had just turned twenty-four and she'd been acting twice her age. No, scratch that. Granny Fran was over seventy and *she* wouldn't have wasted time sitting in her room with a bad book when she had a tropical paradise right outside! Granny Fran probably would have spent the past three days sight-seeing or beachcombing—or sailboarding or parasailing, knowing her adventurous grandmother.

And what had Celia been doing? Moping. She snorted in self-disgust and headed determinedly for the door. She was on vacation, darn it. Her first one in ages. She was going to have fun if it killed her.

Reed Hollander was still sitting by the pool, carefully shaded from the "dangerous" sun, his nose buried in the thick book. Celia stopped and stared at him. Pathetic, she thought with a shake of her head. He was a young man, nice looking, seemed pleasant enough. Yet he was wasting this beautiful day reading a book that looked boring even from where she stood.

Without giving herself time to think about it, Celia walked up to him, reached out, plucked the book from his hands and closed it without bothering to save his place. Later she would wonder at her actions—she *never* did things like this!—but for now, it seemed the right thing to do.

He blinked owlishly at her through his horn-rimmed glasses. "Er . . . ?"

"How old are you, Reed Hollander?" she demanded, staring aggressively down at him.

Looking thoroughly bewildered, he cleared his throat. "I'm thirty-three. As of yesterday, actually."

"Congratulations. And I've recently turned twenty-four. So what the hell are we doing?"

"I'm not sure I—"

"Look around us!" she said, warming to her subject, swinging an arm to direct his attention outward. "There must be a gazillion things to do around here. Everyone else seems to be having a great time. So why aren't we?"

"Well, I—"

"I don't know about you, but I'm not ready for a rocking chair and a shawl. I want to have fun while I'm young enough to enjoy it. And you are going to have fun, too, Reed Hollander."

His eyebrows rose. "I am?"

"Yes. Your parents can thank me later. Now, come on, get up out of that chair. We're going to play."

"But—"

She lifted an admonishing finger. "No arguments," she warned. "You're going to have fun, even if I have to drag you screaming and kicking."

His firm mouth quirked into what might have been the beginnings of a smile. "That should be an interesting sight."

"Want to bet that I won't try it?"

"No," he said hastily, his smile deepening. "I'm sure you would. But it won't be necessary. I accept your graciously extended invitation. I was only going to point out that I don't have a car."

She dug into her pocket and dangled a key ring in front of him. "I do." Damien had taken care of that, of course. "So what are we waiting for?"

"Not a thing." He took the book from her hands and laid it on the table. "Lead the way."

"Don't you want to put your book away first?"

He shook his head. "Anyone who would go to the trouble of stealing it will get exactly what he deserves."

She chuckled. "Then let's go."

He made an old-fashioned "after you" gesture, then followed closely behind her when she moved toward the garage where Damien kept his cars.

She didn't allow herself to dwell on a nagging suspicion that she had just done something very foolish.

Celia was a bit startled to learn that the vehicle Damien had left for her use was a sleek, glossy black Mercedes convertible. She gulped at the thought of being responsible for a car that cost more than she'd make at the bank in three or four years, but she managed to hide her trepidation from Reed.

They were setting out to have an adventure, she reminded herself firmly. Might as well do so in style.

"Nice car" was all Reed said as he climbed carefully into the passenger's seat, folding his long legs in front of him.

"It's Damien's," Celia admitted.

"I thought it might be. He won't mind if you and I . . ."

"Of course not," Celia cut in airily. She started the engine, flinched at the resulting powerful roar, then shoved the gearshift into Reverse.

She nearly gave herself and her passenger whiplash.

"You—er—always drive like this?" Reed asked mildly as they sped away from the resort. He held one hand to the back of his neck, as though checking to make sure her jolting takeoff hadn't done any permanent damage.

Celia gave him a rather sheepish look of apology. "Sorry. I'm not used to this car. I have a sports car back home, but it's just a little four-cylinder. I think this one must be a six."

"Eight," he corrected her, wincing as she narrowly missed a palm tree that leaned toward the road. "Quite powerful, actually. It would be rather easy to lose control."

"Don't worry about it," Celia assured him, spitting a lock of whipping dark hair out of her mouth. "I'm a great driver."

A spray of sand, gravel and crushed shells showered upward when the two right tires left the pavement and hit the shoulder. Celia overcorrected, swerved, cursed beneath her breath and brought the car firmly back under control on the right side of the road. She didn't look at Reed, though she saw that his hands were clenched on his knees, the knuckles conspicuously white.

Reed released his knees to reach for his seat belt. He fastened it with a loud snap. "Yes," he said, just loudly enough for her to hear. "I can see that my life is in good hands."

Feeling a bit guilty that her restlessness had made her reckless, Celia eased up on the accelerator. "Sorry. I'll slow down."

He murmured something that might have been a thank-you. He didn't say anything else until Celia guided the car onto the Queen Isabella Causeway, the curving, two-and-a-half-mile bridge that spanned Laguna Madre Bay to provide access between South Padre Island and Port Isabel on the mainland.

"Do you have any particular destination in mind?" he asked, glancing over his shoulder as they left the resort behind.

"You like history, right?"

"Yes."

"According to the tourist pamphlets I've been looking over during the past couple of days, this area's crawling with it. The Port Isabel lighthouse. Fort Brown. A bunch of battlefields from the Mexican War and the Civil War. Lots of museums and stuff. Any of that sound interesting to you?"

"Yes," he admitted with a smile. "But what about you? Are *you* interested in history? Military history?"

"Not particularly," she answered candidly. "But anything's better than sitting in my room with a dumb book. I might as well broaden my mind, since I have nothing better to do."

Reed chuckled.

Realizing how ungracious she'd sounded, Celia groaned and slapped a hand to her forehead. She placed it back on the wheel quickly, to Reed's obvious relief. Both of them were aware that the long, busy bridge was no place to start swerving again.

"I'm sorry, Reed. I didn't really mean that I've kidnapped you for the afternoon for lack of anything better to do. I just thought since we're both here on our own, and both having trouble finding anything to do at the resort, maybe we could keep each other company for a while. I suppose I should have given you a chance to say something."

"I'm glad you've kidnapped me," Reed assured her. "I'd like to see the local sights with you. As I said, I'm not very good at this vacation business."

Celia slanted him a smile. "Neither am I."

He smiled back at her, and she thought again that he was a very attractive man. She liked his smile and his nice hazel eyes. She wondered if he had anyone waiting for him back home in Cleveland. And if he did, what was he doing here alone?

Their gazes held for a moment. And then Reed cleared his throat, tapped the dash and recalled her attention to her driving. "I think we'll enjoy ourselves more if we arrive in one piece," he suggested teasingly.

Celia laughed and turned her full concentration to her driving. "I'm sure you're right. Hang on, friend. We're off to have fun—even if it kills us."

"What a pleasant thought," Reed remarked wryly, but he seemed to relax when she did.

Maybe this would be fun, after all, Celia mused with a faint smile.

It was always nice to make a new friend.

Chapter Three

Reed proved to be a very pleasant companion for an afternoon. Polite—almost excessively so, at first—considerate, interesting when he finally relaxed enough to carry on a conversation.

He hadn't been kidding about his interest in history, Celia thought at one point during the afternoon. It seemed to fascinate him. Just show him a historical marker or a battered old weapon or a scrap of hundred-year-old paper covered with faded, indecipherable writing, and those nice hazel eyes of his lighted up like beacons behind his sensible glasses.

She had rather expected to be bored. She was almost surprised to find out that she wasn't. Using a map they picked up at a visitor information booth, they scouted out several local tourist attractions. Reed seemed almost comically worried that Celia wasn't having a good time; she assured him repeatedly, and quite sincerely, that she was having a lovely day.

"Celia," Reed said as she drove away from the final museum late that afternoon. "We've been exploring sites of interest to me all afternoon. Surely there's something you'd like to do before we go back to the resort."

Glancing at the many tourist attractions around them, Celia nodded. "Actually, there is."

"What is it?" he asked encouragingly.

She spun the wheel of the Mercedes, swinging into a parking lot. "I want food," she said with a grin. "And not that elegant cuisine served in the Alexander's restaurant. I want something greasy and fattening and totally non-nutritious. A cheeseburger, fries and a chocolate milk shake."

She parked in front of a building decorated with the universally recognized golden arches. "Perfect," she pronounced.

She looked at Reed, who was looking back at her with a solemn expression. She frowned. "Fast food doesn't appeal to you?" *Don't tell me he's a strict vegetarian or a health-food nut.* She groaned inwardly.

"Well, there is one change I'd like to suggest to your menu," he said diffidently.

Probably wanted to add a salad to appease his conscience, Celia thought wryly. "What change would you like to make, Reed?" she asked patiently.

"Could we make those double cheeseburgers? Preferably with bacon? And I really prefer strawberry milk shakes to chocolate."

Celia laughed. That made several times during the afternoon that he'd surprised her with a dry sense of humor. "Double cheeseburgers with bacon," she agreed, reaching for her door handle. "And you may have a strawberry milk shake if you like—but I'm having chocolate!"

After they'd placed their orders at the counter, Celia insisted she pay for the meal. "After all," she reminded him, "I kidnapped you this afternoon. So, it's my treat."

He nodded. "Thank you," he said politely.

She liked it that he didn't argue with her. A lot of guys felt threatened when a woman bought their dinner. Celia sensed that Reed was a man who was completely comfortable with his own worth, his own masculinity. He didn't appear to be trying to prove anything, or to impress her. He was just being himself. And she liked him all the better for it.

They found a booth at the back of the room, as far as possible from the corner in which a small child's birthday party was in noisy progress. Celia bit into her burger with a sigh of delight. "Mmm," she murmured. "That's exactly what I needed."

She looked up to find that Reed was watching her. He hadn't even unwrapped his own burger, yet. "Reed?" she prompted. "Aren't you hungry?"

He blinked. "Oh. Yeah." He picked up his burger and fussed with the paper covering, seeming to avoid her eyes for a moment.

Celia thought in some amusement that he looked embarrassed. Why? Was he worried about table etiquette or something silly like that? At a place where two kids were climbing the light fixtures and another was eating french fries that had fallen on the floor?

He really was a very sweet man. A bit staid, but sweet.

Remember the job, damn it, Reed told himself angrily as he bit off a corner of his dripping burger. *Remember the job.*

He didn't know what strange quirk of fate had made Celia choose him to entertain her during the afternoon; he certainly hadn't been trying to compete with her dashing boyfriend or any of the wealthy guests currently in residence at the resort. But now that she had, instead of taking advantage of the chance to subtly find out more about her dealings with Alexander, he found himself sitting in a fast-food restaurant booth fantasizing about having her wrap her lips around him with the same frankly sensual enthusiasm she'd displayed for her hamburger!

Not smart, Hollander. Damned stupid, in fact.

He was confident that he'd carried out his role believably enough during the afternoon. Celia had no reason to think he was anything other than what he'd told her he was—an ordinary tax accountant with a passion for history. She seemed to trust him.

But she still hadn't given him any clue as to what she was doing at Damien Alexander's resort while Alexander was taking care of business elsewhere.

The thought of Damien Alexander made Reed strengthen his resolve to keep his distance from Celia Carson. No matter how attractive he found her, no matter how invitingly she looked at him, no matter how seductively she walked or how intriguingly she smiled—he still had no intention of making a play for Alexander's woman.

That, he reminded himself flatly, could only lead to disaster. Professionally—and personally, if he wasn't careful.

When they left the fast-food restaurant, Celia mentioned that there was one other thing she'd like to do.

"What is it?" Reed asked, perfectly willing to indulge her.

Celia smiled and pointed to a gaudy, colorful place across the street from the burger joint. "That."

Reed followed the direction of her pointing finger, then frowned. "Miniature golf?"

"Yes. Looks like a great course, doesn't it? Look at that windmill. And the castle. I bet that's a tough one."

Reed was still frowning. "I wouldn't know."

"Haven't you ever played miniature golf?"

He seemed to consider the question for a moment. "If I have," he said at last, "I've forgotten."

"Well, that settles it, then. We have to play. You can go home and tell your parents that you tried something new on your vacation. They'll be delighted," she assured him.

He didn't look convinced. "I don't think I'd be very good at it."

"Don't sweat it, Reed," she told him, tucking a companionable hand beneath his arm. "Everyone's a little nervous the first time. But I promise, I'll be gentle with you."

She gave him a bland, innocent smile when he looked at her with suddenly narrowed eyes. She wasn't sure how he'd react to the double entendre; she hadn't been able to resist finding out.

Reed cocked his head, stroked his jaw, then nodded. "All right," he said. "I'm yours. Take me."

This time it was Celia who lifted an eyebrow in response to the unexpectedly sexy growl in which he'd spoken. "Er—"

"Take me to play golf," he said, his smile wicked. "That's what I meant, of course."

She resisted an impulse to fan her suddenly warm cheeks with one hand. He really did have a tendency to surprise her at times, she thought.

In fact, there were moments when she wasn't at all sure that he was quite as mild-mannered and innocuous as he'd seemed at first.

It was after eight that evening when they crossed the causeway again onto South Padre Island. Reed was behind the wheel this time, Celia having declared that she was tired of driving. As she'd expected, particularly after knowing him for a few more hours, he handled the powerful vehicle competently, confidently—and cautiously.

The same way he'd played miniature golf, she thought with a suppressed sigh. He'd slaughtered her at the game, even though he swore it had been his first time.

From beneath heavy eyelids, she studied the gleam of lights on the now blue-black waters of Laguna Madre. A mile ahead of them, the closely nestled buildings on South Padre Island gleamed brightly against the darkened Gulf horizon. "Pretty, isn't it?" she murmured.

"In a glittery way," he hedged. "I usually prefer a more natural landscape, myself. Moonlight on undeveloped beaches. A campfire glowing in a clearing in the middle of a forest. A fireplace burning in a cabin high up in the Rockies after a snowstorm."

Celia lifted her head from the leather seat and stared at him. This didn't sound like the pragmatic, history-buff accountant she'd spent the afternoon trailing at several historic sites. "Why, Reed," she said. "You sound almost like a closet romantic."

He shifted uncomfortably in the driver's seat. "Nah. I just meant I usually vacation in less luxurious surroundings. Padre's got a lot to offer, of course, which makes it so popular. Did you know there's evidence that the Karankawa Indians wintered here more than four hundred years ago? Which means the island has always been seen as an ideal—"

Celia interrupted him with a groan. "Please. No more historical tidbits. My brain is already on overload with all these perfectly useless facts."

"Like what?" Reed asked, smiling.

"The Port Isabel lighthouse was constructed in the 1850s and abandoned in 1905. The construction of Fort Brown in 1844—"

"Forty-six."

"Thanks. In 1846, then, precipitated the beginning of the U.S.–Mexican War. The last land engagement of the Civil War was fought at Palmito Ranch near Brownsville, a month after Lee's surrender. The battle was won by Confederates who didn't know the war was already over, and afterward the victors became the captives of their former prisoners. That was sort of interesting, actually."

"I thought so," Reed murmured, his voice underlaced with amusement.

"I know you did. You just ate that stuff up, didn't you? I bet you made all *A*s in history in school."

"Yeah, but don't ask about my grades in composition and literature."

"I was good at math and sciences, but history always put me to sleep."

"Then you had the wrong teachers."

"Maybe I did," she agreed, smiling at him. "You made it very interesting this afternoon. Maybe you should have been a history teacher instead of a tax accountant."

Reed's smile seemed to fade in the shadows. Before Celia could decide why, he shrugged and said lightly, "I thought about it. Then something more interesting came up."

Celia lifted her head again. "Tax accounting is more interesting than teaching?"

He cleared his throat. "At times. Are you hungry?"

It took her a moment to switch gears. It had been several hours since they'd indulged in the burgers and shakes. Even now, she shouldn't be hungry—but she discovered that she was. "Now that you mention it, I am rather hungry," she said. "It's hard to believe after all we ate this afternoon, but I could eat again."

"So could I. Will you join me for a late dinner in the resort restaurant?"

"I'd like that."

"Should we change first?"

Celia hesitated, thought about how grubby and windblown she felt after a day of sightseeing in a convertible, and nodded. "I'll make it quick. Meet you in the restaurant lobby in, say, half an hour?"

"You've got a date."

Celia swallowed in response to his wording. She hadn't really thought of this as a date. For some reason it was easier to think of it as a friendly outing between two amiable acquaintances. She didn't bother to correct him. It seemed better to just let it go.

Reed's message light was flashing when he entered his room. His accommodations were nice, but much less luxurious than the suite Celia had been provided. He called the message desk, then dialed the number he'd been given, keeping one eye on the clock. He didn't want to be late for his dinner date, he thought, as he listened to the faint buzz of the other phone ringing.

"Kyle Brown," a familiar voice answered.

Reed didn't bother to identify himself. "What's up?"

"There's been another delivery."

Reed tensed. "Any leads?"

"Nothing new. All arrows still point to Alexander. Every major transaction we can trace during the past two years has taken place in an area where Alexander was conducting business. We've had two sources mention his name in anonymous tips. We have solid evidence implicating at least one of his employees. Rumor still has it there will be an important meeting on Padre Island sometime this week between Alexander and two of his current customers. Apparently, it was put off a few days because of the storm that damaged his resort in the Caribbean."

"Leaving me cooling my heels here when I was expecting to be witness to the meeting two days ago," Reed grumbled.

"As I said, there's every reason to believe the meeting is still on when Alexander gets back there."

"He's due to return in a couple of days," Reed said, repeating something Celia had casually mentioned during the afternoon.

"Yeah. Novotny's discreetly making arrangements to be there."

Reed felt the tension low in his neck, a sure sign that the case was nearing a resolution. All the major players were coming together, and he would be here when they gathered.

"The woman still there?"

Reed shoved a hand through his wind-tossed hair. "Yeah."

"Keep an eye on her. She could be setting everything up on that end."

"Or she knows nothing about any of this," Reed cautioned.

"C'mon, Reed. We know she's been seen several times talking to our suspects in her hometown. And she's been photographed with Alexander on several occasions."

"Dates, not meetings, as far as we know. As for her talking to the other suspects—well, it's a small town. She's lived there a long time, works in the town's only bank. She probably knows everyone there. It could only be a coincidence that she's been seen with our suspects."

"Maybe." Kyle sounded skeptical. "But you know how I feel about coincidences."

"She's spent the past few days taking walks and swimming and sightseeing. She's hardly spoken to any of Alexander's staff. No suspicious meetings. No mysterious disappearances. She claims she's nothing more than a friend of the owner, here on a vacation."

"If she's nothing more than Alexander's newest bed toy, why is she there now, when he's not even in the country? Why would he want her hanging around when he's about to set up a transaction of this magnitude?"

As much as Reed didn't want to think of Celia being involved with Alexander's unsavory sideline, he was even less enthused about hearing her referred to as a "bed toy." He'd spent the whole afternoon with her, damn it. His instincts about people were usually directly on target. And all his instincts told him that Celia Carson was exactly what she appeared to be. Good-natured. Restless. A bit naive. Honest.

But—rare though it had been—he had been wrong before. "Damn," he growled, wishing for a moment that he *had* become a history teacher.

"What's the matter, Hollander? Don't tell me you're starting to share Alexander's tastes in PYTs?"

PYTs. Kyle's dry, uncharitable way of referring to the pretty young things that Damien Alexander had made a hobby of collecting and discarding. Pretty young women like Celia Carson.

Innocent bystander? Eager mistress? Or calculating business associate?

Reed found, to his self-disgust, that he wasn't nearly as certain as he should be about which label best fit the woman he was meeting for dinner in fifteen minutes.

"I've got to go," he said abruptly. "Anything else you wanted to tell me?"

"No. I'll be there when Alexander arrives."

"Right. See you then."

"Have fun, Reed. But watch your back."

Reed growled a response and replaced the phone. He wasted another few minutes cursing himself for forgetting, even for a couple of hours, the careful objectivity he'd always prided.

It was a mistake he wouldn't make again during this assignment, he promised himself.

Dressed in a royal blue silk T-shirt and a gauzy print skirt, Celia entered the restaurant lobby only five minutes later than she'd intended. She didn't see Reed at first, though she quickly spotted the resort manager, Enrique Torres, and his wife, Helen, who were entering the restaurant at the same time as Celia.

"Miss Carson." Torres greeted Celia with an overbright smile probably reserved for VIP guests. "Are you enjoying your stay with us?"

"Yes, thank you, Mr. Torres," she replied. Oddly enough, she meant it this time. She'd had a better time today than she had since her arrival. "Your staff is very friendly and efficient," she added, because he still looked a bit anxious. "I wouldn't hesitate to recommend this resort to any of my friends for their vacations."

His smile relaxed fractionally. "That's very kind of you. Were you on your way in to the dining room?"

"Yes. I've been so busy sight-seeing this afternoon that I've just now gotten around to dinner."

That, too, seemed to please him. The guest was keeping herself entertained. He nodded toward his wife, who was chatting with another guest across the lobby. "Please, won't you join us at our table? Helen and I will enjoy your company."

"Thank you, but I'm meeting someone. As a matter of fact," she added, when a hand fell lightly on her shoulder, "he's here now."

She smiled up at Reed, who returned the greeting with a slight nod. "Mr. Torres, have you met Reed Hollander?"

"Only briefly," Torres replied, extending a hand. "Are you enjoying your stay with us, Mr. Hollander?"

Celia thought with a stifled smile that he must automatically ask that question of all his guests.

Reed shook the manager's hand briefly. "I'm enjoying it more all the time," he said.

Celia glanced up at him, to find him smiling down at her in a way that made his words somehow directed toward her. She felt her cheeks warm a bit, and quickly looked away.

Torres was watching them with a tiny frown between his dark eyebrows. "Er—well, enjoy your dinner. Please let me know if anything is unsatisfactory."

"I'm sure everything will be fine, as always," Celia assured him.

Torres managed another strained smile, murmured a good evening, and returned to his wife, giving them one last, worried look over his shoulder.

"He doesn't like it that I've joined you this evening," Reed commented.

"Don't be silly. Why would he care?"

"Maybe because his boss wouldn't like it?"

"Damien wouldn't care, either," Celia replied firmly, though she wasn't as confident as she tried to sound. "Let's go in, Reed. I'm starving."

She slipped a hand beneath his arm, an almost defiant gesture that earned her a quizzical look from him and another faint frown from Torres. Reed didn't say anything, simply put a hand over hers and led her to the doorway. He kept her hand on his arm as they were escorted to a table by the rather surprised-looking maître d', who'd become accustomed to escorting each of them to tables "for one."

Celia had just noticed how firm and muscular Reed's arm was beneath his thin, white cotton shirt when they reached the table. Surprisingly muscular for an accountant, she mused as she slipped into her seat. Served her right for stereotyping.

The table was Celia's favorite in the beautifully decorated restaurant, which was another indication of her preferential treatment, since the restaurant was fairly crowded on this Friday evening. The table was small, private, candlelit, set cozily into a bay window overlooking the Gulf. The full moon reflected softly off the rolling waves and nearly deserted beach. A night made for romance.

Celia glanced at Reed from beneath her lashes and tried to imagine Damien sitting across from her. Damien, with his thick, precisely-styled blond hair, his gleaming, dark-lashed blue eyes, his flashing dimples and killer smile. The image kept fading in contrast to the reality of the man sitting across from her. Reed Hollander, with his neat dark hair and grave hazel eyes, his horn-rimmed glasses and cautious smiles, his muscular arms and fact-crammed brain.

Reed, who was becoming more intriguing to her all the time.

She mentally shook her head. Talk about confusing situations! Here she was at this glamorous resort with tentative plans to begin an affair with a dashing, exciting man, only to find herself suddenly attracted to another man who was all too much like the men she'd left behind, the ones she'd thought too ordinary to interest her. And she was even less certain than she'd been before that she wanted to become intimately involved with Damien.

Now *this* was a moral dilemma!

"So, what's your decision?" Reed asked from across the table.

Celia blinked at him over her menu, wondering if the man could read her mind. "I—er—beg your pardon?"

He nodded toward his own menu. "Have you decided what you want for dinner?"

"Dinner. Oh, yes, of course. I'll—um—I'll have..." She glanced down at the menu and read off the first entree that caught her eye. "Baked snapper."

"Sounds good," Reed said, closing his own menu. "I'll have that, too."

They placed their orders, selected a wine, were served salads and bread. A noticeable silence fell between them when they were alone again. Celia found her eyes turning once again toward the inviting expanse of moon-washed beach. She could so easily imagine herself walking hand in hand along that beach in that soft moonlight. Problem was, she couldn't seem to decide whose hand she'd most like to be holding.

"You've gotten very quiet," Reed commented, reclaiming her attention. "Tired?"

"A little," she admitted. "I was just noticing how beautiful the beach looks tonight."

He followed her gaze. "It is nice. Would you like to take a walk after dinner?"

She almost choked on a bite of bread. "Maybe," she murmured after taking a quick sip of wine.

"Tell me more about yourself, Celia. All I know is that you live in Percy, Arkansas, and you work in a bank. Have you always lived in Percy?"

"Since I was a toddler," she replied, sternly telling herself to stop being foolish and just talk to the man. "I was born in Little Rock, but then my dad had a chance to go to work for a small counseling center in Percy. He's a psychologist," she added.

"You said you have an older sister?"

"Rachel. She's eight years older than I am, very serious and responsible, but we've always been close. When I was just finishing my junior year of high school, my dad took another job in St. Louis. I couldn't bear to move away before my senior year, so I stayed in Percy with Rachel and her first husband, Ray, and their baby daughter, Paige. It worked out great."

"She still lives in Percy?"

"Yes. Ray died in a car accident a few years ago, leaving her with two small children to raise, Paige and Aaron. She's had a rough time, but she's getting married again soon and she's very happy about it. His name's Seth Fletcher, he's an attorney, and he's crazy about Rachel. I'm thrilled for her."

"Do you have any other siblings?"

"A brother, Cody. He's five years older than I am. He's single, and part owner of a country-western dinner and dance club in Percy. He's a real joker, always cutting up and doing impulsive things to make the rest of us laugh. You'd like him. Everyone does."

Reed studied her face in the candlelight from their flowers-and-tapers centerpiece. "And what about you? Are you more like Rachel or Cody?"

"That should be obvious," she answered wryly. "As much as I'd love to be more like Cody, I seem to be more like Rachel all the time. I mean, Cody would have found lots of things to do here alone. He'd already know everyone, probably would have organized beach parties and volleyball games and exchanged addresses and phone numbers with all the other guests. Rachel, on the other hand, would have taken long walks alone on the beach and read a good book or two—which is basically what I've been doing.''

Reed chuckled. "Not quite. You did kidnap me this afternoon, and you hardly know me. That sounds more like Cody.''

"True,'' Celia said, brightening. "Rachel never would have done anything like that. Of course, Rachel wouldn't be here in the first place. She was really opposed to me—'' Suddenly realizing what she was about to reveal, she stumbled and fell silent, reaching quickly for her wineglass again.

Reed had lifted an eyebrow. "Rachel didn't want you to come?'' he prodded gently, a bit too casually.

Celia shrugged. "She doesn't particularly like Damien,'' she admitted.

Reed definitely looked interested now. "How come?''

Shaking her head, Celia tried to downplay the admission. "It's silly, really. Rachel's never even met Damien. For some reason, they've never been in the same place at the same time.'' She didn't bother to add that she'd invited Damien to meet her family on more than one occasion; Damien had always politely declined, adding ruefully that family gatherings always made him nervous. "She's simply been reading too many juicy scandal sheets. I keep telling her they're exaggerated, but you know how over-protective older sisters can be. Brothers, too. Cody's almost as bad as Rachel.''

"No, I really don't know about older siblings. I was an only child.''

"Your parents' pride and joy, I'd bet,'' Celia teased, relieved to turn the conversation away from herself.

"What makes you think that?''

"Well, they did give you this vacation. Quite a nice birthday present."

"I suppose you're right."

"Have you ever been married?"

Reed seemed startled by the question. "No. Why?"

Celia shrugged. "I know less about you than you do about me now. Only that you're a tax accountant from Cleveland and that you like history. What else would I find interesting?"

"Nothing much," Reed answered self-deprecatingly. "I live a quiet life, on the whole. I have a few good friends with whom I socialize, and a job I enjoy. I like to read and visit museums and historical sites, as you already know. I do a little wood carving, but I'm not very good at it. Just an average sort of guy, I guess."

Celia almost sighed. An average sort of guy. Just as she'd suspected.

She wondered if any of his "few good friends" were women. She wondered if there was any woman who was an especially good friend. She wondered why she couldn't seem to stop wondering.

"You've never been married, either, I take it?" Reed asked after their entrées had been placed in front of them.

"No. Not even close." He probably wouldn't believe how little experience she'd actually had with men.

And all because she'd been waiting so long for one who was so much more than "average."

She suddenly discovered that she wasn't quite as hungry as she'd thought when she'd placed her order. She picked up her fork and made a determined effort to eat, telling herself she was being silly.

What possible reason could there be for her to suddenly feel restless and discontented? As though there was something she needed, but couldn't quite name. And it was especially foolish for her to think that Reed Hollander could do anything about it.

Celia was just beginning to regain her equilibrium when Reed asked, from seemingly out of the blue, "How long have you known Damien Alexander?"

Again, Celia felt herself growing self-conscious, and inexplicably anxious to clarify her relationship with Damien. "Almost a year now. We met when he started coming into the bank where I work. He's thinking about building a new resort near Percy, and he wants to involve the local businesses as much as possible."

"An Alexander resort in Percy, Arkansas?" Reed sounded skeptical. "Forgive me, but that wouldn't have been a location I would have expected."

"I know. Everyone's been surprised that he's even considering the possibility. But it makes sense the way Damien explains it. The area is really beautiful—unspoiled, natural, with several beautiful lakes and rivers available for water sports, lots of golf courses, and mountainsides for hiking and hang gliding. It's reasonably close to Little Rock and Memphis for shopping and dining, only a couple of hours away from the riverboat casinos in Tunica, Mississippi, and from Branson, Missouri for the music shows that are so popular now. Damien says it's a location with a great deal of potential."

"Sounds reasonable," Reed conceded. "I hadn't looked at it that way."

"You've never been to the area," she pointed out. "Arkansas has a lot more to offer than most people suspect—or than the national press has led them to believe, lately."

"Is that why you've stayed so close to home? Because you love the area?"

"That, and to be close to my sister and brother," she replied. "But lately..."

"Lately...?" Reed urged when she fell quiet.

She shrugged. "Lately I've realized that there are a lot of other places to see and experience."

"Places Damien Alexander could show you?"

Celia couldn't quite read Reed's expression. He looked suddenly distant, disapproving. Much like Rachel did whenever she mentioned Damien. And Celia reacted the same way with Reed that she did with Rachel. Defensively.

"Damien and I are friends. We have dinner together when he's in town, see an occasional show in Little Rock, talk on the phone occasionally when he's busy at his other resorts. When I told him I'd heard about this area and had always wanted to see it, he asked me here as his guest. We're hardly trotting the globe together just because I'm visiting one of his smaller resorts."

"Don't be so prickly. I was just making conversation."

Celia cut irritably into her fish. "I wasn't being prickly. I was just...explaining."

"You don't owe me any explanations."

"I'm well aware of that." She avoided his eyes as she concentrated on her dinner.

They picked up the conversation a few minutes later. They kept it light, impersonal, and carefully avoided any mention of Damien Alexander.

After dinner, Reed asked again if Celia would like to take a walk on the beach with him. Maybe visit the lounge, which provided live music for dancing on weekends.

Standing beside him on the path outside the restaurant, Celia hesitated, wistfully replaying her earlier fantasy. And then she shook her head. "I have a few calls to make this evening. Thank you for going sightseeing with me, Reed. I had a very nice afternoon."

"So did I. I'm glad you kidnapped me."

She smiled. "Good night."

"Would you like me to walk you to your room?"

"No, that's not necessary."

He nodded, not bothering to argue. "Then I'll see you around."

"Yes, of course. Good night," she repeated, and turned away. Reed made no effort to detain her.

As she walked alone to her elegant suite, she tried to convince herself that she hadn't wanted anything more from this evening. Or from Reed Hollander.

Her life was complicated enough at the moment.

Chapter Four

Reed ended up walking the beach alone after discreetly making sure that Celia did, indeed, return to her rooms after dinner.

He stayed right at the edge of the gently lapping Gulf waters, his shoes sinking slightly into the wet sand beneath them. He was aware of the fragrance of nearby flowers, the taste of salt in the steady breeze, the sounds of the waves and the glow of full moonlight. He knew he wasn't the only one out enjoying the evening, but the few others kept to themselves, reinforcing the illusion of solitude.

He was well aware that, had he been a bit more tactful with Celia, he wouldn't be walking alone.

He shouldn't have sounded so judgmental when they'd talked about Damien Alexander. Celia had already claimed the guy as her friend; was, after all, here as Alexander's guest. Reed had already known she became defensive about him. But still, he'd found himself going cold and stiff when

Alexander's name came up, and Celia had obviously noticed.

Real smooth, Hollander.

His job was to observe, not to form judgments. He was supposed to subtly pump Celia for useful information, something he had no hope of doing if his behavior set her guard up. Celia wasn't going to let anything slip about Alexander running illegal shipments of stolen military weapons if she was too busy depicting him as just a nice, upstanding guy who'd been viciously maligned by the gossip sheets.

Reed was having one hell of a time getting a handle on her. She'd admitted that she'd been bored, restless with her sheltered, small-town life, which could indicate that she'd turn to the quick money and exciting subterfuge to be found by cooperating with Alexander. Yet he'd seen how uncomfortable she'd been here for the past few days, even with Alexander's entire staff all but standing on their heads to please her.

She hadn't asked for special treatment, hadn't ordered the most expensive items from the restaurant menu, even though it had been made clear that her meals were on the house. She hadn't even visited the expensive gift shop, at least not that Reed had seen.

She'd spent the entire afternoon with him, touring historical sites. And she'd seemed as happy eating hamburgers as she was with Alexander's gourmet cuisine, as comfortable playing miniature golf as lounging by the resort pool. Why? Because she really was bored, lonely, feeling out of place?

Or—he scowled—was it possible that he'd somehow raised suspicions? That Celia had been instructed to find out more about him, the same way he was trying to find out more about her? Had she been pumping him for information when she'd asked questions about him, rather than displaying any personal interest?

The possibility made his fists clench.

Damn it, he should have thought of it before.

Not that he'd told her anything she shouldn't know, of course. His fascination with her hadn't made him that careless.

Movement from his left caught his attention. Without turning his head, he checked it out. A couple stood beneath a scraggly palm tree, locked together, mouths fused, hands roaming. Reed turned his eyes forward and kept walking. And continued to think of Celia.

Celia woke early again Saturday morning, facing another day with nothing in particular to do. Though she'd spent the evening before telling herself to stay away from Reed Hollander in order to avoid any unwanted complications, she found herself thinking of him before she'd even finished her shower. She knew he, too, would be at loose ends today. He would probably be agreeable to spending time with her again.

"Some liberated woman you are," she grumbled at the dark-haired, blue-eyed woman in the bathroom mirror. "Can't you have a good time all by yourself?"

But the problem was, she couldn't. Celia just wasn't a loner.

She could find someone else to spend the day with, of course. Yesterday morning she'd chatted for a few minutes with two middle-aged sisters who were vacationing together, and who'd hinted that they wouldn't mind if she joined them for a shopping jaunt into Mexico or a couple of hours bird-watching on the untamed central section of Padre Island. She'd probably have a very nice time with them.

Of course, she'd had a very nice time with Reed yesterday.

Shaking her head in frustration at her own behavior, she did her makeup, dressed quickly in a navy-and-white, blouse-and-skort outfit, and brushed her hair into a gleaming, straight curtain to her shoulders. She was hungry, she decided. She would think about her plans for the day during breakfast.

She was detained twice on her way to the restaurant. She had hardly left her building before she crossed paths with Enrique Torres, who greeted her warmly and then tried to talk her into joining him and his wife for an afternoon of local sight-seeing. Celia graciously declined, fibbing that she'd already made plans for the afternoon.

Torres was frowning worriedly when Celia walked away; she wondered if he suspected that she would be spending another day with Reed. And if he did, why should he care? Surely Damien didn't expect the resort manager to chaperone any women friends who happened to be at the resort without Damien!

Celia had taken only a few more steps toward the restaurant when the resort social director, Mindi Kellogg, all but chased her down from across the common, calling her name in a shrill voice. "Miss Carson! Miss Carson!"

Celia paused reluctantly, aware of a faint grumble of protest from her stomach. "Yes?"

"I want to personally invite you to join a group of us for an excursion this afternoon. It's going to be so much fun. We're visiting the University of Texas–Pan American Coastal Studies Laboratory at Isla Blanca Park to see the aquariums and the shell collection. From there we'll be stopping at Sea Turtle, Inc. to learn about endangered sea turtles. It's a fascinating afternoon, I can assure you. One of our most popular activities."

"It sounds like a lot of fun," Celia said, "but—"

"If that doesn't interest you, we have a shuttle that will take you to Matamoros, Mexico. It's only a thirty-minute trip. Have you been, yet?"

"No, I—"

The blonde grinned and patted Celia's arm. "Oh, you'd love it. The markets are fascinating, and the museums are very interesting."

"Thank you, Mindi, but I—"

"Or perhaps you'd rather take a guided horseback tour of the island. The stables provide a—"

"No, thank you," Celia interrupted, trying to speak firmly without actually being rude. She was growing increasingly irritated by the staff's efforts to keep her occupied. She didn't like feeling as though her actions were being monitored, her choices limited. "It's very nice of you to offer, but I have other plans for today."

"But, Miss Carson, we—"

"Celia." A familiar deep voice overrode Mindi's squeak of protest. A large, warm hand fell on Celia's shoulder. "I'm sorry I'm late. Must have overslept. Are you ready for breakfast?"

Celia looked up gratefully, meeting Reed's sympathetic smile. "Yes, I'm starving," she said fervently.

He nodded to the openmouthed social director. "Good morning, Miss Kellogg. Nice day, isn't it?"

He left her sputtering an answer as he all but towed Celia toward the restaurant.

"You looked as though you were in need of rescue," he said before Celia could speak, as soon as they were out of the social director's hearing. "What was she trying to do, sign you up for a talent show or something? A bungee jumping tournament?"

"No, she wanted to introduce me to endangered sea turtles or take me shopping in Mexico," Celia corrected ruefully. "I'm sure both would be interesting, but—"

"But not with Mindi standing on the sidelines cheering
you on, right?"

"She is a bit cheerleaderish. I'm sure she means well,
though," Celia added quickly, feeling guilty for making fun
of the other woman.

"Too perky for my tastes," Reed said with a shake of his
dark head. "All that bubbly energy and enthusiasm makes
my teeth hurt."

Celia giggled. "I was trying to be nice," she reproved
him.

He shrugged. "I'd rather eat. Are you really starving, or
was that just an excuse?"

"No, I'm really hungry. I was just on my way to breakfast."

"There's no reason for us to eat alone, is there?"

She hesitated, and looked up to find him watching her
with an intentness that belied his light tone. Since she
couldn't think of any good reason why they shouldn't have
breakfast together—none she could have explained, anyway—she smiled and shook her head. "No."

Reed looked pleased with her answer.

Reed seemed to go out of his way to be entertaining during their leisurely breakfast, and he succeeded. Celia found
herself forgetting her reservations and chatting with him as
easily as an old friend.

They had almost finished their meal before she realized
how closely they were being watched.

The staff was being discreet—sort of. They weren't exactly staring at Celia and Reed. But they were watching,
and Celia wondered if this shift had been told that she and

Reed had been together for dinner last evening. Were they speculating whether she and Reed had spent the entire night together?

The only restaurant employee who didn't seem overly curious was their waiter, a good-looking young African-American with an engaging smile. The service he gave them was nothing more than briskly professional—which was a great relief since Celia was so painfully aware of the more open curiosity from the others.

This was getting ridiculous. She was *not* the personal property of Damien Alexander, despite what his staff might think. Or was she being completely paranoid?

She looked across the table. "I need to get away from this place today, Reed. Are you interested?"

"Tired of being the center of attention?"

She widened her eyes. "You've noticed it, too? That everyone seems to be watching us? I thought—I hoped I was imagining it."

He shook his head. "You aren't imagining it."

"I don't know why they're doing this. It's not as though I'm all that interesting."

"They're guarding the boss's interests," Reed explained with a faint smile that didn't quite reach his eyes.

She frowned. "That's stupid. Damien and I aren't—we haven't even—we're only friends," she concluded awkwardly, wondering how many times she had to repeat it. And whether Reed believed her any more than anyone else seemed to.

Reed studied her for what felt like a long time. And then his smile deepened, becoming just a shade more genuine. "Where would you like to go?"

"Anywhere," she said in quick relief. "How far are we from San Antonio?"

"It would take about three, maybe three-and-a-half hours by car, I think. Why?"

"I've never been there, have you?"

He shook his head in the negative, though he wasn't looking at her, but at the nearly empty cup of coffee in front of him.

"I've heard it's a nice place to visit. Lots of things to do. And the Alamo's there," she added enticingly. "That should be right up your alley."

"You'd think so, wouldn't you?"

"Or we could do something else," she said, uncertain of his reaction to her initial suggestion. "We could drive into Mexico or maybe up the coast to Corpus Cristi or—"

"San Antonio sounds good," Reed said, lifting his gaze to hers. "We should probably leave soon if we're going to have enough time."

Something in his eyes still bothered her. She cocked her head and looked at him closely. "Reed, are you sure you want to? I'd understand if you have other plans. Really."

"I don't have other plans. I'd like to spend the day with you," Reed said, and there was no doubting the sincerity of his voice.

She relaxed. "Good. I'll go get my purse."

"Meet you in fifteen minutes."

She glanced up to find two waiters watching them. She shivered. "Make it ten."

He followed her gaze, then turned back to her with an understanding nod. "Ten," he agreed.

Though she felt rather foolish, Celia was relieved that he agreed with her so easily.

She was growing more anxious by the minute to get away from the Alexander resort, if only for the day.

The drive to San Antonio was a pleasant one. Comfortable. Reed had insisted that Celia bring along a lightweight jacket, knowing the unpredictability of that area in early November, but they quickly discovered that she didn't need the extra warmth. The temperature was in the low eighties when they arrived, not much cooler than Padre Island. Celia laughed and declared that the weather was cooperating with her crusade to make sure Reed had fun on his birthday vacation.

She added that she was glad they'd gotten an early start. There was so much to do, she enthused. So many fascinating things to see.

Though he'd been to San Antonio quite a few times before for various reasons, Reed found himself viewing the city through Celia's eyes, and felt almost as though he were really seeing it for the first time. At the Alamo, for example.

Many tourists were disappointed when they first saw the Alamo. Expecting an impressive structure in a true old-West setting, they found, instead, that the old mission was now shadowed on every side by hotels and shopping malls and tourist booths. The Alamo compound, bordered by a surprisingly low rock wall, contained a museum, a theater, a shrine and a souvenir shop stocked with Alamo key chains, drinking glasses, postcards and faux coonskin caps.

A sign outside the chapel everyone associated with the Alamo—the original mission *San Antonio de Valero*—requested that visitors enter quietly, in respect of those who'd died there. Inside, neatly lettered informational signs hung on the pocked walls, finger-smudged glass boxes held historical artifacts such as Davy Crockett's razor and William Travis's ring, and discreetly placed containers solicited donations from tourists for the maintenance of the grounds, for which the Daughters of the Republic of Texas received no state or government funding.

A uniformed park employee stood behind the reception desk to answer questions until the next scheduled historical lecture. Gawking tourists shuffled around the foot-polished rock floor and read the signs aloud. A tiny Japanese toddler dashed squealing through the main room, pursued by his embarrassed mother.

Reed had been one of those disappointed by his first visit to the landmark. This hadn't looked to him at all like the place where John Wayne had led his fellow actors to a dramatic and glorious defeat in the movie; he'd later learned that the set of the movie still stood as a tourist attraction in Bracketville, Texas. Of course, Reed had only been a teenager still dazzled by that old movie the first time he'd visited the real Alamo. Now, as an adult, he felt more respect for this structure, built in 1758, that had served as such an important symbol since its bloody capture in 1836.

Realizing that he was suddenly standing alone in the center of the chapel, he looked around for Celia. He found her in front of the William Travis display case, reading the famous appeal for aid that Travis had written during his ill-fated stand against a Mexican army of thousands.

"'I shall never surrender or retreat,'" she read in a low, husky voice when Reed moved to stand beside her. "'Victory or death.'"

She looked up at him, then, and her blue eyes were brightened by a sheen of tears. "Can you imagine being so dedicated to a cause that you're willing to die for it?" she whispered. "One-hundred-and-eighty-six men died here, because freedom meant more to them than life itself. They were true heroes, weren't they?"

"And almost six hundred Mexicans died here believing they were preserving the glory of their own country," Reed reminded her gently. "Many of them were just young soldiers with dreams and families and the duty to follow the orders they'd been given. They were no more anxious to die than the men inside these walls, and yet their names aren't recorded here as brave heroes. Obviously, I support the cause of freedom, and greatly admire the courage of the men who died for it. But dehumanizing the enemy is one of the greatest evils of war, one we should always try to resist.''

Celia looked thoughtful. ''I hadn't considered it that way. We tend to view the great historical battles as good against evil, right against wrong. But it all comes down to individuals, doesn't it?''

''This 'history stuff' can be pretty interesting, after all, can't it?'' he teased her gently.

She gave him a smile that made his head swim. ''It is when I'm with you,'' she said.

Reed was forced to clear his throat before he could speak again. ''Ready to move on?''

After one last glance at the display case, Celia nodded. ''I'm ready.''

Celia was disappointed to learn that Sea World was closed in November, even on weekends. ''I would have liked to have seen Shamu,'' she said with a sigh.

Reed fought an immediate impulse to try to arrange a special showing of the famed killer whale just for her. He couldn't do that, of course, even if he wanted to—but for some reason he didn't want to examine too closely, he hated to see her disappointed. ''Maybe you'd like to go to Fiesta Texas, instead?''

She looked intrigued. ''What's that?''

''An amusement park built into an old rock quarry. You know, rides and shows and arcade games and junk food. There's a huge wooden roller coaster that's supposed to be world class. Very popular place. Want to go?''

She seemed surprised at how easily he described the park. "I thought you said you'd never been to San Antonio."

Reed tugged at his open shirt collar. "I've heard about it from friends."

"Oh." She considered the offer for a moment, then shook her head. "Why don't we just explore San Antonio, instead?"

Reed was secretly relieved. Theme parks weren't really his thing. And roller coasters inevitably made him queasy. Still, he would have ridden this one with Celia, if she'd asked. After seeing her tears in the Alamo, there was very little he could have denied her today.

"*Damn it, Hollander, what are you doing?*" he could almost hear his partner asking.

He wouldn't have had a clue how to respond.

They spent the afternoon exploring two of the other old missions in the area—*Mission Nuestra Señora de la Purisima Concepcion* and *Mission San Jose y San Miguel de Aquayo*—and the Witte Museum, which closed for the day before they could begin to do justice to all the exhibits in it. They talked easily and at length about the artifacts they were seeing, Reed sharing his extensive knowledge of history, Celia asking questions and forming her own opinions about the stories he told. Despite her self-proclaimed disinterest in history, Reed could tell that she enjoyed the outing. She walked from one exhibit to another with avid, unflagging interest.

His love of history was one of the few things he'd told her about himself that was true. He really *had* considered becoming a history teacher at one time, until a good friend had persuaded him to give law enforcement a try. He'd displayed a natural aptitude for the job, and had eventually worked his way into the Treasury Department, working in the Bureau of Alcohol, Tobacco and Firearms. Instead of facing classrooms of bored teenagers, he spent his days tracking down illicit shipments of stolen military weapons and ammunition, and those who profited from the sales.

He'd been in danger on more than one occasion, had lost several good friends, but on the whole, he liked his job. Enjoyed the rush, the satisfaction of bringing down those who profited from the loss of human life.

He wasn't enjoying this assignment. He didn't like looking into Celia's seemingly trusting blue eyes and lying through his teeth. He didn't like wondering if she was as naive and upright as she seemed, or if she had let greed pull her into a transaction that could ultimately lead to another bloody disaster like the one in Waco, which Reed still couldn't think about without shuddering. He'd lost friends in that fiasco. He didn't want to lose others in central Arkansas.

Afternoon was fading into early evening when Celia spotted the forty-foot-high cowboy boots outside Saks Fifth Avenue at North Star Mall when Reed drove past while showing her a bit more of the city. A light came into her eyes that Reed hadn't seen at the museums.

He shook his head and turned the Mercedes into the parking deck without even asking if she wanted to stop. There was just something about women and shopping malls he would never understand.

Celia was a window shopper, he quickly discovered. She loved peering into each intriguing display, admiring the merchandise, at times unable to resist touching, but she didn't seem overwhelmingly compelled to actually buy anything. Reed suspected part of her reserve was due to lack of resources, particularly when she gasped audibly at one high price tag.

"Can you imagine spending that much just for a dress?" she whispered, shaking her dark head and tugging him away from the department.

"I don't buy a lot of dresses, personally," he answered dryly, making her giggle.

He smiled in response, but his mind was filled with doubts. Was she hoping to afford dresses like that after concluding her dealings with Alexander? Or was she hoping Alexander would take care of her purchases in the future? And if she was really intent on reeling in Alexander, why the hell was she spending this much time with *him?* Reed hadn't bought her anything except a fajita combo platter for lunch, yet she seemed to be enjoying his company.

Or was she only killing time until Alexander returned?

"Reed?" Celia sounded as though she'd spoken his name several times.

He blinked. "What?"

"Are you okay? You're frowning as though you have a headache, or something."

He gave her a reassuring smile. "No, I'm fine. It's getting late, though, and we have that long drive ahead of us. We should probably head back toward the resort."

"But we haven't even seen the River Walk, yet," she protested. "We were saving it until after sundown, remember? Surely you don't want to leave San Antonio without even seeing the River Walk."

Again, he found himself unable to resist the appeal in her eyes. "I guess it doesn't matter when we get back," he said. "It isn't as though either of us has to get up early in the morning."

Her own smile was blinding. "No, there's no reason at all to hurry. Besides, I'm hungry. I'd love to eat at an outdoor table beside the river, wouldn't you?"

He couldn't do anything but agree.

Celia smiled at him again, and took his arm in a warm, companionable gesture that made his pulse rate climb. "Think you can find the way back downtown?" she asked.

"I think I'll manage," he answered, wishing he didn't sound quite so hoarse.

special.

Chapter Five

As Celia had wanted, they dined at a popular restaurant
on the river. The temperatures had fallen with the onset of
darkness, so she'd worn her jacket, but it was still a nice
evening for dining beneath the old-fashioned streetlamps
that lined the narrow river. Shallow tour boats passed occasionally, some containing tables for more adventurous
diners.

The river was lined on either side with restaurants, clubs,
boutiques, hotels, a specialty mall. The muted strains of
several types of music drifted on the fragrant air, inviting
them to explore and sample. Celia could hardly concentrate on her food for taking in the sights and sounds and
smells and sensations around them.

"Isn't this wonderful?" she asked Reed, smiling across
the table at him.

Looking up from his mesquite-grilled quail, he glanced around and nodded. "It's nice," he said, with the understated simplicity she'd come to expect from him.

Funny how comfortable she was with him, she mused as she turned back to her own grilled shrimp dinner. Hard to imagine she'd actually met him only yesterday. She could hardly believe she'd been so forward with him—dragging him off on an excursion only a few hours after he introduced himself, pulling him away again today. She'd always made friends quickly, but this was different. This was... special.

She studied him from beneath her lashes. Reed was a very nice man, she'd decided. Easygoing. Undemanding. Pleasant. She could hardly imagine him losing him temper, or being deliberately unkind.

Her family would probably love him.

She sighed. If only he didn't remind her of everything she'd convinced herself she didn't want in a man. He was so staid and practical, so serious and cautious. He'd probably be the overprotective type, as well—like her family. Like her late brother-in-law. Nice, upstanding, admirable—but without an ounce of adventure in his soul.

"Celia, if you sigh one more time I'm going to think you've sprung a slow leak," Reed teased her. "What's wrong?"

She shook her head quickly, as though to clear it. "Nothing. I'm just sorry our day is coming to an end. It's been so nice."

"We could always spend the night here, in San Antonio," he suggested cautiously. "See some of the other local attractions tomorrow."

She searched his face, wondering what, exactly, he meant by the invitation. Was he really only suggesting that they extend their friendly sightseeing excursion? Separate rooms, no strings, no expectations?

Or was he hinting that he wanted to spend the night with her? Together. One room. One bed.

She honestly didn't have a clue.

Not for the first time, she regretted her sheltered upbringing, blaming that inexperience for her inability to understand Reed now. She wasn't quite sure how to respond. She didn't want to lead him on—nor did she want to make assumptions that could prove embarrassing for both of them if she was wrong.

It seemed safest to smile, shake her head, and say, "That sounds really nice, but I guess we'd better go back to the resort. My family might call, and they'd worry if I wasn't there."

He nodded, apparently unaffected by her decision. "Fine. We'd better plan to leave here no later than 10 p.m. Even then, it will be well after midnight before we get back to the island."

"All right. Will you be too tired to drive? I'm afraid I don't drive very well late at night."

"I'll drive," he assured her.

"You won't be too tired?" she persisted, and then wondered if she wanted him to talk her into staying, after all.

He shook his head. "I've been known to keep late hours—especially during tax season," he added with a slight smile. "I'll be fine. Now, how about dessert?"

True to their plans, they left San Antonio behind at just after 10 p.m. Buckled into the passenger seat, Celia was rather quiet during the early part of the trip. Reed reached out and tuned the radio to a soft-rock channel, leaving her to her thoughts as he concentrated on his own.

He wasn't immune to the pleasures of driving the expensive, powerful car—nor to a faint sense of guilt at helping himself to the property of a man he fully intended to destroy.

"Celia?" he asked after they'd been traveling for nearly an hour in near silence.

"Mmm?" She sounded half asleep, though her eyes were open.

"When were you planning to go home?"

"I've got another week of vacation," she murmured. "I hadn't really intended to spend two full weeks here, but of course I didn't know Damien would be called away so quickly. I considered leaving this weekend, but Damien wants me to stay a few more days."

Reed felt the muscles tense at the back of his neck. He really hated the way Celia said the other guy's name in such a comfortably familiar manner. "I'm sure he was disappointed that he couldn't be here with you this past week," he said noncommittally.

"He said he was. I understood, though. As I pointed out to him, there was no way he could have predicted the storm that hit his resort in the Caribbean. I'm sure he assumes I've been having a great time relaxing and being pampered by his staff at the resort."

"He doesn't know you very well if he thinks you'd be content for long to sit around doing nothing." Reed couldn't help pointing it out.

Celia shrugged. "He doesn't know me that well, actually. We met some time ago, but we haven't spent much time together. One of the purposes of this visit was so that we could get to know each other better."

"Testing the waters, as it were?" he asked, keeping his tone bland.

There was a short silence before she answered. "Just getting to know each other better," she repeated, a bit curtly.

He told himself to shut up. Reminded himself that his only interest in Celia's relationship with Alexander was a professional one. And still he heard himself saying, "I think you should go home, Celia. Tomorrow, preferably."

She turned her head to stare at him. "What are you talking about?"

Cursing himself for a fool, he doggedly continued, "Alexander isn't your type. He goes through pretty young women like you the way some people devour a can of peanuts."

Celia groaned loudly. "Not you, too. I would have thought that you, at least, would be above believing gossip and rumors."

"You have to admit the guy lives in the fast lane, Celia. He isn't like the people you know back home in Percy. This isn't just an average, ordinary Joe we're talking about."

"I know he isn't average and ordinary," Celia retorted heatedly. "That's one of the things I like most about him!"

Reed exhaled in frustration. "Look, I know this is none of my business—"

"You're right," she cut in flatly. "It isn't. Damien is my friend, Reed. I like him. And I don't think it's right of you to put him down when he isn't here to defend himself—especially when you're driving his car!"

That effectively silenced him. Reed tightened his hands on the steering wheel and stared grimly at the road ahead. The road to Damien Alexander's resort.

After a few minutes, Celia reached out to touch Reed's arm, startling him. "I'm sorry," she said quietly. "I shouldn't have snapped at you. I know you're only concerned about me—the same way my family is, I suppose.

But you should all realize that I'm old enough to know what I'm doing, and to take care of myself. I'm not under any delusions about Damien. I know exactly what he is, but I like him. He's my friend. Okay?''

"I'm sorry I interfered," Reed answered stiffly.

"Don't sulk, Reed. You're my friend, too, and we've had such a lovely day. Don't spoil it, please."

He sighed and patted her hand where it rested on his arm. "Sorry. I won't say any more about it."

"I appreciate it. I have enough mother hens watching out for me, Reed. I really don't need another one."

It was the first time in his life Reed had been called a "mother hen." And he found that he hated it.

There was nothing familial about his growing feelings for Celia. Nothing rational, or cautious, or calculated. He wanted her, regardless of whether or not she'd been sleeping with Damien Alexander. He was even losing interest in how deeply she might have been involved with the arrangements for the weapons sale. Trying to find excuses for her—her youth, her naïveté, her vulnerability.

That was the sort of thinking that had gotten friends killed. The kind that could get *him* killed if he didn't stop it.

He shot a sideways look at Celia. She had laid her head back on the seat and was looking pensively out the windshield. She looked tired. A little sad. Sweet.

You're an idiot, Hollander. A thick-skulled, hormone-driven, prize-winning idiot. And if Kyle knew about this, you'd never hear the end of it.

The thought of his cynical, blunt-spoken partner made him look sharply forward again. He spent the remainder of the drive reminding himself that he had a job to do. When it ended, he would never see Celia Carson again. He would do well to keep that in mind.

* * *

Celia was asleep by the time they reached the resort, had been for almost an hour. Reed roused her gently, then half led, half carried her to her door. She gave him a sleepy smile as he slipped the key into the lock. "I had a very nice time today, Reed," she murmured, sounding like a schoolgirl coming home from a movie date. "Thank you."

"My pleasure." He pushed the door open and nudged her through. He shot a quick look around the sitting room, taking in the quiet elegance. Alexander provided very well for his special guests, he couldn't help thinking grimly.

Celia stood in the center of the luxurious room, swaying a bit on her feet. "It's very late, isn't it?"

"Very. Get some rest. I'll see you tomorrow."

"Okay. Will you be having breakfast?"

"Probably."

"Maybe I'll sleep late," she said around a yawn.

He smiled. "Sounds like a good idea."

"What about you? Aren't you tired?"

"Like I said, I don't need much sleep." He tilted her chin up with one hand and studied her lightly flushed, heavy-eyed face. "Good night, Celia. Sleep well."

"Good night, Reed." She smiled up at him, trustingly. Too trustingly.

Deciding he was getting rather tired of being treated like a big brother, Reed bent his head and deliberately covered her mouth with his own.

Celia hesitated only a moment before responding. Her lips moved tentatively beneath his, and then with growing confidence. He deepened the kiss, allowing himself one lingering, appreciative taste of her before he finally, slowly drew away. "Good night," he repeated, hearing his own huskiness.

And then he left quickly, while he still could.

Celia was still standing openmouthed in the middle of the sitting room when he closed the door behind him. His last glance at her showed him that she suddenly looked wide awake.

Celia woke Sunday morning still tired, a bit achy... and thoroughly confused. She'd come to this resort to learn more about herself, and what she wanted. Now she felt even further from the answers than she'd been before.

Reed Hollander had kissed her. And something inside her had changed.

Shaking her head in quick rejection of that fanciful thought, she stepped beneath a hot, stinging shower. She lingered for a long time beneath the steamy spray, refusing to allow herself to think about Reed, or Damien, or anything else in particular. By the time she finally emerged from the bathroom, she felt somewhat more relaxed, more like herself.

She was also a bit homesick.

On an impulse, she pulled on a bathing suit, then donned a striped T-shirt and denim cutoffs over it. Maybe she'd spend some time on the beach today, she thought. Alone? Well—that remained to be seen.

And then she reached for the telephone, trying to decide who to call. Her mother? No, not when she was in this state of mind. Her mother would only worry. Rachel wouldn't be much better, though Celia wouldn't have minded hearing her older sister's calm, practical voice. Cody...well, as much as Celia loved her brother, she didn't know what she would say to him.

Almost without realizing her intentions, she found herself dialing a number that was as familiar to her as her own.

"Granny Fran?" she said a moment later. "Hi, it's Celia."

"How nice to hear from you," her grandmother said sincerely. "Are you back from your vacation?"

"No, I'm still in Texas. I just thought I'd call to say hello."

"I'm glad you did. Are you having a nice time?"

"It's a beautiful resort. You would love all the flowers. The weather's been perfect—can you believe it's warm enough for swimming here?"

"Sounds lovely, dear, but you didn't exactly answer my question. Are you having a nice time?"

"For the most part," Celia hedged. "It hasn't exactly turned out the way I expected."

"Oh?" Her grandmother sounded concerned. "Mr. Alexander isn't being a good host?"

"He's not even here. Hasn't been since I arrived." Celia gave a quick summary of the emergency that had called Damien away, and her conversation with him the day before. "He should be here tomorrow morning."

"I suppose you're looking forward to seeing him."

"Yes, of course," Celia answered, but only after a momentary hesitation.

"Sounds as though you may have changed your mind," Frances observed perceptibly.

Celia sighed. "I don't know. I really didn't have any specific plans when I came here, hadn't made any decisions about what direction I wanted my relationship with Damien to take. I just thought I'd take it a day at a time, get to know him a little better, learn more about his lifestyle. But then I met Reed, and now I'm confused again."

"Reed?"

"Yes." Celia moistened her lips. "He's a, er, another guest here. He's an accountant from Cleveland, vacationing alone. We've been doing some sightseeing together."

"And..."

"And...he's very nice. You'd like him, I think. He's rather quiet, and serious and courteous. He has a thing for history, and he's been teaching me a little about the history of this area. He makes it all sound very interesting."

"An accountant with a passion for history?" A note of amusement crept into Frances's voice. "Quite a change from your dashing jet-setting friend, Damien."

Celia grimaced. "I know. They couldn't be more opposite. I should be bored to tears when I'm with Reed, the way I am with so many of the guys back home. And yet..."

"And yet?" Frances prodded gently.

"I'm not."

"I see."

Celia ran a hand through her hair. "I wish I did."

Frances laughed softly. "Maybe you're just starting to realize that you aren't quite ready to tie yourself into a serious relationship, with Damien Alexander or anyone else at the moment. You're still a young woman, Celia. You have time to 'shop around' a bit before you make your selection."

"This from the woman who's been reminding me that I'm not getting any younger?" Celia teased. "Aren't you the one who has told me several times that you were married and had both your children by my age?"

"I just don't want you to make a decision you might regret," Frances replied, her own amusement gone. "I want you to have what I had, darling. A man you can love, who will love you in return. A soul mate."

"And how am I supposed to know when I meet this 'soul mate'?" Celia asked, as bewildered now as she'd been all morning.

"You just will. It won't necessarily be instant recognition, or a blinding flash of revelation, but there will come a point when you'll know. That's the way it happens in our family."

"Maybe I'll be the exception to the family tradition," Celia said wryly.

"I don't think so. I think there's a very special someone waiting for you, my darling. Someone with whom you will be very happy."

Celia chuckled and shook her head. "You always make me want to believe in impossible things, Granny Fran."

"'Why, sometimes I've believed as many as six impossible things before breakfast,'" her grandmother quoted, and Celia smiled mistily at the happy memories of sitting at Granny Fran's knee, listening to her read from *Alice's Adventures in Wonderland.*

"I love you, Granny Fran."

"I love you, too. Do you feel better?"

"Much." And it was true. Still confused, but better. She glanced at the clock on the nightstand and gasped. "Here I've kept you talking and you're going to be late for church."

"I won't be late. I'm already dressed. I've enjoyed talking to you, dear."

"Still, you'd better be going. I'll call you when I get back home, okay?"

"All right. Have a good time. And remember—you'll know when it's right for you."

"I hope you're right, Granny Fran," Celia murmured after disconnecting the call. "I really hope you're right."

It had been very late when Reed had finally gotten to sleep, which meant he slept later than he'd intended Sunday morning. He was awakened by the buzz of the telephone on the nightstand. He snatched it up, more than half expecting the caller to be Celia.

Instead, it was his partner's voice that greeted him. "Alexander's making arrangements to leave the island first thing in the morning."

"Which means he'll be back here tomorrow afternoon," Reed interpreted.

"You got it. Novotny's booked on a flight that leaves tomorrow evening. We have information that all the players should be gathered there by Wednesday at the latest. It's going down, partner. You ready?"

"I've been ready for the past week," Reed growled, running a hand over his stubbled jaw. "What do you think I've been doing here all this time, working on my tan?"

"Rumor has it you've been working on Alexander's woman. How *is* the PYT, Reed?"

"Who the hell's been watching me?" Reed demanded, sitting abruptly upright in the bed.

"No one's been watching you, Hollander. But we do have another agent there who's waiting for the meeting, remember? I talked to him yesterday—when I couldn't find you."

"I was out."

"So I heard. Seems you've been helping yourself to Alexander's fancy car as well as his lovely bed toy."

"Stop calling her that, damn it!"

There was a notable silence on the other end of the line. "What's going on, Reed?" Kyle asked more quietly.

"Nothing, okay? I just think everyone's misjudged Celia. My hunch is that she's nothing more than an innocent bystander, maybe a carefully planted pawn to make everything seem like business as usual for Alexander. She's in the wrong place at the wrong time, that's all."

"If you're right—and I still wouldn't put any money on it—then she sure as hell doesn't need to be there now."

"I know that. She won't even consider suggestions that she should go home now. She thinks Alexander's a great guy. Won't listen to a word against him."

"You are being discreet, aren't you, Reed?" Kyle sounded genuinely worried. "One wrong word, one hint of our presence there, could blow the whole operation."

"I know how to do my job," Reed answered coldly, very close to being genuinely angry with his longtime co-worker. "I just don't want to see anyone get hurt."

"That goes for you, too, my friend. It's not like you to lose your head over a—"

"*Don't* call her a PYT," Reed cut in. "And stop fretting, Kyle. I know what I'm doing."

And wasn't *that* a whopper of a lie? he asked himself as he hung up the phone a few moments later. He hadn't been fully in control of his actions since Celia Carson had taken that book out of his hands and "kidnapped" him.

He needed to be thinking about his job, preparing for the expected meeting—and yet all he could do was think of Celia. Wonder when he could be with her again. When he could kiss her again. And whether she'd cooperate as sweetly next time, when she was fully awake.

"Damn, Hollander," he muttered, shoving his sleep-tousled hair off his forehead. "What the hell *are* you doing?"

Celia was sitting on the side of a spectacular fountain in the resort's central courtyard, watching rainbow-hued koi swimming lazily in the shimmering pool, when a shadow fell over her. Her heart tripped and she looked around quickly, expecting to find Reed standing behind her. She couldn't lie to herself and pretend that she hadn't been hoping he would find her here. She'd been surreptitiously watching for him all morning, and had been discouraged that she hadn't yet seen him, even when she'd breakfasted alone in the restaurant.

Damien's secretary was standing over her, patiently waiting for her to notice him. "Oh," she said, trying to keep the disappointment out of her voice. "Hello, Evan."

"Mr. Alexander called," the dark young man said. "He said to tell you he'll be here early tomorrow afternoon."

Celia nodded. "Thank you. Was there anything else?"

"No, that's all. Umm...you have no plans for this afternoon?"

"Nothing in particular," she replied with a shrug. *Where are you, Reed?*

Evan cleared his throat. "Mr. Alexander was quite concerned that you haven't been enjoying your stay with us."

"He shouldn't have been. I've been treated very well here. I couldn't ask for better service," Celia assured him.

"Is there anything I can do for you now?"

"No, thank you. I was just enjoying the fountain. It's beautiful."

"Mr. Alexander had it shipped here from Italy."

Of course he had. Celia resisted a smile that Evan might have misinterpreted and tried to look suitably impressed.

"There's a complimentary showing of the new Julia Roberts film for resort guests this evening in the theater. Hors d'oeuvres and cocktails will be served...even popcorn, I believe," Evan added with a slight smile. "It begins at eight."

"Thank you. Maybe I'll go. I've been wanting to see that film."

He looked disproportionately pleased by her words. "I'm sure you'll enjoy it. I've heard it's excellent."

Celia smiled and nodded, wondering what he expected her to say next.

He shifted his weight, looked suddenly self-conscious, and tugged at his neatly knotted tie. "Well," he said heartily. "I'd better get back to work. There's some paperwork I have to finish this afternoon."

"On Sunday?"

"Oh, yes. Mr. Alexander is a very busy man," Evan said gravely. "He can't be bothered with all the detail work that I handle for him."

"But don't you ever take time off?"

"Of course I do. But with him having been gone this week, we're all a bit behind. I'll take extra time off when we catch up."

"You're a very dedicated employee, Evan," Celia told him, as somber as he was. "Damien's lucky to have you working for him."

Evan permitted himself a smile. "I consider myself very fortunate to be working for Mr. Alexander. All his employees feel that way. Now, if you'll excuse me, I must get back to it."

Amused, Celia watched Evan hurry away. Nice guy, she thought, but borderline hypertensive.

"Blind loyalty. Nice quality in an employee, if you can find it," Reed said dryly from behind her.

Celia swung around so quickly she almost ended up in the fountain. Reed reached out to steady her with a hand on her arm. "You startled me," she accused him unnecessarily. And undeservedly, she reminded herself guiltily. Hadn't she just been hoping he would appear?

"Sorry." But he didn't look particularly repentant. Actually, he looked great. His close-fitting, pale blue knit shirt emphasized his dark tan and nicely developed muscles, and the loose-fitting jeans hinted that he was in excellent condition below the waist, as well. At the moment, he didn't look at all like her concept of the average tax accountant.

"What are you doing?" he asked, while she was still surreptitiously admiring him.

She cleared her throat and looked hastily toward the fountain. "I was just watching the fish."

Reed glanced at the koi, then across the compound, and then turned back to her. "Cheerleader alert."

Celia blinked, then suddenly understood. She looked over her shoulder. Mindi Kellogg, the determinedly cheerful social director, was making a beeline toward them across the compound, clipboard in hand. "Oh, God. Now what?"

"Want to get out of here?"

"Yes," she said immediately.

He held out his hand. "Let's go to the beach."

"Sounds like an excellent idea." She placed her hand in his.

Chapter Six

Even though it was a weekend, the beach was pleasantly uncrowded. Reed claimed a large umbrella and two beach chairs, making one of his typical comments about keeping Celia out of the sun.

"You're tanned," she remarked, nodding toward his brown arm. "Why are you so concerned about me getting some sun?"

"You're lighter skinned," he replied promptly. "Statistics show that people with fairer skin tend to burn more easily, leading to a higher incidence of cell damage and skin cancer. One out of every—"

"Enough." She held up her hand in laughing protest. "I should have known an accountant would have a wealth of statistics to support his arguments."

Reed gave her an apologetic smile. "Job hazard."

"Yes, I'm sure. But if it makes you feel any better, I slathered myself in sun block this morning. The water-proof kind that's supposed to last for hours."

He nodded gravely. "Regular use of sun block is a smart habit, of course. But it still doesn't hurt to be careful."

"Are you ever *not* careful, Reed?" she asked just a bit wistfully.

He seemed to give her question deep consideration before he murmured, "Most of the time I am."

"And just what happens when you're not?" she asked, trying to tease.

He didn't smile. "I'll let you know."

That didn't make a lot of sense to her. She started to ask him to explain, but he forestalled her by asking if she was hungry. "We should have arranged to bring a picnic basket."

She shrugged. "We'll get fast food later. I'm not hungry now, are you?"

"No. Is that a bathing-suit strap peeking out of the neckline of your T-shirt?"

She smiled. "Yes."

"Want to swim?"

She glanced at his shirt and jeans. "You're hardly dressed for it."

In answer, he stood, kicked off his shoes and peeled off his shirt and jeans, revealing brief black swim trunks beneath. "Race you to the water," he said, and loped toward the surf.

Celia was left lying beneath the umbrella, her mouth open, her eyes wide.

For an accountant, she thought dazedly, Reed Hollander had one hell of a great body.

The water was cool, she discovered when she waded into the lapping waves until the water reached her knees. Reed was already some distance out, swimming steadily. He motioned for her to join her.

Celia hadn't mentioned it to him, but she'd never been swimming in saltwater before. She'd waded into plenty of freshwater lakes and creeks back home, had her toes nibbled by fish and turtles, dodged a water snake or two—but those were familiar creatures. She knew nothing about saltwater creatures, except what she'd read.

She pictured crabs and stingrays and jellyfish and fish with sharp teeth. She knew all of them were native to this area. Did they come this close to shore?

The sand shifted beneath her feet with another wave and she stumbled for balance. Her right foot came down on something hard. Something that moved. She squealed and jumped.

Reed was at her side instantly. "What is it?"

"I think I stepped on a crab."

He relaxed. "Hermit crab, probably. They're harmless."

"Oh." She minced cautiously a few feet deeper, letting the water lap at the bottom of her scarlet maillot. And then she stopped again. "Reed?"

He was watching her with an odd light in his hazel eyes. "Yeah?"

"Are there—er—sharks or anything around here?"

He laughed.

She scowled at him and planted her fists on her hips. "Don't laugh at me."

He motioned some distance down the beach, to a family of four or five kids who were splashing through the water like playful dolphins, while their parents watched closely from the sand. "Would those people let their kids swim out here if there were sharks?"

Feeling stupid, Celia shrugged. "I don't know."

He shook his head. "Don't tell me this is your first time all week to come out to the water."

"Well, yes," she admitted. "I've been swimming in the pool."

"You can swim in a pool back home in Arkansas," he teased, tugging at her hair. "You really aren't the adventurous type, are you, Celia?"

She sighed deeply. "I'm trying to be," she reminded him.

His sudden grin was positively wicked. She didn't have time to interpret it.

A moment later, she was underwater, having been bodily lifted and tossed lightly into a cresting wave.

She came up spitting salt and blinking furiously, her eyes stinging from the unfamiliar grittiness of the water. "Reed!" she wailed, slinging wet hair out of her face. "That was a really lousy thing to do."

He was still laughing. "Just trying to be of service, ma'am," he drawled. "You can't be adventurous half an inch at a time."

Her open palm hit the water at a slashing angle. His laugh turned to a sputter when the resulting stream hit him squarely in the face. And then he dove for her.

A laughing, gasping water battle ensued. Celia was at a definite disadvantage, due to her smaller size and her unfamiliarity with rolling waves and shifting sand. But she held her own, she decided in satisfaction.

Taking advantage of a perfect opportunity, she hooked a foot behind Reed's leg and tugged. He went down like a rock. But not before catching hold of her and dragging her with him.

They came up together, laughing, rolling in the waves, clinging to each other for balance.

And then the laughter faded.

Reed regained his footing slowly, his gaze locked with Celia's.

Her eyelashes beaded with water, her hair streaming down her back, she became suddenly aware of the feel of his wet, slick skin beneath her palms. He was warm. Hard. Strong.

His tan extended over every inch she could see of him. Water clung to the light dusting of hair that spread across his chest and narrowed downward toward his swim trunks. His wet hair clung to his head, darkened to almost black. Without his glasses, his hazel eyes were bright and piercing. Almost as though they could see right into her.

Celia was mesmerized, unable to move if she'd wanted to. Waves shoved gently against her, but Reed held her steady. She felt safe. And yet, at the same time, she felt deliciously panicky, her pulse racing, her skin tingling, her breathing shallow and rapid.

It seemed inevitable that he was going to kiss her. If he didn't, she thought she'd surely shatter from disappointment.

He didn't disappoint her.

He drew her closer, giving her every opportunity to pull away. She didn't even try. Her breasts brushed his chest, then he pulled her closer still, their wet bodies plastering together. The water lapped around Celia's rib cage, hitting Reed just above his waist. If there were any crabs or stingrays or jellyfish—or even sharks—Celia no longer cared. For all she knew just then, she and Reed could have been standing on a deserted island.

His mouth was cool, wet, salty. His tongue was warm and seeking. Celia parted her lips and welcomed him inside.

She didn't worry about who might be watching them. She didn't think about Damien. She didn't even ask herself what might happen next.

She simply enjoyed.

Reed drew away first. He sighed, kissed her nose, then lifted his head. "Celia?"

She was still drifting, her cheek resting now against his pounding heart. "Mmm?"

"Let's have a taco."

She blinked and frowned. "What?"

He loosened her arms from around his neck. "Lunch," he said firmly, not quite meeting her eyes. "I'm starving."

How could he possibly think about food? Here she was in his arms, a quivering bundle of soggy hormones, and Reed was talking tacos!

It took a moment for her to recover enough to appreciate his common sense. This was certainly not the time, or the place for necking, she reminded herself as she stumbled back toward the beach with him, steadied by his arm around her waist.

Maybe before the day ended, they would find the right time. And the right place.

She swallowed hard and concentrated on getting back to the beach umbrella without having her suddenly unsteady knees buckle beneath her.

They bought tacos and ate them on the beach. Celia tossed the trash into a convenient waste can, but kept the bag from the fast-food Mexican restaurant. "I want to find some shells to take home to my niece and nephew," she told Reed. "Want to help me?"

He agreed. "How old are your niece and nephew?" he asked, his eyes on the sand at his feet as they strolled along the edge of the water.

Celia pounced on a promising-looking shell, then tossed it aside in disappointment when she discovered that it was broken on the bottom. "Paige is eight and Aaron's six."

Reed handed her a pretty little pink shell. "Do you spend much time with them?"

Celia admired the shell, wishing she knew more about the creature that had made it. "This is a pretty one. Paige will love it. And, yes, I do spend quite a bit of time with them. Actually, I spoil them terribly, according to Rachel. I just can't resist buying them cute clothes and toys I know they'll like. They always thank me so sweetly. Rachel fusses at me, but she doesn't really mind. She's such a good mother that she's able to compensate for my indulgences. She keeps warning me that I'll have to change my ways when I have kids of my own, or I'll find myself with a houseful of greedy little monsters."

"A houseful?" Reed asked with a smile. "Is that how many you're planning?"

"Just a figure of speech. I think two or three would be plenty for me," Celia replied, rinsing off a gray shell she'd dug out of the sand. She was pleased to find it in excellent condition. She added it to the sack.

She glanced up at Reed. "What about you? When are you going to settle down with your own little brood?" she teased.

He grimaced. "Now you sound just like my mother. She's been dropping broad hints about grandchildren since I graduated from college. She even comes right out and demands some occasionally. I told her I have no intention of having kids until I find someone I wouldn't mind raising them with—and that just hasn't happened, yet."

Celia nodded in sympathy. "I know the feeling. I don't want to get married and raise children until I'm absolutely sure I'm ready. How could I teach them anything about life if I haven't even experienced it myself, yet?''

Reed was watching her with that thoughtful, assessing expression again. She blushed, suddenly aware of how personal the conversation had become. She turned away. "Here's another one," she said quickly, bending to dig up a shell and hoping her activity would hide her sudden embarrassment.

It was very late that afternoon when they returned to the resort. The paper bag clinked with the shells they'd gathered for Paige and Aaron. Both Celia and Reed were windblown, slightly sunburned and liberally coated with sand. Celia's hair had dried in a salty tangle, and her makeup was long gone. She didn't care.

She'd had a blissfully wonderful day.

Reed hadn't attempted to kiss her again, but there had been a new warmth in his eyes when he looked at her—which he seemed to do a lot. His touches had been casual—brushing back a lock of her hair, steadying her on the sandy beach, a touch of hands when he handed her a particularly nice shell—but each time, he seemed in no hurry to break the contact. He'd lingered just long enough to make her fully conscious of his warmth, his strength, before he drew away.

He walked her to her suite, but he made no attempt to enter. Celia was tempted to ask him in for a drink from the fully stocked wet bar, but she found herself hesitating, uncertain how he would take the invitation. Not quite sure what she wanted, herself. After those kisses in the surf, she wouldn't blame him for thinking she was offering more of the same—and then some.

But was she really ready for that?

While she hesitated, Reed touched her cheek, brushing away a bit of sand. "Have dinner with me tonight," he said, and it wasn't exactly a request.

It would be their last night together, Celia thought, suddenly pensive. For the first time in hours, she remembered Damien. He would arrive tomorrow, and she would be obliged to spend time with her host. She sensed that there would be no more leisurely afternoons with Reed once Damien appeared, determined to entertain her and make up for lost time.

The thought of saying goodbye to Reed elicited a tug of sadness somewhere deep inside her.

She was growing more confused with each passing hour. She wondered if Damien's presence would make her more certain of what she wanted—or if he would only confuse her more.

"Celia?" Reed said, sounding impatient. "Dinner?"

"Yes," she said recklessly. "Give me a couple of hours to shower and change and rest a bit. I'll meet you in the restaurant at seven-thirty."

He nodded, and the lines around his mouth seemed to relax slightly. "There's a live band in the lounge this evening. Maybe we'll listen to them a while after dinner— dance a bit, perhaps."

She thought of the film that would be shown in the resort theater, the one to which Evan had personally invited her. Popcorn and a movie—or dancing with Reed? She realized there was little contest. "That sounds nice," she said.

"Then I'll see you at seven-thirty."

"Fine." She placed her hand on her doorknob.

Reed hesitated, his gaze focused intently on her mouth. She could feel her lips tingling, almost as if he'd already kissed her. She resisted a strong urge to moisten her lips with her tongue.

The taut moment seemed to stretch for a very long time. And then Reed took a quick step backward, and hooked his thumbs in the back waistband of his jeans. Keeping his hands out of trouble, perhaps?

"Later," he said gruffly, then turned and walked away.

Celia had already closed herself inside her suite before she finally remembered how to breathe normally again.

On an impulse, Celia dressed up that evening. Her sleeveless white dress fit closely at the bodice, then flared softly from the hips to sway flirtatiously at her knees. She added strappy white sandals, glittering earrings and bracelet, then swept her dark hair up and secured it with a sparkling rhinestone clip. It was an outfit she'd purchased with Damien in mind; but tonight she wore it for Reed's benefit.

The woman in the mirror looked very different from the windblown beachcomber of the afternoon. Celia studied her reflection thoughtfully, wondering which image came closer to the Celia Carson she wanted to be.

Jeans and T-shirts and fast-food restaurants suited the life she lived at home in Percy, and she'd been happy in that life. Most of the time. Expensive dresses and sparkling jewelry were more of what she could expect should her budding relationship with Damien Alexander continue to develop. She'd almost convinced herself that she wanted that more glamorous, more adventurous life-style. Until she'd met a so-called "average" tax accountant named Reed Hollander.

She sighed and shook her head. Was she really so fickle, to come to this island half prepared to begin an affair with one man only to find herself craving kisses from another? Who would believe that she, who had always been so careful, so fastidious, would find herself in this situation?

Part of the problem, she decided, trying to be objective, was that she wasn't entirely sure what Reed wanted. He'd certainly made himself available to spend time with her—not that he'd had any better offers, apparently. He'd been a perfect gentleman, for the most part, and yet something about the way he looked at her . . .

The frown that darkened his face whenever Damien's name came up almost seemed to indicate that he was jealous. But why? It wasn't as though he and she were anything more than friends—casual ones, at that. After all, they hardly knew each other.

But did she really know Damien any better?

She groaned and slapped a hand against her forehead. She could drive herself crazy this way! She should have listened to Rachel, and stayed at home where she belonged.

"Yeah, right," she muttered aloud. "Might as well join a convent."

All in all, that might just be the safest choice, she thought with a wry grimace.

The resort lounge was a tropical paradise of exotic flowers, shadowy corners, flickering lights and strategically placed rock waterfalls. The polished, wooden dance floor was in the center of the room, small tables arranged in cozy grottos around it. A band played from a stage nearly hidden in lush greenery.

Celia felt almost as though she'd just stepped out of Texas and into the Caribbean.

"This is the first time I've been in here," she told Reed when they were seated at a table in a secluded corner. "It's beautiful."

"Staged romance," he said dismissively.

Celia frowned at him. "Is there *anything* about this resort that pleases you?" she demanded, exasperated by his attitude.

He reached out to touch her cheek. "Yes. You're here."

She blushed. She was very glad to see the cocktail waitress who approached their table at that opportune moment.

They placed their drink orders, then looked at each other again across the tiny table.

"Did I remember to tell you how nice you look this evening?" Reed asked.

"Yes," Celia answered with a smile. "But thank you again."

Reed looked very nice, himself, in a charcoal dress shirt and black dress slacks. He seemed to favor dark colors, on the whole. Maybe because someone had told him how good they looked on him.

Celia looked quickly toward the dance floor. "It isn't very crowded tonight. Most of the other guests must have chosen to see the film."

"They didn't have the option of spending the evening with you," Reed said.

She blinked. He had been saying outrageous things like that all evening. "Reed, are you flirting with me?" she asked, unable to hold it back any longer.

He smiled. "Yes."

"Why?"

His smile turned to a chuckle. "Why are you so surprised?" he countered.

"Well . . . because," she answered lamely. "We've spent several days together and you haven't flirted with me before." Unless, of course, one counted those kisses—which she supposed she should.

"Let's just say I need the practice," he said lightly, then pushed his chair back. "Dance with me?"

Looking at him a bit warily, she stood and placed her hand in his outstretched one.

The song was a slow, bluesy number. Only three other couples were on the dance floor, locked closely together, oblivious to spectators. Ignoring them in return, Reed smiled down at Celia and took her in his arms.

He held her close, but not so tightly that she was uncomfortable. His hand rested discreetly at the small of her waist, his palm warm through the thin fabric of the white dress. His other hand clasped hers, firmly, almost possessively.

She trembled.

"Are you cold?" Reed asked solicitously, leading her into a slow, swaying rhythm.

"No," she whispered, then managed to regain her voice. "It's been a while since I've danced," she added, as though in explanation of her hesitancy.

He made a tight turn, his feet meshing expertly with hers. "It's been quite a while for me, too."

She looked at him skeptically. "You don't dance like you're in need of practice."

He gave her a slow smile and then rested his cheek against her hair. "That's because I'm dancing with you," he murmured.

"You don't flirt like you're in need of practice, either," Celia muttered, her pulse rate fluttering like crazy.

She'd never thought herself a sucker for a corny line—but it looked as though she'd been wrong. At least, she found herself unable to resist being affected by Reed's lines, which should have sounded silly, but somehow didn't.

He began to hum softly along with the music.

"Unforgettable." Her favorite song. Her knees went weak in response to his sexy tenor.

He sang, too?

It was growing increasingly obvious that she had badly misjudged Reed Hollander.

It was late when Reed walked Celia to her suite. She was wide awake this time, tingling with anticipation of the kiss she was sure would come. After a magical evening of music and candlelight and champagne and dancing, how could she expect anything else?

She was still confused, except for one thing. She knew she wanted Reed to kiss her tonight. Wanted it with an intensity that was almost frightening.

Her key in hand, she looked up at him at the door. She opened her mouth to say something—anything—but before she could speak, he fulfilled her prediction by covering her mouth with his own.

There in the hallway, he kissed her with a hunger that first overshadowed, then inflamed her own. She wrapped her arms around his neck and kissed him back.

His arms locked around her waist, dragging her closer. His tongue surged between her parted lips, coaxing and demanding a response. His heart beat powerfully against hers. Though it seemed impossible, he was obviously as deeply affected by the embrace as Celia was.

It was a very long time before he lifted his head. Celia was trembling again—and she thought Reed was, too. His eyes glittered, and his breath was rapid and uneven.

"You can't know how long I've been wanting to do that," he muttered, pressing his lips to her temple, her cheek, the corner of her mouth.

Celia caught her breath, clinging to his shirt, drawn to his warmth, his strength. Oh, he didn't kiss like a tax accountant, she thought inconsequentially. He kissed like...like a dream.

"Would you..." She had to stop to clear her throat to speak coherently. "Would you like to come in for a drink?"

He went very still. His eyes locked with hers. "Are you sure?" he asked.

"Just...just a drink," she whispered, her heart racing now in what felt very much like panic.

He winced, then shook his head. "I can't promise not to touch you again if I come in."

She bit her lip. She wasn't sure she was ready to actually go to bed with the man, but she wouldn't mind a few more of those delicious kisses. If Reed could be content with that...

Her fingers laced tightly in front of her, she asked hesitantly, "Can you promise to leave when—umm—if I ask you to?"

She searched his face while he considered her question. His now familiar face. The face of a man she instinctively trusted. When he nodded, she almost sighed in relief. "Yes," he said quietly. "That I *can* promise."

She smiled shakily and opened the door. "What would you like to drink?" she asked as they stepped through together. And then she stopped in her tracks. "Oh."

It was impossible to miss seeing the flowers. The bouquet was enormous, seeming to fill the room, dwarfing the small table on which they'd been placed. The heavy scent of roses and assorted other blooms filled the air. The card had been placed on the table, propped against the crystal vase, clearly readable to both Celia and Reed from where they stood.

"Darling, I'll be with you tomorrow. I can't wait. Damien."

Celia looked quickly up at Reed. His face could have been carved from granite. His eyes were dark, shadowed. Unreadable when he looked back at her.

"It's getting late," he said, his voice flat. "I'd better go."

"But..."

"Celia." He took her shoulders in his hands. "Will you go home? Tomorrow morning, before he arrives?"

Bewildered by the sudden change in him, Celia shook her head. "I—I can't, Reed. I told him I'd be here."

He dropped his hands. "Then I guess I'll see you around. Maybe."

"Reed," she said when he turned toward the door. "Don't do this."

He looked over his shoulder, first at her and then at the flamboyant bouquet. "You're going to have to make a choice, Celia. You know where to find me. If you want me."

With that, he was gone.

And Celia began to cry.

He'd been a jealous idiot. Again. Reed paced restlessly down the beach, oblivious to the fragrances or the sounds or the moonlight that had seemed so romantic before. Now they only reminded him of Celia. And of how stupidly he'd acted with her.

Darling. The words of the note had emblazoned themselves on his mind. *I can't wait.*

How could Celia fall for that crap? Was she really so utterly unaware of the kind of man Damien Alexander was? Had she had so little experience with men that she didn't recognize a slick, well-practiced line when she heard one? And how the *hell* could she fall into his arms the way she had today when she was still planning to spend the rest of the week with Alexander?

He'd known plenty of women who didn't mind dallying with one man while waiting to warm the bed of another. He just couldn't make himself believe Celia was like that.

What did she want? Why was she here? Why did she tremble when he touched her if she was thinking of someone else?

But she hadn't been thinking of Alexander tonight, Reed thought with a sudden vicious satisfaction. Until she'd seen those flowers, Alexander had been as far from her thoughts as he was from her presence. She'd been thinking only of Reed.

And he'd blown it. Again.

He should have stayed with her. Made love to her until she couldn't even imagine being with anyone else. Until she hadn't the strength to say any name but Reed's.

And then, first thing tomorrow morning, he'd have put her on a plane headed for Little Rock. Toward safety. And when this was all over, no matter what she'd done, no matter how deeply involved she'd been to this point, he'd have followed her. And made sure that from now on, any trouble she got in would be with him.

He turned impulsively toward her rooms, deciding to do just that. And then he stopped and slammed a fist into his hand, knowing he wouldn't.

He remembered the look in her eyes when he'd stormed away from her.

And he remembered every word of that damned note.

He muttered a curse that echoed eerily on the deserted beach. And then he began to pace again.

Chapter Seven

Celia woke with heavy eyes the next morning, after a restless night's sleep. She wasn't at all pleased with the reflection that met her in the mirror. She looked worn, dispirited—sad.

She didn't look like a woman taking a carefree vacation, that was for sure!

She didn't want Damien to find her looking like this when he arrived. He would only ask questions, and Celia didn't know what she would have said to reassure him. What could she tell him? That she'd met another man while Damien was away? That she'd suddenly found herself falling for the guy, even though she knew he wasn't right for her? That she'd all but thrown herself into his arms, only to have him throw her right back out of them?

She'd cried from embarrassment and confusion and weariness, she told herself firmly. Certainly not from any deeper or more serious reasons. Her pride had been bruised, but her heart was intact.

Or, at least, that was what she told herself as she climbed defiantly into the shower and turned the water directly onto her tear-streaked face.

Damien arrived early that afternoon, accompanied by his usual entourage. The group included Maris Cathcart, a loyal secretary in her late forties who often traveled with Damien; Jim Bennett, a very large man usually introduced as head of security, but whose primary function was that of bodyguard; and Damien's "right-hand man," Mark Chenault.

They had all met Celia during business trips to Arkansas. Maris greeted her with the distant politeness that Celia had always suspected hid a streak of jealousy. Jim nodded and mumbled something unintelligible—his usual form of conversation. Mark displayed the rather condescending indulgence he always showed her. She had never really liked him, though Damien had repeatedly assured her that Mark was invaluable to him.

His thick, gold-tipped hair attractively disheveled, Damien flashed the brilliant smile that so often graced the society pages. His dimples deepened, his teeth gleamed, his blue eyes sparkled; Damien Alexander was a man who almost pulsed with energy and enthusiasm. And wealth, and power, both of which he seemed to take casually for granted, even as he wielded them so skillfully.

"Celia! I can't tell you how glad I am to finally join you—or how sorry I am that I kept you waiting so long," he said as he caught her hands in his and gave her a melting look. "Can you ever forgive me?"

She smiled and leaned forward to return his light kiss of greeting. "We've discussed this before, Damien. I don't blame you for being called away. I understand completely."

Waving the others off, he tucked Celia's hand beneath his arm and led her in the direction of her suite. "Have you been completely bored, darling, or has my staff managed to entertain you during the past week?"

"Your staff has been wonderful," she assured him. "I couldn't have asked for more attentive, or more gracious service. Please be sure to thank them all for me."

Damien's eyes glinted with amusement. "A nice evasion of my question."

She shook her head reprovingly. "I haven't been bored. I've been doing some sight-seeing. Actually, I've been spending time with one of the other guests who was vacationing alone. His name is Reed Hollander, from Cleveland. He's a history buff—you wouldn't believe how many battlefields and museums I've visited in the past few days."

Celia spoke lightly and confidently. She had no intention of having Damien's overly watchful staff tell him about the time she'd spent with Reed—as she suspected someone would. She hadn't been sneaking around with Reed; and she'd be darned if she would allow anyone to make their brief time together seem so sordid.

Damien opened the door to her sitting room and gave her a searching look. "Reed Hollander, huh? Competition?" His tone was light, but she could tell he wasn't pleased. The sudden glint in his eyes reminded her that Damien was known in some circles as an intimidatingly powerful man.

Her heart fluttered, but she answered easily. "Don't be silly. Reed's a friend. Just as you are," she added as she entered her suite ahead of him. The huge bouquet he'd sent her still seemed to dominate the room. Celia avoided looking at it. The memories those flowers evoked were still too disturbing, too raw.

Damien gave an exaggerated sigh. "Can I help it if I continue to harbor hopes that you and I will soon become much more than friends?"

He really was gorgeous, Celia thought almost dispassionately. Charming, smooth, fun to spend time with. And if he tried to kiss her now, she'd probably hit him. She wished she understood why.

As though he'd read her thoughts, Damien patted her hand and released her. "I've brought you something," he said, reaching into the inner pocket of his lightweight jacket.

She frowned warily at him. She'd made it clear from the first time they'd had dinner together that she would not accept expensive gifts from him. She'd wanted him to know that it wasn't his money that interested her; she would have liked Damien even if he'd been penniless. He made her laugh. She'd never been bored with him. Those points, alone, would have guaranteed their friendship.

Her frown turned to a smile when she saw her gift. It was a small wood carving—no more than six inches high. A clever little palm tree appeared to be bent by a strong wind; a tiny man clung to the trunk of the tree with both hands, legs straight out behind him, a comical, wide-eyed look on his tiny face.

"It's adorable," Celia said, cupping the carving in her hands.

"My manager carved it. As soon as I saw it, I begged him to let me buy it for you."

Celia was startled. "The manager who had both legs broken beneath a fallen tree?"

Damien nodded ruefully. "He carved this in his hospital room. He can't stand being inactive for long."

"He must have a wonderful sense of humor."

"Some would say a sick sense of humor. That's why I like the guy so much," Damien admitted with a grin.

Celia laughed, greatly relieved that Damien hadn't brought her the expensive gifts he was known to lavish upon his "lady friends"—for want of a better term.

"I'm going to make up for every day I haven't been here with you," Damien announced, almost rubbing his hands together in anticipation. "We'll go snorkeling, horseback riding... have you been parasailing, yet?"

Celia tried to imagine Reed dangling from a parachute over the Gulf. Or herself, for that matter. She laughed. "No, Damien. I haven't been parasailing. And to be honest, I'm not sure I want to try."

"Nonsense. You'll love it. I also happen to have two brand-new, top-of-the-line Jet Skis in my boathouse. We'll take those out tomorrow morning. Do you like to fish? We can spend one day out on the boat. I'll have the chef prepare a gourmet picnic for us. Last time I was out, I caught a trophy-size marlin. Of course, you can't expect that every time, but..."

He continued in that vein for some time, eagerly describing all the wonderful things they would do together, all the fun they would have. Celia listened politely, nodding occasionally and trying to look as enthusiastic as he was about the sports he loved. She'd never tried most of them—tennis and swimming were the only sports she participated in regularly at home—but she'd wanted excitement and adventure, hadn't she?

It looked as though she was about to find them.

Saying he was sure Celia was growing tired of the Alexander's amenities, Damien took her to a different restaurant that evening, an exclusive French restaurant at the top of one of the other hotels. Apparently, Damien had a standing reservation, since he was warmly welcomed and escorted immediately to a very nice table.

Celia had dressed up again, this time in a little black dress she wore with a crystal-beaded silver jacket she'd borrowed from Rachel. It was an outfit Damien had seen before, but she hadn't felt like wearing the slinky white number she'd worn for Reed only last night. She wasn't sure she would be in the mood to wear that dress again for a very long time.

Damien was still planning their next few days together during dinner. "I will have to work a little, of course," he said with a dismissive wave of his hand. "A couple of meetings with potential investors, some paperwork for the insurance company. I'll try to clear most of it away early to leave us the rest of the days free."

"I don't want to keep you from your work. I'm quite capable of entertaining myself for a few hours a day."

"Have you talked to your family while you've been here?" Damien asked inconsequentially.

"Only to Granny Fran. Why?"

Damien's eyes glinted in the candlelight. "I thought maybe Rachel would have called to see if I've thoroughly corrupted you, yet."

Celia giggled. "She would be afraid to ask."

Damien gave an exaggerated sigh. "What would I have to do to convince your sister that I'm really a very decent, trustworthy guy?"

Celia pretended to give his question some thought. "Join the priesthood, I think," she answered at length.

Damien widened his eyes and managed to look amused and horrified at the same time. "Anything but that."

Celia laughed. "That's exactly what I thought you would say. Forget it, Damien, Rachel will probably always believe that you're a jaded, heartless seducer."

With a rueful grimace, Damien shook his head. "If I'm such a master of seduction, how come I haven't gotten past first base with you, hmm?"

Tossing her head, Celia grinned. "Maybe because my sister trained me so well?"

"Remind me to thank her sometime," he murmured gloomily.

Amused, Celia turned her attention to her exquisitely prepared dinner. This, she reminded herself, was why she liked Damien so much. He made her laugh.

Unfortunately, he'd never made her tremble.

Damien suggested dancing after dinner. Celia forced a smile and told him that would be lovely. Her mind filled with images of dancing with Reed; she pushed them ruthlessly away, feeling vaguely guilty for thinking of him when she was out with Damien.

What an awkward situation she'd gotten herself into, she thought in exasperation as she and Damien went into the lounge and found a table. How Cody would laugh that his little sister, who so often complained of boredom, was now finding herself unexplainably involved with two men—one a well-known millionaire, the other a history-buff accountant!

She tried to imagine what Rachel would say. She almost shuddered at the thought. Rachel would be a nervous wreck over the whole situation. She would have to remind Celia how little she trusted Damien, how sordid his reputation was, how worried she was that Damien would use Celia and then abandon her, leaving her ego in shreds and her heart battered.

And then she would surely point out that Celia really didn't know Reed any better than she did Damien. Sure, he *said* he was a straight-arrow accountant, a fine, upstanding citizen, Rachel would say, but how did Celia really know any of that was true? For all she knew, Reed could be a . . . well, an ax murderer or something.

"What's so funny?" Damien asked after he'd ordered drinks. He was giving Celia a quizzical look across the little table he'd found for them.

She blushed, realizing she'd laughed aloud at her imaginary conversation with her sister. "Oh. Sorry. I was just thinking about Rachel."

Damien looked exasperated. He motioned around them to indicate their cozy, romantic surroundings. "I'm trying to seduce you and you're thinking about your sister? You really aren't helping me out here, Celia."

She only laughed again, not taking him particularly seriously. Damien was always saying things like that. "I was just picturing what Rachel would say if she could see us now," she prevaricated.

Damien winced. "Don't even tell me," he begged. "Your sister is really terrible on my ego."

"Damien, sweetie, your ego couldn't be dented with a jackhammer," Celia retorted sweetly, making him laugh.

They danced until almost midnight. Damien danced with more skill and style than Reed had, his steps expert and dashing. He murmured teasing sweet nothings in her ear at times, his flattery so charming and outrageous that Celia giggled, making other couples smile indulgently at them. She had a lovely time.

But never once did she tremble in Damien's arms. Damn it.

Damien had his arm around Celia's waist as he led her down the hallway toward their suites. He'd had a bit too much champagne in the lounge; his steps were just perceptibly unsteady.

He nuzzled Celia's temple with his lips as they approached their doors. "I don't suppose..."

"No," she said with a smile, completely sober. She'd had only one glass of champagne, herself.

He hefted a sigh. "I didn't think so. I fully expected to pay for standing you up for a week. You've been plotting this for days, haven't you, darling?"

Celia frowned. "I'm not exacting revenge, Damien. I'm just not ready to—"

"That's all right, Celia," he cut in magnanimously. "You don't owe me explanations. No means no, right?"

"Right. But—"

"Get some rest. We have a busy day ahead of us tomorrow. I'll clear away my paperwork and meet you in the lobby—say, ten o'clock? You might want to wear a bathing suit under a beach dress or something. Shall I have breakfast sent to your room?"

Trying to follow his quick changes of topic, Celia nodded. "That would be nice."

"Anything in particular?"

"Surprise me."

He laughed and kissed her cheek. "I like the sound of that."

She brushed a quick kiss across the corner of his mouth and stepped quickly away before he could press for more. "Good night, Damien."

He struck a pose. "Good night, sweet Celia. 'Parting—'"

She groaned. "Please don't quote Shakespeare. It's been such a nice evening. Don't blow it with a smarmy ending."

He chuckled. "No wonder none of my patented lines work on you. You never let me finish any of them."

She put a hand in the middle of his back and gave him a slight shove toward his own suite. "Good night, Damien."

He left her with his usual good grace. As she let herself into her own rooms, Celia was wryly certain that Damien still believed she was subtly punishing him for keeping her waiting for so long. As much as she liked him, she was aware that he was a rather vain man who was quite certain it was only a matter of time until he charmed his way into her bed.

There'd been a time when she'd suspected the same thing. Now...

Now she wasn't so sure.

Hidden in shadows at the end of the hallway, Reed watched Celia and Alexander part, obviously for the evening. He discovered that his fists had doubled at his sides; with some effort, he relaxed them.

He wasn't sure what he would have done if Celia had kissed Alexander at her door, the way she'd kissed Reed only the night before. If she'd given Alexander that sweet, shy smile and invited him inside.

He suspected that he might have torn Alexander's face off.

He was extremely grateful that he hadn't been put to the test.

He couldn't quite figure out what was going on between Celia and Alexander. He'd seen the easy camaraderie between them, the comfortable flirting. And he hated it. But...

He frowned, trying to analyze their behavior. There had been a notable lack of passion—though perhaps not for lack of trying on Alexander's part. Celia was the one who seemed to be taking pains to keep their relationship friendly and platonic.

If she had no intention of becoming Alexander's lover—and Reed wished he could be certain of that—then what *was* she doing with the guy?

Had Kyle been right all along? Was Celia here on business, just as Novotny and Perrelli and the others would be?

Was Celia involved with the ruthless survivalist cult who were allegedly depending on Alexander to supply them with enough weapons and ammunition that they could invade a small country, if they chose to do so? Was she a member of the inner circle, or only using them for her own financial reasons?

Reed couldn't have said at that moment which role he hated most for her—mercenary arms dealer or Alexander's pampered mistress.

He only knew it was all he could do to keep himself from pounding on her door right now and taking her in his arms. Forcing her to admit that the passion that seemed to be missing between her and Alexander had been present between her and Reed from the first time their eyes had met that morning beside the pool.

His fists clenched again at his sides. It took all the willpower he possessed to turn then and walk away.

Away from Celia Carson, whoever—whatever—she might be.

Celia changed into her nightgown and carefully hung up her dress and her sister's jacket. It had been a very pleasant evening. She should have been thinking of Damien, and his insistence that they would become lovers before she left his resort.

Instead, she found herself thinking of Reed. Again.

She hadn't caught a glimpse of him all day. Had he left? Gone back to Cleveland and his predictable, comfortable accounting practice?

The thought filled her with a quick flood of panic.

Never to see him again.... Never to see his slow smile or hear his deep, reassuring voice....

Her eyes filled with tears.

She blinked them away angrily. She would *not* cry over Reed Hollander again. He was the one who'd left so curtly last night, after they'd spent such a special evening together. He was the one who'd practically thrown her tentative overtures back in her teeth.

All because he was jealous of Damien.

Jealous? She mulled the word over for a moment, wondering if it was accurate. Reed had certainly acted jealous, but were his reactions only those of a piqued ego? Or had the few days they'd spent together meant as much to him as they had meant to her? Had he, too, been aware of something growing between them?

She groaned. Why was it that the very man who should have been everything she *didn't* want was keeping her restlessly pacing her room tonight? Damien was right across the hall, perfectly willing to indulge her with the sort of passionate, exciting, adventurous and carefree affair she'd fantasized about during her long, generally boring workdays. All she'd have to do was cross that hall right now, and he would welcome her with open arms and no strings. Anything she wanted, for however long they both wanted it.

Reed, on the other hand, was a man who probably had a whole pocketful of strings. She remembered their tentative conversation about children. Had he been telling her something then? Testing her, feeling her out about his own hopes for the future?

He was a one-man, one-woman guy if she'd ever met one. Four-bedroom house in the suburbs, two-point-three kids. Dog. And if his reactions to Damien's flowers were any indication, he was the possessive sort. The kind who would treat his mate very well, but keep a rather close eye on her, too.

Was that really what she wanted? An average sort of life with an average sort of guy? The kind of life her mother lived? It was all her sister had ever really wanted, first with Ray, and now with Seth—but Celia had always thought it would take more to satisfy her.

Because she was afraid to analyze the answers to those searching questions, Celia pushed them firmly out of her head and climbed into bed.

Her dreams were vivid, eerily realistic. In them, she walked slowly through a tropical paradise of palm trees and waterfalls, heavily scented flowers and exotically feathered birds. It wasn't commercial Padre Island; the place in her dream was a romantic, secluded island retreat.

There was a man at her side. She didn't look at him, but she held his hand. He drew her into the shadows of a spectacularly flowered tree and cupped her face between his hands. Her eyes closed. He kissed her with a hunger and a passion that made her moan in her sleep and clutch the sheets in feverish fingers.

In her dream, she felt his hands on her skin. On her back, her breasts, her thighs. She felt his muscles beneath her palms, rippling and iron-hard. And she was vaguely aware of her own surprise that an accountant would have a body like that.

Accountant...

The face in the dream suddenly became clear. Reed Hollander lifted his head and gave her a smile that sent a shiver all the way down her spine. He kissed her again, and she wrapped her arms tightly around his neck, clinging as though she'd shatter if he released her.

Locked together, they lowered themselves to the thick, plush grass beneath them. Reed reached for the elastic neckline of the colorful peasant top she wore in her dream, and she arched into his touch. "Reed," she moaned. "Oh, Reed."

She woke with Reed's name still echoing in her mind. Had she said it aloud? Probably.

Her cheeks were wet again. She swiped at them impatiently, calling herself an idiot. She'd never dreamed about Damien that way—what was it about Reed that made her act like an infatuated adolescent?

She really should have stayed in Arkansas, she thought, flopping angrily onto her back.

She should have stayed where she belonged.

Chapter Eight

Celia's erotic dream contributed strongly to her flustered discomposure when she came face-to-face with Reed the next morning. She had just left her building, having decided to take a walk around the resort while Damien finished his paperwork. Reed was leaving the restaurant, probably having just finished his breakfast.

Celia came to a dead stop on the sidewalk. She felt a blush begin somewhere around her waist and surge upward to the roots of her hair. She hated herself for reacting that way, but she kept remembering the dream. And those kisses outside her door—and the hesitant invitation she'd extended to him afterward. The one he'd rejected so coldly when he'd seen Damien's flowers.

If Reed shared her inner turmoil, his feelings did not show on his face. The sun glinted off the lenses of his horn-rimmed glasses, hiding his eyes almost as effectively as dark glasses would have done.

"Good morning." He could have been exchanging greetings with a total stranger.

She struggled to keep her own voice as cool. "Good morning."

"Going in for breakfast?"

"No, I had breakfast in my room this morning."

A muscle twitched in his jaw. "Oh."

It occurred to her that he was probably thinking she'd had breakfast with Damien. She automatically opened her mouth to dispel the notion, then changed her mind. It was none of Reed's business whether she'd breakfasted alone, she reminded herself. So why was she feeling so damned defensive about it?

He glanced down at the floating sundress she wore over her bathing suit. "Big plans for today?"

"We're going parasailing, I think," she said wryly.

"Parasailing." He repeated the word with a slight lift of one eyebrow.

"It sounds exciting." She had flushed again, remembering how he'd teased her for being a bit wary of the water when she'd gone into the Gulf with him.

But Reed only nodded. "Much more exciting than another war museum, I suppose. Or miniature golf."

She moistened her suddenly dry lips. "Reed—"

He took a step away. "I have a few things to do this morning. Have fun."

The hand she'd instinctively lifted toward him fell to her side. "Thank you," she said tonelessly.

He started away, paused, then looked over his shoulder. "Celia?"

"Yes?"

"Be careful."

She watched him walk away, looking almost as though he'd regretted the words. What had he meant by them? That he wanted her to be careful parasailing?

Was she only imagining that there had been some deeper meaning behind the warning?

"Celia! There you are." Damien joined her with a broad smile, looking like a model from a catalog in his swim shorts and sporty T-shirt, a jaunty cap on his golden head. "Ready for adventure?"

Celia glanced one last time at Reed's disappearing back, then turned determinedly to Damien. "Yes," she said. "I suppose I am."

Celia had thought museum-hopping with Reed had been wearing. That was before she spent a day with Damien, the sports fanatic. The guy was tireless. He was almost fifteen years older than Celia, but it was all she could do to keep up with him. She'd thought tennis and swimming kept her in decent shape—but Damien had the body and the stamina of a teenager. He only laughed good-naturedly when her endurance—or her courage—deserted her.

Celia's legs felt like wet spaghetti by the time they returned to the resort to change for dinner that evening. Damien was still a bundle of energy.

"What would you like to do tonight?" he asked as they parted at her door. "Dancing again? There's a great disco where the young crowd hangs out. Much less sedate than the lounge we visited last night."

Celia wondered what he would say if she told him she thought she'd spend the evening in the whirlpool bath with a nice, dull book. Instead, she smiled and said, "That sounds like fun."

"Great. We'll go after dinner."

She forced a smile. "Great."

He kissed her quickly, told her he'd meet her in an hour and a half for dinner, then headed for his own suite, whistling what Celia thought was an old Bee Gees disco number between his teeth.

Celia walked straight through the sitting room of her suite, entered the bedroom, and fell facedown on the bed, not caring that her clothing was still wet, sandy and salty. Damien could certainly afford to replace the bedspread, if necessary.

Funny, she'd never noticed until she'd shared an entire day with him that he spent a great deal of time talking about his own wealth. Someone less charitable than she might have even called it bragging.

Not that she hadn't had a good time. It was just that occasionally with Damien she felt like little more than another part of his entourage of bodyguard and boat crew, secretaries and yes-people.

It had been different with Reed. She'd always felt that she had Reed's full attention. That he enjoyed just being with her, regardless of whether they were doing anything exciting or impressive or physically challenging.

He never boasted of his own accomplishments—in fact, he rarely talked about himself at all, but he'd always seemed to enjoy listening when she spoke. Damien sometimes—just sometimes, she amended a bit guiltily—seemed anxious for her to hush so he could talk about himself some more.

She supposed it was understandable. So many people hung on Damien's every word—were *paid* to do so, in fact—that he'd probably gotten a bit spoiled by it. Most people were almost comically impressed by his wealth and his charm and his fame and his power.

Maybe Celia had been a bit impressed, in the beginning. If so, the novelty was wearing off. Now she wanted to know what Damien was like beneath the flash. Whether she liked him as a person—and whether he valued her in the same way.

It was Damien she'd considered starting a relationship with—not his money. Lately it was getting more difficult to separate the two in her mind. Because he defined himself so strongly in terms of wealth—or because there wasn't that much behind the dashing facade?

She sighed and ran a weary hand through her salt-stiffened hair. She had only a little over an hour in which to shower, change and somehow find the energy—and the enthusiasm—to go dancing.

It was going to take a miracle.

Celia and Damien didn't dine alone. Four other couples joined them—an influential business magnate and his trophy bride, a minor television star who was spending a few days at the resort with a model who was not his equally well-known wife, Enrique Torres and his quiet wife, Helen, and Mark Chenault, Damien's personal assistant, who was accompanied by a striking young blonde introduced only as "Kimmi."

Damien, of course, sat at the head of the large, rectangular table. Celia sat on his left, next to Mark Chenault. Torres, as resort manager, had been seated at the other end of the table.

Still a bit winded from the active day, Celia was rather quiet during dinner, content to observe the others. It seemed to her that they all genuinely liked Damien, though they treated him with an obsequiousness that she found vaguely annoying at times. Honestly, she thought at one point, did no one *ever* dispute him? Not even in friendly argument? She had certainly done so a few times, and he'd handled it well enough.

Damien ordered obscenely expensive champagne, and the party grew progressively noisier. Mike Smith, the waiter Celia particularly liked, smiled when he poured champagne into her glass and she whispered that she wouldn't be needing it refilled. Not much of a drinker, Celia sipped that one glass slowly, making it last while the others quickly finished the first magnum and called for another.

The conversation swirled around her, and she held up her end well enough, but the topics changed so rapidly that there was little chance to discuss anything in detail. She found herself thinking of the long, quiet talks she and Reed had shared over meals. Hardly exciting... but nice. Very nice.

A funny little tickle at her nape accompanied her thoughts of Reed. Taking a sip from her champagne flute, Celia glanced over her shoulder. Only to find Reed watching her from a solitary table across the room.

Reed's silence and stillness—his aloneness—seemed more noticeable in contrast to the chattering, laughing crowd around Celia. Their gazes held for a moment across the dimly lighted room. The bubbly champagne seemed to go flat on her tongue, leaving the bitter taste of regret in its place.

"Celia." Damien spoke as though he'd been trying to gain her attention.

She looked quickly around at him, breaking the visual bond with Reed. "Yes?"

"We're heading over to the disco now. Have you finished your dessert?"

Celia looked down at the empty dessert plate in front of her and wondered what had once been on it. "Yes, I'm finished."

Damien grinned. "Ready to get down with some disco?"

She lifted a brow. "Get down?" she repeated.

"You know," the now rather tipsy actor said, leaning toward Celia from his place across the table. "Boogie-oogie-oogie."

Kimmi giggled, her manner decidedly star-struck. "That sounds so funny. Are you quoting something?"

"The song's before your time," Damien said with a wry roll of his eyes. "Before yours, too, I guess," he added to Celia. "What were you—five, six when disco was popular the first time?"

"True, but my late brother-in-law liked disco," she explained. "He played his old Bee Gees albums all the time during the year I lived with him and Rachel. Some of it's not bad."

Mark Chenault gave an exaggerated shudder. "I don't know how any of you can listen to that stuff—even for a laugh. I'm a classic rock man myself. The Doobies, Creedence, Black Oak, the Allmans—now *that's* music."

"I like contemporary country, mostly," Celia admitted. "Garth Brooks, Vince Gill, Wynonna, Collin Raye."

A brief silence followed. If there were any other country music fans at the table, no one said so. The conversation quickly returned to the dance club they'd be going to after dinner.

To Kimmi's obvious distress, Mark begged off. Damien smoothly invited Kimmi along, anyway.

"I'm sure you'll have plenty of chances to dance," he said, looking pointedly at Mark, who only shrugged and told Kimmi to go if she felt like it.

Everyone else planned to go, except Enrique and Helen, who laughingly declared themselves much too old for such nonsense—though neither of them could have been more than five or six years older than Damien. Celia rose with the others, laughed perfunctorily when the inebriated actor stumbled into his giggling date, and wondered what in the hell was wrong with her. This should be fun, darn it. Wasn't that why she was here?

She glanced back over her shoulder as they left the restaurant. Reed's table was empty.

There was a corresponding emptiness somewhere deep inside her that she was finding increasingly difficult to ignore.

Though the others may have been prepared to party until dawn, Celia asked Damien to return her to the resort at eleven. "I'm exhausted," she admitted, earning an indulgent smile and a smooth apology from him for attempting to do too much in one day.

She was rather startled when he kissed her at her door with more passion than he usually exhibited. His arms closed around her in a hold that made her more claustrophobic than responsive. They'd kissed before, of course, and she'd always enjoyed it. But tonight . . .

"I'm sorry," she murmured, drawing away with an effort. "I'm really tired, Damien."

Something flashed through his eyes that might have been annoyance. He replaced it quickly with compassion. "Get some rest," he urged her. "We'll meet for breakfast in the restaurant—say, nine o'clock?

"I have several meetings tomorrow, so I can promise you a slower pace," he added with a smile. "Maybe tomorrow evening we'll drive into Matamoros for a quiet dinner and to listen to some good mariachi music."

"That sounds like fun. Good night, Damien."

She closed herself into her suite before his response was fully out of his mouth. She stood there for a moment, listening. Damien's footsteps faded down the hallway. He hadn't gone into his own suite.

She let out a breath, feeling as though something had changed between them that evening. Perhaps Damien's patience was running out.

She sensed that the time was rapidly approaching when she was going to have to make a decision once and for all whether she wanted to become intimately involved with Damien Alexander.

She suspected that she'd already made that decision, even though she hadn't yet found the courage to admit it. To Damien, *or* herself.

She took her time changing out of the emerald dress she'd worn for dinner, donning her nightgown, brushing her hair. Face and teeth scrubbed clean, she padded out of the bathroom to her bed.

The telephone caught her eye, and for a moment she longed to pick it up and call someone just to talk. Granny Fran. Rachel.

Reed.

She shook her head impatiently. This was ridiculous. How could she make up her mind about Damien when she couldn't stop thinking about another man? One who was little more than a stranger to her, at that.

She crawled beneath the covers, sighed wearily and willed her heavy-limbed body to sleep.

She wasn't successful. Half an hour later, her eyes were still wide open, focused unblinkingly on the darkened ceiling. Her mind swirled with doubts, questions, self-recriminations. She would never get to sleep this way, she thought impatiently, punching the pillow to vent some of her frustration.

Another fifteen minutes passed with excruciating slowness.

Finally, Celia muttered a curse that would have earned her a stern rebuke from her mother, threw back the covers and shoved herself out of the unwelcoming bed.

"This is stupid," she muttered, but she dragged the nightgown over her head and threw on a T-shirt and a pair of shorts.

Maybe a walk alone on the beach would clear her head, let her mind relax so her aching body could do the same. Walking alone at midnight was perhaps not the safest thing to do—but wasn't she here in the first place because she was tired of living cautiously and sensibly?

The beach was deserted, as she'd expected—and hoped. The wet sand looked black at night, especially when the moon played hide-and-seek with fast-moving clouds that hinted at rain. Sandals held loosely in her left hand, she walked along the surf's edge for a time, letting the water lap over the tops of her feet. Unbound, her hair blew free in the stiff breeze. She used her right hand to hold it out of her face. The taste of salt was strong on her lips, the smell of brine and fish heavy in the air.

She closed her eyes for a moment and enjoyed.

The muted sound of men's voices brought her eyelids up quickly. She looked warily around, tensing in automatic self-protection.

Two men were walking toward her, some distance away, apparently deeply involved in conversation. From what she could see in the moonlight, neither man was dressed for beachcombing; they both seemed to be wearing jackets and dress slacks and shoes that weren't made for scuffing in sand.

She had seen them first, but they spotted her just as she recognized them. One was Mark Chenault. The other was a dark-haired, olive-skinned man Celia vaguely remembered seeing around the resort for the past few days—another guest, she'd assumed.

Mark spoke first, after a moment that seemed to hold taut surprise. "Celia? Is that you?"

"Yes." She walked toward them. "Hi, Mark."

"What are you doing out alone so late?"

"I couldn't sleep. I thought a stroll in the fresh air would clear my head." She glanced curiously at the other man, but Mark made no attempt at introductions.

Instead, Mark frowned and motioned around them at the empty beach. "You really shouldn't be out alone in the middle of the night, Celia. Our security is good, but it still isn't particularly safe for a pretty young woman to wander around on a deserted beach."

"But it isn't quite deserted, is it?" she asked sweetly, resenting his unwanted lecture. "You're here."

His frown deepened, exaggerated by shadows into an ominous glare. He seemed to struggle to speak pleasantly and solicitously. "If you'd like to continue your walk, why don't I call someone to accompany you? One of the staff, perhaps, if Damien is unavailable."

"Thank you, but if I had wanted company, I would have found it," Celia answered, speaking with the same forced courtesy. "And, anyway, I was just about to go back in."

"Looks like rain," the other man said, squinting up at the rapidly disappearing moon.

The darkness grew heavier. Celia backed a step away from the two men. It wasn't that they made her nervous, she assured herself. Just . . . uneasy.

Probably because she'd never really liked Mark and the other man was a stranger, she assured herself. She certainly didn't consider herself at any risk from either of them.

"Well," she said, holding her sandals in front of her, "Enjoy your walk."

"Good night, Celia."

She murmured a response to Mark, nodded pleasantly at the other man, then walked away without looking back. She was aware that they watched her for a few minutes before they turned and continued their walk and their conversation.

"Rather late for a friendly little visit on the beach, isn't it?" The low growl came out of the shadows of her building. Having been engrossed in watching Mark and the other man disappearing down the beach, Celia jumped several inches at the unexpected voice coming from so close to her.

"Reed!" she gasped, when he separated himself from the dark concrete-block wall. She pressed a hand to her pounding heart. "What the hell—? You scared me half to death!"

"What can you expect when you go wandering around in the middle of the night by yourself?" he returned unrepentantly. "And what the hell were you doing out there with Chenault and Perrelli?"

"Contradicting yourself, aren't you?" she taunted, her irritation rapidly growing. "First you criticize me for being alone, then you demand to know why I was with someone else."

She suddenly realized that he'd named the men with whom she'd been speaking. "How do you know Mark Chenault?" she asked. "And who's Perrelli?"

In the harsh glow of an overhead security light, Reed's face was a harshly carved mask. She thought she saw a muscle jump in his jaw—something she'd grown to recognize as a sign of self-annoyance. "Never mind," he said. "You'd better get inside. It's late."

She planted her fists on her hips, ignoring the sandals that still dangled from her left fist. "I will not be talked to like a child who is out past her bedtime," she informed him coldly. "I'll go in when I damned well feel like it."

He loomed over her, dressed in dark, snug-fitting clothing that emphasized his size and strength and made him look like anything but an innocuous tax accountant.

She realized that he wasn't wearing his glasses. His face looked harder, more angular without them. At that moment, he was someone she didn't even know.

She'd thought he was going to snap at her again. Instead, he remained silent for a long, tense moment, then let out a gust of breath and took a step backward. "You're right, of course," he said stiffly. "You have every right to be out here if you want."

Her satisfaction at his concession mingled with the new awareness of him. An electrically charged awareness that made her skin tingle, her pulse race, her breath quicken. It wasn't fear making her react this way now, she decided.

Not entirely, anyway.

She reached hesitantly out to him. "Reed?"

He glanced from her hand to her face, his own revealing nothing of his thoughts. "Yes?"

"I've missed you," she said with a candor that wasn't particularly prudent.

A ripple of some emotion—or was it only a shadow?—passed over his face. And then he took her hand. His voice was much gentler this time. "Have you?"

"Yes."

He touched her cheek. She wondered if her skin felt as hot to him as it did to her.

"Did you enjoy your parasailing?" he asked inconsequentially.

"I chickened out," she said wryly. "They were strapping me into the harness when I suddenly knew I couldn't go through with it. I kept picturing myself falling into the open mouth of a shark. Stupid, I know. The others laughed at me."

Damien, thankfully, had been very patient with her. A bit condescending, but she supposed she couldn't blame him for that when she'd been so silly.

Reed searched her face as though looking for another meaning to her words. And then he smiled faintly. "What happened to that adventurous streak of yours?"

"It decided it liked having both feet attached to something steady. Like a boat. Or, even better, solid ground."

Reed chuckled. And then he bent his head and kissed her.

It wasn't like the last time. There was heat—but it was firmly reined. Reed permitted himself no more than a leisurely taste of her lips, and granted her only an unsatisfying sample of his own, before he stepped away.

"Go home, Celia." The gentleness was gone from his voice again. Might never have been there.

She blinked, trying to clear her mind. The change of mood was too abrupt for immediate comprehension. "To my room, you mean?"

He shook his head. "Home. To Percy, where you're safe."

Her chin lifted. Was he calling her a coward? Telling her she didn't belong here? Reminding her that she wasn't the adventurous type—and never would be? "I'm not ready to go home," she answered flatly.

He stepped back into the shadows, and she had the oddest sensation that he dissolved into them. As though he had never been real, but only an illusion. She shook off the strange fantasy impatiently. He was real, all right. And he was proving to be as irritating as he was disturbing.

"Think about it," he suggested. Before she could answer—whatever she might have said—he was gone, vanished into the darkness as smoothly and silently as a passing breeze.

"What the—?"

Go home, Celia.

Why did he keep telling her to go home? One could almost get the impression that he didn't want her here, she thought with a weary attempt at humor.

She wasn't going home, of course. Not just yet. Something was keeping her here.

She no longer even tried to convince herself it had much to do with her obligation to her host.

Chapter Nine

Celia dressed in bright colors the next morning, pairing a red silk shell with a bright purple raw silk vest and skorts and a red, purple and yellow tie belt. Her earrings were a tinkling cascade of red and purple stars and she wore a chunky red-stained wood bracelet and red flats.

Maybe, she thought with a final glance in the mirror, the bright colors of her clothing would detract from the paleness of her complexion. Nearly sleepless nights always left her looking rather washed out.

Though she'd hurried, she still reached the restaurant ten minutes later than she'd agreed to meet Damien there. She was greeted with the usual fawning enthusiasm and led immediately to Damien's table. She was less than three feet away when she came to a sudden stop, her jaw dropping at the sight of the man sitting at the table with Damien and Mark Chenault.

"Chuck?" she said uncertainly, though there was no doubt of the man's identity. "Chuck Novotny?"

The middle-aged man she'd known for years from her hometown seemed as startled as she was. He started to say something to Celia, then turned to Damien, instead. "What is *she* doing here?"

Standing to hold Celia's chair, Damien lifted an eyebrow at Novotny in subtle reproof of the discourtesy. "Celia is my guest. I assume you two know each other."

"Of course we do," Celia explained, taking her seat. "Percy is a very small town, Damien. There are few people there I don't know. Chuck's a longtime customer of the bank where I work."

Now that she'd had a moment to think about it, she realized why Chuck was at the resort. The Novotnys owned the spreading acres of lakeside property that Damien found most tempting for his potential Arkansas resort.

Everyone in town had speculated about whether Chuck would sell the land that had been in his family for many generations. Chuck was a shrewd businessman, notoriously miserly and money-hungry, but he was a very conservative, almost reactionary man who caustically, and vocally, rejected "modern values"—often in long, vitriolic letters to the editor of the statewide newspaper.

Celia had always gotten along well enough with the man—generally exchanging little more than distantly courteous greetings upon passing—but her brother detested Chuck. How many times had Celia heard Cody refer to Chuck's ilk as "a bigoted, big-mouthed, smallminded bunch of fascist rednecks"?

Cody was usually the most laid-back and tolerant of men, his many friends made up of a widely diverse selection, but he was uncharacteristically intolerant of Novotny and his cronies. Celia, on the other hand, had always just considered Chuck a compulsive grouch—annoying, but basically harmless.

"Chuck's here to look over the resort," Mark explained, breaking the brief silence that had fallen over the table as Damien took his seat again. "Perhaps you know that he's been a bit concerned that an Alexander Resort near Percy would disturb the natural beauty of the area and destroy the peace and tranquillity the local residents have enjoyed for so many years. We want him to see several of our resorts around the country, beginning with this one, to see that we make every effort to adapt to the traditions and environment of their settings."

Celia thought Mark sounded like one of the PR brochures some ad agency probably composed for the chain. She couldn't imagine what comparisons Damien could make between the rural foothills of her hometown and the glittery tourist mecca of South Padre Island, but she smiled and nodded as though she understood completely.

"It's really a lovely resort, Chuck," she said helpfully. "The staff is all very nice."

Chuck grunted and gave her a glare of disapproval. Because he didn't approve of women speaking? Celia wondered flippantly. Or—more likely—because he considered her a shameless hussy for being here as Damien's guest, without benefit of a chaperon or a marriage ring.

Chuck couldn't know, of course, that nothing had happened between her and Damien…and the narrow-minded, judgmental man wouldn't believe her if she tried to tell him. Not that she considered it any of Chuck's business whether she was sleeping with Damien and all his staff, for that matter.

Mark pushed his chair away from the table and waved to indicate his empty coffee cup. "Since we've finished our coffee, Chuck, why don't you and I tour the facilities now and leave Damien and Celia to their breakfast? I'm sure I can answer any questions you might have about the operations of the Alexander resorts."

"Aren't you having breakfast?" Celia asked, having assumed they'd be dining together.

Chuck lifted one corner of his too-heavy mouth. "I had my breakfast several hours ago. I've never been one to lay in bed half of a morning, even when I didn't have to work."

Celia choked back a reply, settling for a slight nod.

Damien shook his head in dismay when they were alone. "Cantankerous old coot, ain't he?"

Celia giggled at Damien's bad Southern accent. "He is that," she agreed. "But, as I keep telling Cody, he's harmless."

"Cody doesn't care for the man?" Damien asked idly.

"For some reason, he despises him. Always has."

"I see. I'm—er—sorry if it embarrassed you for Chuck to see you here. I'd forgotten to mention that he would be here. It never occurred to me that there would be any awkwardness attached to you both being here at the same time."

It probably *hadn't* occurred to him, Celia thought wryly. The women Damien usually dated probably never worried about chaperons and reputations—in fact, their reputations were considerably enhanced because they *were* sleeping with Damien. She assured him breezily that Chuck's attitudes were his own problem and didn't bother her in the least.

Apparently she sounded convincing. Damien smiled, patted her hand, then changed the subject. "So, what would you like for breakfast? I was thinking of having the chef's special pecan waffles."

Their waffles had just been delivered to the table when a stunning redhead sauntered past the table, her golden-tanned, five-foot-ten body shown to perfection by a cling-ing, shoulder-baring sundress. Damien stopped what he was saying in midsentence, his eyes riveted to the woman who gave him a sultry smile as she passed the table, ignoring Celia completely.

Amused, Celia watched as Damien suddenly recalled his companion. "Uh—sorry," he said. "What was I saying?"

Celia glanced after the redhead. "Old friend?"

"No," Damien admitted with a rueful smile. "I don't know her. She must be a newly-arrived guest."

"She seems to be dining alone," Celia observed, watch-ing as the woman was seated by the usually ultra-efficient maître d', who seemed to be making an effort to keep from falling over his own feet. "Should we ask her to join us?"

Damien laughed. "You probably would, at that."

Celia grinned. "I love watching men make complete idiots of themselves. Even when it's some other woman causing them to do so."

Turning his shoulder on the other woman's table, Da-mien focused his full attention on Celia. "Now, darling, that's not fair," he said in his patented whiskey-smooth murmur. "I've been making a complete idiot of myself over you for months now, and look where it's gotten me."

"Nowhere?" she asked sweetly.

"I wouldn't say that," he replied, smiling in satisfac-tion. "You're here, aren't you?"

"Hmm. You know, Damien, you were right. These waf-fles are heavenly."

Damien laughed again.

Celia's own smile faded when she saw Reed enter the restaurant. She hadn't expected to see him this morning. He usually breakfasted earlier. She'd hoped he would do so today.

Meeting her eyes across the restaurant, Reed nodded impersonally, never slowing down as he followed the now brusquely businesslike maître d' to a solitary table near the redhead's. Reed was wearing his glasses again, Celia noted, and his accountant's casual wear of neatly pressed shirt and dark slacks.

Most women would probably be more impressed by Damien's magazine-cover good looks and sharply tailored, latest-style clothing. Celia was beginning to think she wasn't at all like "most women."

"Your sight-seeing friend, isn't it?" Damien asked, proving he was as observant as she had been a moment earlier.

Celia deliberately dragged her attention away from Reed. "Yes."

"Should we ask *him* to join us?" The offer seemed to be a sincere one.

Celia shook her head. She didn't at all like the idea of sharing a table with Damien and Reed. "Let's not."

Damien looked pleased. "Good. I don't want to share you, either."

She realized that he'd misinterpreted her refusal, but she made no effort to correct him. Instead, she encouraged him to tell her more about his plans for the central Arkansas resort.

She succeeded nicely in changing the subject. Damien was always eager to talk about himself, and the resorts of which he was inordinately proud. Fortunately, he was never boring about it, and he encouraged her questions and comments, seeming to value her input.

Celia listened attentively, genuinely interested in the project which could be such a huge financial boon for her hometown area. She was satisfied that Damien never realized how often her gaze wandered to Reed's table.

She was watching when the sexy redhead accidentally knocked over a full glass of water, spilling the contents over her linen tablecloth. The woman jumped up with a startled cry, narrowly avoiding having the water in her lap. Half the restaurant's staff converged on the table to assist her as she stood there looking embarrassed.

Having been seated so close by, Reed stood and motioned courteously toward the empty chair at his table. Celia continued to watch as he introduced himself to her with the diffident smile she so easily recognized.

To Celia's hidden dismay, the woman accepted Reed's invitation to join him. Mike, the waiter Celia associated with especially helpful and friendly service, made sure the woman was comfortably settled at Reed's table and took their orders, then left Reed and the woman to get acquainted.

"Your accountant friend is certainly quick to take advantage of an opening, isn't he?" Damien asked, sounding both amused and admiring.

"Isn't he, though?" Celia agreed curtly.

Damien lifted an eyebrow at her tone, but smoothly resumed the conversation about his tentatively planned resort.

Celia had to work harder than ever to pay full attention to her companion and keep her eyes away from the chatting couple across the room.

She saw them again later in the afternoon.

Damien was in one of the business meetings he'd warned her about, and Celia had taken the opportunity to rest in her room for a while before they were to leave for Matamoros. Tired, but not expecting to sleep, she lay on her bed and closed her eyes. When she opened them again, nearly two hours had passed.

Yawning, and considerably refreshed from the nap, she stood and padded barefoot to the window, letting the fresh breeze blow the remnants of sleep from her mind.

It was then that she saw the couple walking on the beach, deep in conversation. A tall, dark-haired man. A tall, flame-haired woman. Reed and the clumsy woman from the restaurant, Celia realized, her fingers going tight on the windowsill.

As Damien had said, Reed certainly wasted no time.

Celia's temper flared. Had he given this woman the old "poor little me, I'm vacationing all by myself" routine? Had he passed himself off to *her* as a slightly shy, socially awkward type?

Was he planning on taking *her* to his boring museums and then making them seem far less boring, the way he had with Celia?

"That—that—" She sputtered, unable to think of a word scathing enough to fit her mood at the moment.

Reed and the woman had already passed out of her sight before she cooled down enough to think rationally. Why *was* she so furious? It wasn't as if Reed was being disloyal to her. For all he knew, she was sleeping with Damien Alexander. He'd made it clear that he hadn't liked it, but she'd made it equally clear that she wasn't asking his opinion.

Now it seemed she was being paid in kind. Reed was a single, unattached male who had every right to get friendly with a stunning, drop-dead gorgeous redhead, if he was fortunate enough to manage it. Why should Celia hate it so much?

But she did. Oh, how she hated it!

She pressed icy hands to burning cheeks, appalled at the realization that had just hit her.

She was going to have to talk to Damien, she thought with a pang of reluctance. And she was going to have to make it soon.

She'd already taken advantage of his gracious hospitality badly enough. There was no excuse to prolong a flirtation that she now knew was going nowhere.

She'd come to Damien's resort in search of what she thought she wanted, only to meet a man who represented everything she'd thought she *didn't* want. How ironic that she had changed her mind now...when it might be too late to do anything about it.

Unable to stay alone in her room any longer, Celia changed into a soft cotton blouse and a long, tiered, printed-cotton skirt that seemed appropriate for an evening in Mexico. She brushed her hair and pulled it back with a bright bandanna for a headband and donned leather huaraches. And then she went in search of Damien.

He wasn't in his rooms. Following her instincts, she headed for his offices.

The offices took up one entire wing of this building. A large, teal-and-cream area held desks for Damien's secretaries, Evan and Maris, who were huddled over a stack of computer printouts when Celia entered. Both looked up when she came in.

Evan rose quickly to his feet. "Is there anything I can do for you, Miss Carson?"

"Don't let me disturb your work," she said. "I was just looking for Damien."

"Mr. Alexander is in a meeting," Maris explained coolly, glancing at the closed, heavy oak door that led into Damien's office.

"Oh." Feeling like an interloper, Celia took a step backward toward the outer door. "Well...just tell him I'll be around whenever he's ready for dinner, will you?"

Maris nodded and turned her attention back to her work.

Evan was a bit more courteous. With an apologetic smile, he explained that he and Maris were preparing for a large convention that was to take place at the resort the week after Thanksgiving. He offered Celia a cup of coffee, which she politely declined. She left quickly.

At loose ends, she wandered around the resort, watching the other guests, picturing the facilities invaded by conventioneers, finally ending up back at the koi pond that drew her so often. She watched the colorful, contented-looking fish and found her thoughts turning to her family.

In St. Louis, Celia's mother was deeply involved with charities and her bridge club while her husband pursued his career as an adolescent psychologist. Back home in Arkansas, Rachel would be making plans for her wedding, which was to be held on New Year's Eve. The children, Paige and Aaron, were in school, counting the weeks until Christmas holidays. Cody was busy with his work and his friends. Granny Fran was probably already baking for her annual, extravagant Thanksgiving dinner.

Hard to believe Thanksgiving was only a little over a week away, Celia mused, aware of the tropical heat around her. The whole family would be together then, crowded into Granny Fran's house, as always. Aunt Arlene, who was a few years older than Celia's father and had been widowed for many years, would come with her successful, plastic-surgeon son, Adam. Celia's parents would fly in from St. Louis, and Cody, Rachel, Paige and Aaron would certainly all be there.

Rachel's fiancé, Seth, would join them this year—a new member of the close-knit clan. That would probably be the only noticeable difference, Celia thought wryly. The menu would be the same as always—turkey and dressing, homemade cranberry sauce, home-canned green beans cooked with pork seasoning, homegrown sweet corn, mashed sweet potatoes covered with toasted marshmallows, butter-dripping yeast rolls and a dessert table filled with pumpkin pies, pecan pies, coconut pies, chocolate pies. A diet counselor's nightmare; a food lover's dream.

Granny Fran would be happy as a pig in sunshine—as Frances herself would say—surrounded by her loved ones, thriving on their compliments of her weeks of preparation, assuring everyone it had been no trouble at all. Aunt Arlene would complain of her health and sigh delicately because no one truly understood her pain. Adam would make a few subtly barbed comments and try to hide his impatience to get back to work. Dad and Mom would fuss over their grown children's health and shamelessly spoil their grandchildren, while Rachel kept a close eye on the kids and Cody played outrageous practical jokes on everyone.

And Celia—Celia would mingle and laugh and chatter as she always did, wishing she understood how she could be so happy and so restless all at the same time.

From a secluded corner across the resort compound, Reed watched Celia watching the fish. She looked lonely, he couldn't help thinking. It was all he could do to keep himself from crossing the distance between them and taking her in his arms.

If only he could be sure . . .

His fists clenched at his sides when Celia was suddenly joined by two men, Mark Chenault and Chuck Novotny. The three fell into conversation in which Celia participated with apparent ease.

Reed knew exactly why Novotny was here—and it had nothing to do with selling property to Alexander Resorts. In reality, Novotny was the buyer, and weapons the merchandise. Reed wasn't sure how deeply Chenault was involved, though he knew Chenault was Alexander's trusted personal assistant and would probably do anything his employer requested. But what about Celia?

He was growing increasingly certain that there was no physical relationship between Celia and Alexander—at least, not during the past few days. Reed had been watching them very closely. Usually with clenched fists.

So why was she here? Why would Alexander invite her here at the same time Novotny was at the resort? Was he using her for cover? Hoping it looked more natural for one to be here if the other was? Or was she more of a business liaison between the man who would like to make her his mistress and her longtime, hometown acquaintance?

The doubts were driving Reed crazy. His partner was beginning to get seriously concerned—and so was Reed, for that matter.

For the first time in his law-enforcement career, the woman he'd been ordered to watch was becoming more important to him than his duty.

Celia was relieved when Damien arrived and Mark and Chuck made their departure. She'd tried to be friendly when they'd come upon her, but it had taken a great effort on her part. She was still stinging from her curt encounter with Mark the night before, and Chuck still tended to treat her with condescending disapproval because she was there, at all. If he weren't such an important customer of the bank where she worked, she'd be tempted to tell him to stuff his antiquated, unsolicited opinions.

"I wish I'd known you disliked Chuck so deeply," Damien said after watching Chuck leave with a curt nod for Celia. "I certainly would have delayed my meetings with him until after your visit."

"You shouldn't have to reschedule your business plans just because of me," she assured him. "It doesn't bother me that Chuck's here. He would probably have heard about my visit, anyway. You know how gossip travels through a small-town grapevine."

"He and my assistant seem to be getting along well enough, don't they? I asked Mark to keep Novotny entertained while he's here—softening him up for the negotiations, of course—and he seems to be doing a fine job."

"Yes, he's been showing him all around the resort. I think they'd even been to the storage rooms behind the conference center before they joined me here. I'm sure Chuck's impressed by the efficiency of your operation. I certainly have been."

"Thank you," Damien said with a smile that didn't quite reach his eyes. "You said you saw them in the storage room area?"

Celia shook her head. "They were coming from that direction. I just assumed—"

Damien shrugged. "It doesn't matter, though I can't imagine why Chuck would have been interested in seeing holiday decorations and extra resort supplies."

Celia smiled. "I can. Chuck's just naturally nosy. He's probably examined every inch of this place, whether it has anything to do with him or not."

Damien dismissed Novotny with a wave of his neatly manicured hand. "I'm sorry I kept you waiting," he said, changing the subject. "Evan and Maris told me you'd stopped by the office."

"Yes. I didn't realize you were still in meetings. I love this koi pond, Damien. It's lovely."

"There's one at each of my resorts," he said, looking pleased. "I find it relaxing to watch them."

"So do I."

"See?" he said, putting an arm around her shoulders. "I knew we had a lot in common."

She couldn't help smiling. "Watching fish isn't exactly a shared philosophy of life, Damien."

"True. But it's a start. Are you ready for an evening in old Mexico?"

She assured him he was. And then she wondered how she would find a way to tell him that she wouldn't be sleeping with him during the few days she had left of her vacation—or ever, for that matter.

It wasn't going to be an easy topic to work into their dinner conversation, she thought dryly. But somehow, before the evening ended, she had to find a way.

As it turned out, the opportunity for a serious conversation with Damien never arose. They were accompanied by two other couples on their night out in Matamoros, so Celia never found the right moment during dinner or dancing afterward.

She didn't know why Damien had invited the other couples when he'd seemed so anxious to be alone with her. He hinted to her that they'd sort of invited themselves along. Celia knew that wasn't exactly true; Damien wasn't the sort of man to be manipulated. If the other couples had invited themselves, it had been because Damien encouraged them.

As he had before, Damien dominated the dinner conversation, keeping everyone laughing at his outrageous stories, generally acting the gracious, entertaining host. Celia was beginning to suspect that he was deliberately keeping her from having a serious talk with him that evening.

Had he started to suspect what she wanted to tell him? Was he hoping the outrageous flattery and megawatt smiles he showered on her during the evening would change her mind?

Her suspicions grew stronger when Damien drove her back to the resort. Even though they were alone in his car, he kept up that cheery monologue, hardly giving her time to say a word. Whenever he stopped for breath, he turned the radio up loudly enough to fill the void.

She promised herself that she would talk to him as soon as they returned to her suite. It was well past time that she got this settled—whether Damien wanted it to be or not.

They had just gotten out of Damien's car when Evan appeared, a deep frown creasing his usually smooth forehead. "Mr. Alexander. Thank goodness you're here."

Damien sighed heavily. "What is it this time, Evan?"

"It's that television actor, Mr. Alexander," Evan replied with a slight curl of his lip. "He's gotten drunk or high and started hitting the young woman with him. The police were called, and now the press has been alerted. The woman is not his wife, of course, and his wife is a well-known actress, as well, so..."

"...so," Damien cut in, "it's going to get ugly."

"I'm afraid so, sir. The man is already talking about lawsuits against us—though what he could possibly sue *us* for, I can't imagine."

Us, Celia noted. Evan certainly took his job personally.

Damien turned to her with a look of apology. "Celia, I'm sorry—damn, I've been saying that a lot to you lately, haven't I?"

"Yes," she said with a sympathetic smile. "And it really isn't necessary. I know you have to deal with this."

"It may take hours, damn it."

"I'm sure it will. Let's just call it an evening, shall we?"

Damien looked torn, his eyes going from Celia to Evan, who stood impatiently nearby. He exhaled deeply. "Okay. We'll talk tomorrow—even if I have to bolt the door and disconnect the telephones to do so!"

Which meant, of course, that Damien was finally ready to have that serious talk that he'd been avoiding all evening, Celia interpreted.

She wasn't sure whether to be more relieved or disappointed that the confrontation had been delayed. It wasn't something she was looking forward to, even though she was sure Damien would make it as painless as possible for her. He was too nice a man to cause an unpleasant scene just because she'd decided she didn't want to be his lover.

Still, it wouldn't be easy for him. He was a man of considerable ego—and with some justification for being that way. He couldn't be accustomed to being rejected.

She assured Damien that she was perfectly capable of seeing herself back to her suite. She reminded him that he was needed in his office immediately.

"Before the press descends," she added, watching a spasm cross his face in reaction. She knew how Damien felt about the gossip sheets, though he courted them when he deemed it professionally advantageous.

Damien nodded and brushed his mouth hastily across her cheek. "Tomorrow," he promised, and rushed away. Evan was at his employer's side, not even sparing a backward glance for Celia.

Celia was on her way to her suite when she suddenly changed her mind. She stopped in the middle of the path, her gaze drifting to the tall building in the center of the compound, the twelve-story, multibalconied complex in which Reed was staying. She knew his room number; he'd mentioned it on one of their outings in case she ever needed to call him.

Was he in his room now? It was just after 10 p.m. Not late—but rather early for a single man on vacation to turn in alone.

Or *was* he alone? she wondered with a hollow feeling deep inside. She pictured him on the beach with the beautiful redhead and then in his room with her in his arms.

The image made her heart ache.

She suddenly knew she couldn't go to bed without knowing whether Reed was spending the evening with the other woman.

She could call his room. Ask if he wanted to join her for a nightcap in the lounge.

Or she could show up at his door and hope for the best.

She stood for several long, indecisive moments at the door leading into her building, her eyes locked on the lighted windows of Reed's building. And she remembered what he'd said to her when he'd left her Sunday evening, after their romantic evening had been so abruptly interrupted by Damien's flowers.

You're going to have to make a choice, Celia. You know where to find me. If you want me.

She wanted him. But finding him would take more courage than anything she'd ever done in her entire life.

She took a step toward his building. And then another. And she prayed during that long, slow walk that she wasn't making an enormous mistake.

Chapter Ten

Celia must have stood in front of Reed's door for ten minutes trying to work up the nerve to knock on it. She knew he was inside; she could hear the television playing and the sounds of someone moving around.

But what if he wasn't alone?

She crossed her arms in front of her and rubbed her hands up and down her goose bump-dotted forearms. Surely he was alone, she mentally argued. He wouldn't be watching CNN during a romantic interlude, would he?

But then, again, knowing Reed, he just might, she thought with a feeble attempt at humor.

She drew a deep, shaky breath and rapped her knuckles lightly on the smooth wood door—so lightly she wasn't even sure he could hear her over the sound of the television. If he didn't immediately respond, she'd consider it a sign and she would leave.

Her heart jumped when the door suddenly opened. She placed a hand against her chest as though to slow its pounding.

Reed wasn't wearing his glasses. He wasn't wearing a shirt, either, only his usual dark slacks. His tanned chest looked even sexier than she'd remembered from the beach. Funny how she only now noticed the few intriguing scars beneath the dusting of dark hair.

Her heart beat even harder, making it difficult for her to breathe. She attempted a smile. "Hi," she said in a voice that bore little resemblance to her own.

His eyebrows rose. "Hi." There was a hint of a question behind the greeting.

"I was—er—in the neighborhood and I thought I'd stop by." She tried to sound flippant, but she was horribly afraid she only sounded stupid. She bit her lip.

Reed looked at her a moment, then stepped back. "Come in."

His room wasn't nearly as luxurious as hers. It looked very much like any room in any nice hotel—king-size bed with a green and burgundy paisley spread, coordinating wood-framed prints on deep green walls, thick carpeting, glossy wood wardrobe-entertainment center, desk, table and chairs.

At least Damien had resisted the temptation to decorate in tropical colors and rattan. This was much more home-like and restful, in Celia's opinion. Not that she cared about the decor of the room. It was the man who'd been staying in it who fascinated her.

She wasn't surprised to discover that Reed was very neat. Not a thing was out of place in the room, no personal belongings scattered around, except for the shirt draped over the back of one of the chairs, the shoes sitting in perfect alignment beside the bed and the discarded glasses on the nightstand.

She turned to face him as he closed the door behind her. "I hope I'm not interrupting anything."

He made a wry face and motioned toward the empty room and the flickering television. "As you can see, I wasn't spending a particularly eventful evening. You aren't interrupting anything except the late news."

She glanced at the TV. "Anything interesting going on in the rest of the world?"

"No." He snapped the set off.

So much for that subject. Celia slid her damp palms discreetly down the sides of her skirt. "I—umm—wanted to talk to you."

He motioned toward one of the chairs. "Have a seat."

Reed settled onto the end of the bed, crossing his right ankle over his left knee, apparently prepared to listen. Celia perched on the very edge of the chair and wondered what the hell she should say now.

He didn't make it any easier for her. He simply watched her, his hazel eyes intent on her flushed face.

Celia cleared her throat. "Damien was called away this evening. There's been an altercation here at the resort and he's trying to avert unpleasant press coverage."

"What does that have to do with me?" Reed asked bluntly, the mention of Damien's name making him scowl.

"Nothing. Well, not exactly. I was—I wanted—"

She stopped, shook her head in self-disgust and began again. "I had intended to talk to Damien tonight about . . . well, about us."

"Us?" Reed repeated. "You and me?"

"No. Damien and me."

Reed's scowl deepened. "Well?"

"I wanted to tell him that I like him a great deal. As a friend. But that's all it can ever be between us. Friends. Not—not lovers."

Reed sat without moving for a moment, though his scowl had vanished, replaced by a faint look of confusion. "What are you trying to tell me, Celia?"

Her fingers clenched so hard in her lap that her knuckles ached. "You—you said I knew where to find you. If I wanted you."

His eyes narrowed. Something flared in them. Heat? Surprise?

"Well?" he prodded, still without moving.

It was the hardest thing she'd ever had to say. "I want you."

Her voice was little more than a trembling exhalation, but Reed heard it. And he moved with a speed that belied the rigid control he'd exhibited thus far. Almost before Celia knew what was happening, he had her out of the chair and in his arms, his mouth locked tightly to hers.

It was almost as though a neon sign went on inside Celia's head. That suddenly, that clearly, that certainly... she knew. *This is right. This is what I've been looking for.*

All the excitement that had been missing in other men's kisses, she found in this one. All the passion she'd only dreamed of experiencing before, she felt now. The feelings were almost overwhelming.

She was aware of his lips, hard and firm against hers. His tongue, wet and seeking. His chest, warm, broad, strong against her flattened breasts. His legs, long and braced, supporting both of them.

She was fully aware that he wanted her as badly as she wanted him.

If there was this much adventure to be found in his kiss, how much more would she discover when they made love? And was she really brave enough, really ready to find out?

He lifted his head, shifted his mouth to a new angle and kissed her again, his hands cupping her hips to lift her higher against him.

Yes, she decided, wrapping her arms around his neck. She was brave enough. And she was more than ready.

Still kissing her, Reed moved, lowering her to the bed and following her down. He lay half on top of her, his legs tangled with hers. He kissed her eyes, her nose, her temples, her throat.

"Celia," he murmured, his big, warm hands cupping her face. "I can't believe you're here."

She managed a thin, shaky laugh. "You can't know how hard it was for me to come."

"I can imagine." He touched his lips to her flushed cheek. "I'm glad you didn't chicken out this time."

She remembered telling him about the parasailing fiasco, and she laughed softly. "I guess I found my sense of adventure, after all. But I'm still scared," she had to admit.

"Don't worry," he murmured, gathering her closer, his lips only a breath above hers. "I'll keep you safe."

She wasn't entirely sure she wanted to be safe tonight. She wanted excitement, adventure, passion, exhilaration. And she wanted to find them all with Reed.

Somehow, she knew she wouldn't be disappointed with his lovemaking. Instinct told her that Reed would provide her with everything she'd always hoped to find.

The tiny buttons of her thin cotton blouse opened easily beneath his fingers. His lips followed the slowly widening opening.

Celia's hands clenched on his bare shoulders. "Reed," she whispered, just to hear his name.

He murmured something incoherent and nuzzled the top of her right breast. She sighed.

He reached the top of her lacy bra, paused, then nudged it aside. A moment later, his lips closed gently around her nipple. Waves of reaction crashed through her, cresting somewhere deep inside her. Celia moaned and arched upward, her hands locked in his hair to hold him more tightly against her.

How could she have imagined that anything could feel this good, this perfect? This right?

He slid one hand slowly up her bare leg, beneath the full cotton skirt that was bunched around and beneath her. His palm was so hot; it seemed to burn a path upward. She reveled in the heat. His fingers stroked her hips, then moved steadily inward, toward the tiny triangle of satin that was all she wore beneath the skirt.

She drew her leg upward, dimly aware that she must have kicked off her huaraches without even realizing it. Her bare toes curled into the bedspread.

It occurred to her that there was something he should know before this went any further. She didn't want him to be disappointed, wanted him to know that she was willing, but uncertain of what to do to please him. And, oh, how she wanted to please him!

His fingers brushed against her through her rapidly dampening panties and she knew she'd better speak now. She had to—before she completely lost the power of speech. "Reed?"

He brought his head back up and kissed her. "Mmm?" he asked, his lips moving softly against hers.

His fingers moved again, and she shuddered in reaction. Her thighs tightened instinctively around his caressing hand. "I—there's something I need to tell you."

He touched the tip of his tongue to her lower lip, then rubbed his own lips over the moistened area. "Can't it wait?"

He slipped one finger beneath the hem of her panties.

Celia gasped. "No," she managed. "I don't think it can."

He sighed, but drew his hand away. Slowly. Still holding her close to him, he raised his head and studied her flaming face. "What is it, Celia?"

She moistened her tingling lips. How to begin? "I haven't been sleeping with Damien," she said.

One corner of his mouth quirked—whether in surprise or satisfaction, she wasn't sure. "Good."

She wasn't certain he fully understood. "I've never slept with Damien."

He smiled and rubbed his thumb against her lips. "Even better."

"Reed," she said, growing frustrated. She clutched his shoulders and looked steadily up at him, willing him to understand without making her draw a verbal picture for him. "I've never slept with *anyone.*"

He went very still. After a moment, he said, "I'm assuming you're using the word sleep as a euphemism."

"Yes," she admitted.

"Are you telling me—you're a virgin?" The word seemed almost as hard for him to say as it would have been for her.

"Yes," she repeated, trying to read behind the open astonishment in his expression. "Is that okay?"

He blinked. "What do you mean?"

"I mean—it doesn't bother you, does it? I know I'm older than most . . . well, you know . . ."

"Virgins."

"Yes." She didn't know why she was having so much trouble getting that out tonight. It had never particularly bothered her before. "I've waited because I wanted it to be right, and it wasn't before," she felt compelled to explain.

Reed still looked a bit dazed. "But it feels right now?"

She took a deep breath. "Yes," she said on an exhalation, her hand sliding down his chest to savor the feel of him. "It feels right now."

He didn't say anything for a very long moment. And then he groaned. "Damn."

She started to ask what was wrong. Before she could get the words out, she found herself alone on the bed. Reed was halfway across the room. And he didn't look as though he intended to come back.

Celia raised herself unsteadily onto her elbows. "Reed?"

"I was thinking about having a drink," he said, opening the discreetly placed liquor cabinet provided by the resort. "Would you like one?"

Celia stared at him. "A drink? Now?"

He opened a miniature bottle and poured amber liquid into a glass tumbler. "Now seems like a real good time to me."

"But—"

He tossed down the drink, set the empty tumbler on the cabinet top, ran a hand through his hair and finally turned back to face her. "I'll put on a shirt and walk you back to your suite."

At first she'd been startled by his behavior, but now she was starting to get angry, an anger spurred by intense disappointment. She spoke slowly, deliberately. "What if I don't *want* to go back to my suite?"

Reed sighed. And then he walked to the side of the bed and touched her cheek. "You don't understand."

She jerked away from his fingers, finding that her skin was still too sensitized for casual touches. A moment later she was on her feet, facing him defiantly as she rebuttoned her shirt. "You're right," she snapped. "I don't understand. You're throwing me out because you've learned that I'm a virgin?"

It was easier to say that time; maybe because she was too mad to even be embarrassed by the intimacy.

Reed shook his head. "I'm not throwing you out. I just don't think this is the best time for us to go to bed together."

"*You* don't think?" she repeated, her temper flaring even more in response to his overly patient tone. "And what about what I think?"

He reached out and took her hands. "We were moving too fast, Celia. We've only known each other a few days. You need time."

Her chin went up. He sounded so much like her sister or her brother—and all those others who'd tried to convince her that they knew what was best for her.

She tugged at her hands, but he tightened his grip. "Look," she said, still tugging futilely. "If you don't want to go to bed with a virgin—with *me*—just say so. But don't give me this song and dance about it being for my own good!"

He pulled her effortlessly back into his arms. And then he kissed her until she went limp against him, until she wouldn't have been surprised if smoke had come out of her ears.

"Don't even suggest," he said in a low growl, "that I don't want you. I want you so much it's eating me alive. I've wanted you from the first minute I saw you, damn it.

So much that I almost... almost lost my head," he finished, sounding as though he'd started to say something else and had changed his mind at the last minute.

"Would it really be so bad to lose your head just once?" she asked wistfully, her cheek against his pounding heart. "Do you always have to be the careful, logical accountant, Reed?"

He inhaled, his chest swelling against her. His hand tightened at the back of her head. When he spoke, his voice wasn't quite steady. "This isn't the right time, Celia. I'm sorry, but you have to trust me on this one."

There didn't seem to be anything else she could say. She drew slowly away from him, her arms crossed in front of her. "Then I guess I'll say good-night."

He reached for his shirt. "I'll walk you back."

"That won't be necessary."

"Damn it, Celia, I said I'd walk you back!" It was as close as he'd come to really losing his temper in front of her.

Celia nodded stiffly, determined not to show him that his anger intimidated her a bit. Hurt pride and dull disappointment warred within her. She fought to hide both when she spoke. "If you insist."

He swiftly donned his shirt and shoes. Celia noted that he left his glasses lying on the nightstand, but she didn't say anything about them. She assumed he could see well enough without them to walk her to her room.

"Let's go," he said without looking at her.

She nodded and followed him to the door.

They crossed the compound in silence. A few others moved around them, but Celia made no effort to recognize anyone. No one else mattered to her just then. No one except the distant, complex man at her side.

Reed checked the corridor that led to her suite, seeming relieved that it was empty. He walked her to the door and waited until she'd unlocked it before he spoke again. "I want you to go home, Celia. If you'll agree, I'll make the arrangements for you so that you can leave first thing in the morning. I have a few business matters to clear away, but then I'll be in touch with you. I promise."

She could have screamed. "Why do you keep trying to send me home?" she demanded, barely remembering to keep her voice low.

"Do you really blame me?" he demanded, swinging a hand toward Damien's door. "You're here with *him*."

"Oh," she said, biting her lip.

She should have realized that Reed would be bothered by those circumstances, being the kind of man he was. Was *that* the main reason he hadn't made love to her tonight? Because she was here as the guest of another man? It made sense—or was her battered ego only grasping for straws?

"I suppose I've been taking advantage of Damien's hospitality," she admitted. "But how could I have known I would meet you here? It's not as though I came here expecting to meet anyone else."

Reed touched her cheek. "I know. I wasn't prepared for you, either."

She covered his hand with her own, searching his unreadable expression. "I'm going to tell him tomorrow. And, if it makes you feel any better, I'm going to offer to reimburse him for my stay here. He probably won't let me, but I feel as though I should offer, anyway."

Of course, she'd probably have to get a loan from the bank where she worked to cover the expenses, but she supposed it would be worth it.

Reed was frowning again. "You don't have to see him again. You could leave him a letter."

"I'll do no such thing! I could never do anything so rude and ungrateful."

He made a face. "No, I suppose you couldn't, at that. But, Celia, about Alexander—"

A door opened abruptly down the hallway. Jim Bennett, Damien's beefy security man, suddenly appeared. "Who's there?"

"It's me, Jim," Celia assured him hastily. "Everything's fine. Don't wake Damien."

"Mr. Alexander is still in his office," Bennett replied, looking suspiciously at Reed. "You want me to give him a message?"

"No, thank you. I'll talk to him tomorrow."

Bennett nodded curtly, shot Reed one last glare, then disappeared again.

"I'll see you tomorrow," Reed said, nudging her into her room. "Get some rest. And, Celia—"

"Yes?"

He kissed her roughly. "Be careful."

He left before she could ask why he'd felt the need for that particular warning again. Something in his voice made her think he really was worried about something . . . but what? Damien's possible reaction to her discussion with him? Surely not. Despite Damien's exaggerated reputation, there had never been any hint that he was a violent man.

Tired now, Celia locked her door and headed into the bathroom. She shook her head at the disheveled reflection in the beveled-edge mirror. She'd wanted excitement on this trip, and she was certainly finding it.

So, how come she still felt like the world's oldest living virgin?

Disgruntledly shaking her head, she changed and climbed into bed. Alone. As usual.

* * *

After briskly walking for almost an hour on the beach, Reed decided that maybe—just barely—he had himself under control enough to go to bed. He wasn't expecting a good night's sleep—not after sharing that bed so briefly and so unsatisfyingly with Celia—but maybe he'd get a few hours' rest.

He was going to need them.

A virgin. He shoved his hand through his breeze-tossed hair and stared blindly out at the darkened horizon. How could he have known that Celia was so innocent?

Oh, sure, there'd been moments when he'd suspected...but he'd always convinced himself he was an idiot to even consider the possibility. At her age, with her looks, her yearlong friendship with Damien Alexander—well, it just hadn't seemed possible.

"I've waited because I wanted it to be right, and it wasn't before."

"But it feels right now?"

"It feels right now."

He groaned as the conversation replayed itself in his head. He'd known then that he couldn't make love to her. Not yet. Not with so many lies between them.

Maybe he'd really known even before, when he'd opened his door to find her standing there looking so nervous and trying so hard to be breezy and nonchalant. It had taken a great deal of courage for her to come to him. A lot of trust.

He had discovered that he couldn't take advantage of either.

A brief, humorless laugh escaped him. Funny, he'd never considered himself to be particularly noble, or selfless. He'd never wanted to be a candidate for sainthood. But tonight he'd known without question that Celia Carson deserved more than a quick tumble with a man who'd lied to her from the first time he'd spoken to her.

He fully intended to be the one to give her everything she deserved. Everything he had to give. But, first, he had to tell her the truth. All of the truth.

And then, somehow, he had to convince her to forgive him.

He thought of her quick temper and winced. It wasn't going to be easy.

He turned and headed quickly toward the resort. He really needed to get some rest if he was going to be on his toes the next day.

Someone spoke from the shadows just as he reached the walkway beside his building. "I wondered if you were coming back tonight."

The familiar murmur made Reed frown as he squinted to see the dark form that blended so well with the landscaping. "Kyle? What are you doing out here at this hour?"

"I was waiting for you."

"Why? What's going on?"

"Let's just say, I wanted to make sure you came back in one piece. Taking a big chance tonight, weren't you?"

Reassured that nothing was wrong—at least, not seriously—Reed sighed wearily. "I don't know what you're talking about."

"You know damned well what I'm talking about." For the first time, Kyle sounded angry, though the conversation was carried on in cautious whispers. "We have a job to do, Reed. The guys we're after play hardball. What do you think will happen to you if Alexander finds out you're fooling around with his playmate while you're waiting to catch him red-handed in a gun swap?"

Reed immediately became defensive. "Alexander's busy tonight. He doesn't even know I've been with Celia."

"You don't think his bodyguard will tell him he saw you together outside her room?"

Realizing that Kyle must have been watching him all evening, Reed scowled furiously. "Damn it, where were you? And why were you spying on me?"

His partner responded in a heated whisper. "You're risking everything, Reed! Perrelli's here, Novotny's here, Alexander's finally here—everything is in place for the exchange we've been expecting for weeks. One wrong move on our part, even the slightest reason for one of them to get nervous and call the whole thing off, and we've blown weeks of work. Do you want that to happen because you've started thinking with your gonads instead of your head? Are you trying to screw up the whole deal just to keep one PYT out of jail?"

"She's not involved with this, damn it! And stop calling her—"

"Will you keep your voice down!" Kyle hissed, reminding Reed that they were hardly in an ideal place for a conference.

Reed managed to rein in his temper. "I'm going to bed," he said evenly. "We'll finish this tomorrow. But get one thing straight. Celia isn't a part of this. She's an innocent bystander—a civilian—and we're keeping her out of it. If you do one thing to jeopardize her safety, I'll—"

"You'll what?" Kyle challenged, as coldly as Reed.

"I'll quit."

There was a long, tense pause. When Kyle spoke, it was in a different tone. "You've fallen that hard?"

"I've fallen that hard," Reed replied evenly, and without embarrassment.

Kyle took a sharp breath, then let it out slowly. "All right. I'll do what I can to help you. But I hope to God you're right about her, Hollander."

"I'm right." Reed had never been more certain of anything in his life.

Without another word, Kyle vanished noiselessly, expertly into the shadows. Reed went to his room.

He spent a very long, restless night, remembering the way Celia had looked, the way she'd felt, the way she'd responded when he'd had her beneath him for that all too short time.

The maître d' was busy with another guest when Celia arrived in the restaurant the next morning. She was greeted, instead, by her favorite waiter. "Good morning, Mike," she said with a smile.

His own smile was bright, friendly, natural—a nice contrast to the fake smirks the overly efficient maître d' had perfected. "Good morning, Ms. Carson. Are you joining Mr. Alexander's party for breakfast?"

"His party?" Celia repeated. She had thought Damien would be waiting for her alone.

She peeked into the dining room and saw that Damien sat at a large table in one corner with Mark, Evan, Maris, Enrique and two other people she didn't know, but recognized as employees of the resort. Damien was talking, the others were listening intently.

"That looks like a business meeting," Celia said, moving back a step. "I don't think I'll interrupt."

"Mr. Alexander assured us that you were to be brought to his table when you arrived," Mike said.

Celia shook her head. "I'd rather—"

"—have breakfast with me." Reed stepped smoothly to her side and finished the sentence for her.

Celia smiled up at him, hoping their interested observer couldn't tell that her heart rate had just gone into double time. "Good morning."

"Good morning." A total stranger could surely hear the special warmth in Reed's voice, would probably recognize the seductive glint in his hazel eyes, even behind the lenses of his glasses.

Celia, of course, didn't miss either. Her breathing accelerated along with her pulse. Why couldn't he look at her like this when they were alone, darn it? When she could do something about it?

Mike was watching them with a grin that he hastily suppressed when she glanced at him. "I could show you to a table for two," he suggested. "Or—"

He glanced around them and lowered his voice. "There's a great little place just a short way down the beach. The Sandcastle. Flakiest pastries on the island—but don't tell anyone I said so, of course."

"Sounds good to me," Reed said promptly, and held out a hand to Celia. "Shall we?"

Celia looked from him to Damien, who was still absorbed in his meeting and hadn't seen her. She was torn between what she felt obligated to do, and what she wanted to do. For one of the few times in her life, self-interest won out over deeply ingrained Southern manners. "I'd love to," she said, and placed her hand in Reed's.

She felt like a student slipping away from school in the middle of the day. She giggled as they stepped outside.

Tucking her hand into his arm, Reed led her toward the beach walk. "What's so funny?"

"Nothing," she said, curling her fingers into his forearm. "I'm just...happy."

Okay, so she wasn't exactly being subtle about her feelings for him. She figured it was already too late for that. And there was so little time left before she had to go back to her real life. Would Reed still be a part of her life after this vacation ended? She'd wondered, and worried, about that for half the night. And she'd always arrived at the same conclusion.

She would be devastated if he said goodbye to her and walked out of her life for good.

He smiled down at her, looking perfectly content to be with her. For now, at least. "I'm glad you're happy," he said softly. "You deserve to be."

After a moment he asked, "Does this mean you've forgiven me for the way I behaved last night?"

She promptly blushed. She really was going to have to do something about this tendency of hers to show every fleeting emotion on her much too expressive face! "I, er, I suppose so."

"I know I acted strangely," he said, a bit awkwardly. "It was just—well, you took me by surprise."

She peeked up at him through her lashes. "Showing up at your room, you mean?"

"That—and what you told me afterward."

"Oh." Her blush deepened. "That I was—er—"

"Yeah."

It seemed that neither of them could say it this morning. Celia wondered why. And then she decided it was because the matter was too important to speak of lightly. She and Reed would not be casual lovers. Something very important was growing between them. Life-altering. And, oh, how she hoped she wasn't the only one who felt that way about it!

"I understand," she assured him, though of course she didn't quite understand. She'd been trying ever since to decide exactly why he'd suddenly changed his mind about making love to her. Even in her inexperience, it had been obvious that he had wanted her. That he hadn't wanted to leave her at her door last night.

Had he considered himself being noble? Even if his intentions had been honorable, she couldn't be grateful that he'd left her to toss and turn all night with an empty, unsatisfied ache inside her. Nobility was all well and good in its place, but it could certainly lead to frustration.

As if he'd read her mind, Reed gave an odd little groan that strangely echoed her feelings. "If you only knew how many times I called myself a fool last night for taking you back to your own room," he muttered. "If I'd thought a cold shower would have helped, I'd be an icicle by now."

It helped, a little, to know that he'd shared her frustration. She laughed and moved closer to his side. "I called you a few choice names, myself, last night," she admitted.

"I don't blame you." He suddenly sounded grim. "You'll probably call me a few more before the day is over."

She frowned and looked up at him, intending to ask him to explain that strange statement. He distracted her by turning to her and kissing her until she forgot how to form words, much less ask a coherent question.

He finally released her. While she recovered her breath, he polished the smudged lenses of his glasses on a spotless white handkerchief. Celia noted that his hands weren't quite steady.

At least she wasn't the only one trembling, she thought with some measure of satisfaction.

Chapter Eleven

The Sandcastle was a quaint little place built on the beach between two towering hotels. It was busy, but there was a table available for them. Celia interpreted that as another good sign, then mentally chided herself for snatching at straws again. Both she and Reed ordered coffee, croissants and fresh fruit, remembering the friendly waiter's advice about the pastries.

"He's a nice guy," Celia commented after the busy waitress had poured their coffee and left with their orders.

"Who is?"

"Mike. The waiter at the Alexander," she clarified.

"Oh." Reed grinned briefly, then nodded. "Yeah, I'm sure he is."

Celia glanced idly around the room. A short, dumpy woman with bottle-red hair sat alone at a table in one corner. Though she bore little resemblance otherwise, the red hair reminded Celia of the woman with whom Reed had shared breakfast yesterday. Followed by a leisurely stroll on the beach.

She cleared her throat and stirred her coffee, focusing her gaze on the circling spoon. She had no right to quiz Reed about the woman, of course. After all, she had been breakfasting with another man at the time.

"What's wrong, Celia?"

She looked up quickly in response to his perceptive question. "What do you mean?" she stalled.

"You've started frowning. Something I said?"

"No. I was just—umm—thinking."

"What about?" he persisted.

She sighed. "I should have known not to try to hide anything from you. You and I have been very honest with each other, haven't we, Reed?"

Something crossed his face—a more suspicious person than she might have called it guilt. She told herself she must be mistaken.

"Er—" he said, then started stirring his own coffee, though he hadn't put anything in it.

"We *have* been honest with each other, haven't we, Reed?" she repeated, watching him closely, suddenly uneasy.

"Stop trying to change the subject. Why were you frowning?"

Maybe she *was* just trying to change the subject. She made a face and confessed. "I was thinking about that redhead."

Reed looked confused. "What redhead?"

"The one you had breakfast with yesterday. And then—well, I saw you walking with her. She's very beautiful."

"Oh." A glimmer of amusement flashed through his eyes. "That redhead. Yeah. She's beautiful."

"Tall, too."

"Mmm."

"She's certainly in good shape. Probably lifts weights or something."

"Yeah." Reed sipped his coffee, then murmured over the rim of his cup, "Nice pecs."

Celia kicked him beneath the table.

Reed sputtered and laughed. "Sorry—but you made it so easy. She and I went for a short, friendly walk together and then she went to the health club to work out. That's all there was to it."

Of *course* she went to work out, Celia thought as the waitress set her buttery croissant in front of her. Celia hadn't set foot in the health club, herself. Those machines always looked like instruments of torture to her. "I'm sure she's very nice," she muttered after the waitress left the table.

"The redhead? I don't know. She seemed like a real barracuda to me," Reed mused, looking amused at a private joke.

Celia thought of kicking him again, then decided to let it go. "Sorry," she said stiffly. "It's none of my business, of course. It's not as if I was jealous or anything."

"I've sure as hell been jealous of Alexander."

The blunt admission rather surprised Celia, though she'd suspected it. She twisted her napkin in her lap, wondering what to say in response.

As Reed himself had pointed out last night, this was happening very fast between them—whatever it was. They'd known each other such a short time. Less than a week! And yet Celia had been fully prepared to make love with him last night.

She ate in silence for a time, then set her fork down and looked across the little table. She'd already forgotten the dumpy woman across the room—and all the other patrons, as well. She and Reed might have been alone in the crowded little diner, for all the attention she spared her surroundings. "Reed?"

He swallowed the last bite of his croissant. "Yes?"

"I'm a little nervous," she admitted frankly. "Of—well, of this thing between us. It's all new for me."

He reached out to take her hand. "I'm scared as hell," he said, his expression rueful, his tone sincere. "Trust me, Celia, this is new for me, too."

"I do trust you," she said with a little smile of relief that she'd gotten that out of the way. "I have from the beginning."

Reed's smile faded. "We have to talk."

"I know. There are so many things we still have to learn about each other. And such a short time left," she said, fretting. "I have to be back at work at the bank Monday. I suppose you have to get back to your job, too."

"Celia, about my work." He hesitated.

"Can I get you folks anything else?" the waitress asked, appearing suddenly beside their table, recalling them abruptly to their public surroundings.

Reed released Celia's hand and sat back in his chair. "No, not for me. Celia?"

She shook her head, curious about what Reed had started to tell her.

The waitress nodded and slipped their tab onto the corner of the table. Reed picked it up, glanced at it, and laid a bill on top of it. "Are you finished?" he asked Celia.

"Yes."

He glanced at his watch. "Let's go for a walk."

"All right." She set her napkin on the table and rose.

Hand in hand, they strolled down the beach. There were quite a few people out this morning, Celia noted. Joggers, fishers, sunbathers, early picnickers. Some college-age guys playing fetch with a couple of big dogs. Mothers trying vainly to keep their children coated with sun block.

November, she reminded herself with a slight shake of her head. Sometimes the contrasts between here and home were very disconcerting. Made her wonder anxiously if anything she'd found here would survive the return to reality.

Reed led her back in the direction of the resort. He said little, but kept glancing at his watch. Finally he sighed, stopped and ran a hand through his hair. "We have to talk."

"Yes." He'd said that already, and she'd already agreed, but she didn't bother pointing it out. Something was obviously bothering Reed. Something important.

Why was it so hard for him to begin? What wasn't he telling her?

Celia felt her nerves knot somewhere low in her middle. "What is it, Reed?" she prodded, hoping to help him.

He looked again at his watch. "Damn it, there isn't time."

She couldn't understand his sudden obsession with the time. "Why? What do you have to do today?"

"I have to, er, make some calls. Business," he added vaguely. "I'm sorry."

Why was it that men kept saying that and leaving her this week?

Celia wryly shook her head. "You don't have to apologize," she assured him. Those words were starting to sound a bit too familiar. "I understand."

"I want you to go to your suite and wait for me," he said, and the suggestion sounded suspiciously like an order. "It may take a while, but I'll call as soon as I'm free."

"Why should I have to stay in my suite just because you're busy?" she demanded, turning to face him. "There might be other things I'd rather do."

Reed looked frustrated. "Celia, you don't understand."

"Don't start that again! Either tell me what you're trying to say, or drop it."

He grumbled something unintelligible and pulled her into his arms. "I just want to keep you safe."

She spread her hands on his chest and looked up at him, trying to read his expression. "You're right. I don't understand. Safe from what, Reed?"

"From Alexander."

She frowned. "From Damien? You can't be serious. Damien isn't going to hurt me. His pride might be a bit piqued, but he's really a very nice man. To be honest, I think he already knows nothing's going to happen between us. If either of us had really been serious about it, something would have already happened by now."

Reed groaned. "How can you be so naive?"

That made her mad. She tugged against him, trying to free herself from his arms. "Don't talk to me as though I'm a dim-witted child, Reed! I hate that. I may not be overly experienced, but I am not naive. I'm perfectly capable of taking care of myself."

"You don't—"

"And *don't* tell me again that I don't understand!" she exploded, shoving harder against him.

Reed held her easily. "I'm sorry," he said, pulling her closer. "Celia, I'm sorry."

She went still, wanting to believe, but suspicious of the ease with which he'd conceded. "You're sorry you called me naive?" she clarified.

"Yes. And I'm sorry I tried to give you orders. I suppose you could call it a bad habit," he added with a twisted smile.

"Then it's one you're going to have to break," she told him bluntly. "I don't like being told what to do."

"I've already figured that out," he assured her wryly. "And I'll work on it."

She nodded stiffly. "You'd better go make your calls."

"I know." He placed a hand at the back of her head and held her face tipped up to his. "I don't want to leave you."

She softened. How could she not? "I don't want you to," she admitted.

He kissed her, lightly at first, and then harder. Deeper.

Celia wrapped her arms around his neck and responded with everything inside her.

Reed was breathing heavily by the time he drew reluctantly away. He muttered a curse, looked at his watch again, and groaned. "I have to go. I'll walk you to your suite."

"No. I'll walk myself."

He didn't seem to like it, but they parted at the koi pond. Reed headed for his building, Celia lingered for a moment to watch the fish and work up her nerve to go in search of Damien.

This was something she had to do, she told herself firmly. The sooner, the better. No matter what Reed said.

Celia found Damien in his office, for once unguarded by his ferociously protective secretaries. He looked up from a stack of paperwork when she appeared in the doorway. He rose immediately to his feet.

"Celia! There you are, I've been looking for you."

"Have you?" She closed the office door behind her. "I hope you weren't worried."

"I was, a bit," he admitted, rounding the desk. "I thought you'd be joining me for breakfast."

"I saw you in the restaurant. But you were surrounded by your staff and you all looked so serious I hated to interrupt your meeting."

Damien looked regretful. "We did have an impromptu meeting this morning. I'm afraid my staff had gotten a bit lax in handling press matters. I had to remind them of some basic rules when dealing with the paparazzi."

"Did it get ugly last night?" Celia asked sympathetically.

He made a face. "Almost. I think we avoided a scandal. But only barely."

"Did your unpleasant guest leave?"

"Yes. He did so at the urging of local police. His, er, lady friend chose not to press charges."

Celia frowned. "She shouldn't have let him get away with beating her. He'll only do so again the next time he's angry with her—or someone else."

Damien shrugged. "There was some indication that she took the first swing. With a chair. I don't think either of them could be considered blameless in the incident."

Celia shook her head in disgust. "Only goes to show that fame and fortune can't buy class," she murmured.

Damien chuckled. "Sweetheart, people have been telling me that for years."

Unamused, she immediately became defensive on his behalf. "But, Damien, you would never act that way. I mean, you're obscenely rich, but you've never abused your power. Not in front of me, anyway," she added conscientiously, knowing there were sides of Damien she'd probably never seen.

Damien opened his mouth, closed it, then burst out laughing. "Is it any wonder that I enjoy being with you? No one else talks to me the way you do."

"Well, Damien, surely you *know* you're obscenely rich," Celia said, grinning at him now. She always enjoyed teasing him; mostly because he responded so good-naturedly. "It's not as if I'm telling you anything new."

He slung an arm around her shoulders. "Say the word, my darling, and all I have will be yours. Except, of course, my Rolls. That I don't share with *anyone.*"

Celia shook her head, matching his tone. "All or nothing, Alexander. If I can't have the Rolls, then the deal's off."

He sighed heavily. "All right, you win. You can have the Rolls—but only if I get *you* in return."

Though she was still fairly sure he was teasing, Celia felt her amusement fade. She took a deep breath. "That's what I wanted to talk to you about."

"My Rolls?" he asked, still smiling, though his eyes had turned serious.

She shook her head. "Us."

He sighed and released her. "I see."

Celia placed a hand on his arm and looked up at him anxiously. She didn't want to hurt him; she wasn't even sure she could. Still, she chose her words carefully. "I like you very much, Damien. I want you to know that I consider you one of the nicest men I know."

He looked startled. "Lord, Celia, you make me sound like your favorite uncle!"

She winced. She'd forgotten to take into account that male ego thing. "I didn't quite mean it that way. I was trying to say that I consider you one of my very best friends."

He grimaced. "Uh-oh. I know where this is leading."

"Now, Damien, don't make this difficult for me," she chided him. "It's hard enough as it is."

"I think I've already gotten your point. You're trying to tell me that you only want to be friends with me, right?"

"Right." She patted his arm. "I'm sure if you think about it, you'll agree that it's the best decision for both of us. Let's face it, Damien, I'm just not your usual type. Your life is glamorous and exciting and sophisticated—and I'm none of those things. I couldn't even go parasailing with you."

"I could have taught you to be more adventurous," he assured her. "You just needed more time."

She smiled and shook her head. "No. I've had enough time to know that as fond as I am of you, friendship is all there could ever be between us."

She thought of Reed and pictured herself surrounded by a brood of little accountants who looked just like him—tiny horn-rimmed glasses and all. Average. Ordinary. And she could honestly say she wanted nothing more out of life now than to share it with him.

"It's that guy, isn't it? The one you met while I was away. The one you had breakfast with this morning." Damien spoke with uncanny insight, and the line of his jaw seemed harder than usual.

Celia was startled. "How did you know who I had breakfast with this morning?"

"Never mind that. Are you dumping me for him?"

She frowned at his uncharacteristically belligerent tone. "I'm hardly dumping you, Damien. There's never been anything more than friendship between us. One doesn't dump a friend. As for Reed—well, that remains to be seen."

"And it's none of my business," he interpreted.

"Right," she said, though she spoke gently.

He covered her hand with his own. "I'm sorry, Celia. I certainly don't mean to pry into your business. I'm just disappointed. I had hoped that you and I...well. You know."

"Oh, Damien." She rested her head against his arm for a moment, touched by the look in his eyes. "You know it wouldn't have worked out. I'm much too traditional for you. Within a few weeks you'd have been off looking for much more exciting companionship. You know you don't want to tie yourself down to one woman when there are so many waiting to go out with you."

"I suppose you're right," he conceded, a bit reluctantly. "Still, it might have been different this time. For once, I could almost understand the appeal of that old one-man, one-woman thing."

"You can't even say it without shuddering," she accused him, not quite accurately. Actually, he had sounded more sincere than she'd ever heard him.

Surely Damien hadn't really been thinking of permanence with her! She'd never even imagined that he'd wanted more from her that a lighthearted affair—which, to be honest, was all she'd ever envisioned having with him. That, of course, had been before she'd forced herself to accept that she just wasn't the "lighthearted affair" type. Something her sister had told her all along.

"You know me very well, don't you, love?" Damien said, more lightly now. If his feelings really were seriously injured, he hid it well. Celia was relieved that he'd made it that easy for her. She suspected that she'd bruised his ego worse than his heart. He would recover quickly, if he suffered at all.

At least, she hoped that was the case. She didn't like the idea that she'd hurt someone she considered a friend.

He motioned her toward the overstuffed sofa against one pecan-panelled wall. "Can I get you something to drink?" he asked as he stepped behind the well-stocked bar on the far wall and tossed ice cubes into a tumbler for himself.

"Just fruit juice, if you have it," Celia said, taking a seat on the couch.

She watched as he poured bourbon for himself and the juice for her.

He carried both over to the couch, and sat beside her. "So," he said briskly. "Tell me about this guy, Hollander. What do you know about him?"

"I thought we just agreed that this wasn't your business," she reminded him with a smile.

"Humor me. We're friends, remember?" He gave an ironic twist to the word friends. "I'm feeling responsible. If you hadn't come here at my invitation, and if I hadn't stood you up for almost a week, you never would have met the guy. I'll never forgive myself if he turns out to be a con artist or a lowlife."

"No self-respecting con artist would run a scam on me," Celia said with a laugh. "What would he hope to gain? I told him from the beginning that I work as an assistant loan officer in a small-town bank. He surely doesn't think I'm rolling in money."

"He knows you're a friend of mine," Damien corrected her. "And, as you pointed out, I am, er, obscenely rich. Suppose he's using you to get to me in some way."

"He isn't," Celia said flatly. "Reed isn't interested in your money, Damien. It has bothered him very much that I'm here as your guest. Neither of us wanted to take advantage of your hospitality.

"In fact," she added, remembering something else she'd wanted to discuss with Damien, "I insist that you have your staff bill me for the time I've spent here. It's only right."

Damien was shaking his head before she even finished speaking. "Absolutely not."

"Now, Damien—"

"Not another word about it, Celia," he said warningly. "I invited you here as my guest. Because I care for you, not simply to get you into my bed—though that would have been nice," he added with an exaggerated wistfulness that made her smile. "I just hope you've had a nice time, despite the series of misfortunes that kept us separated during most of your visit."

"It's been wonderful," she assured him. "And, Damien—it wouldn't have made any difference if you'd been here," she felt compelled to add. "I think I knew even when I left Percy that you and I would never be—well, you know."

"I know," he said glumly. "Why do you think I haven't pushed harder for more than a good-night kiss at your door? Why do you think I've been working so hard to avoid this 'little talk'? I was sort of hoping you'd change your mind after you'd had a few more days to bask in my charm."

She giggled.

He exhaled deeply. "Would you mind changing the subject, sweetheart? My ego's taken just about all the damage it can handle for one morning."

Celia smiled affectionately at him. "Don't worry, Damien. I'm sure your ego will make a full and fast recovery. If nothing else, Mark's little friend Kimmi would just love to play nursemaid to your wounded sensibilities."

Damien perked up a bit at that. "He is rather ignoring her, isn't he? Poor kid is probably feeling terribly neglected."

"I'm sure she is. Do you think Mark would mind too badly if you stepped in for him?"

Damien grinned. "Mark is paid not to mind that sort of thing."

Celia rolled her eyes. "What was that I said about you never abusing your power? I take it back."

"Now, Celia—"

"Now, Damien—"

They laughed together. And, if the laughter was a bit strained now, they both pretended not to notice.

They chatted politely for another half hour. And then Celia stood, judging the time to be right. "I'll let you get back to work. You looked quite busy when I came in."

"I had planned on letting the rest go and spend the day with you," he answered. "But—"

"Take care of your work, Damien," she said gently. "I'm sure I'll find something to do."

"I'm sure you will," he agreed, and his voice was a bit harder than usual. He masked it quickly with one of his bright smiles. "So, how long will you be staying? Still planning to go back to Arkansas Friday?"

Two more days, Celia thought with a quick surge of dismay. Would she and Reed be saying goodbye then? "I'm not sure," she admitted. "My plans are rather vague at the moment."

Damien nodded. "Stay as long as you like," he said. "The invitation still stands for the full duration."

She squeezed his hand. "Thank you. You're a very sweet man, did you know that?"

He rolled his eyes. "There goes that 'favorite uncle' tone again. I have to tell you, Celia, I'm just not used to having beautiful young women talk to me quite that way. I can't say that I like it."

"I'll work on it," she promised with a smile.

"I'd appreciate it. So, how would you and your new friend like to join me for dinner this evening? I'd like to meet the guy."

Celia was startled. She wasn't at all sure how Reed would feel about having dinner with Damien. She wasn't entirely sure how she felt about it, herself.

"I'll ask him," she temporized.

Damien nodded. "I just want to talk to him. I've always been a good judge of character, you know. I wouldn't be where I am if I weren't. If I sense any reason at all to worry about this guy, if there's the slightest chance that he'll hurt you, I'll—I'll—well, I'll do something about it," he promised flatly.

"Now *you* sound like a favorite uncle," Celia accused him in mild exasperation. "Don't you start overprotecting me, Damien. It really just isn't in character for you."

"You might be surprised," he murmured, and kissed her cheek. And then he escorted her to the door with a bit too much haste.

Celia dialed Reed's room number when she returned to her suite. She half expected the line to be busy, since he'd been so concerned about the calls he needed to make. Instead, the phone rang several times on the other end before she finally conceded he wasn't in his room.

Now what? she wondered. Should she go looking for him? Or wait here, as he'd asked—make that, as he'd ordered her.

Because she was growing increasingly tired of taking orders, she decided to go out. She glanced in the mirror to make sure her loose, oatmeal-colored top and slacks were still neat. She decided she looked a bit colorless. Her restless night and her difficult talk with Damien had left her rather pale.

She dug in her bag for a bright scarf—a favorite silk one that her grandmother had given her for her birthday. She brushed her hair, pulled it back and tied it at the nape with the colorful strip of fabric. The patterned scarf seemed to add color to her face. Satisfied with her appearance, she headed determinedly for the door.

Reed would soon learn that she wasn't an inanimate object to be stashed in her room until he had time to play with her.

It was past lunchtime. Perhaps Reed was in the restaurant, she thought. She wasn't checking up on him, she assured herself somberly. She just wanted to tell him that she'd been completely honest with Damien. That he needn't feel now as though they were slipping around behind their host's back.

The officious maître d' greeted Celia in the restaurant lobby. "Miss Carson. Table for one, or will Mr. Alexander be joining you?"

"No. Actually, I'm looking for Mr. Hollander. Have you seen him?"

The man's thin eyebrows rose. "No. He hasn't been in."

Disappointed, she nodded. "Thank you."

"Shall I show you to a table?"

"No, thank you." She stepped back and allowed an elderly couple to take her place. The maître d' greeted them by name and ushered them solicitously to a table.

"Hi, Ms. Carson. Joining us for lunch today?"

Celia glanced around to find Mike Smith emerging from the employee door, buttoning his neat white jacket as he approached her, obviously just beginning a shift. "No, I'm not hungry," she said. "I was trying to find Reed—Mr. Hollander. Have you seen him, Mike?"

"Not since the two of you left for breakfast this morning," Mike replied. His dark eyes searched her face. "Is anything wrong, Ms. Carson?"

"No." She forced a smile. "I've just misplaced him, that's all."

"I'm sure he'll turn up."

She nodded. "I'm sure he will."

"Want me to tell him you're looking for him, if I see him?"

"Yes, thank you."

Celia didn't bother looking in the health club or bar. Reed had never shown any more interest than she in either facility. She did check the pool, thinking he might be sitting under an umbrella with one of his history books. He wasn't. Nor did she see him at the tennis courts or the koi pond.

She looked thoughtfully at the long, flat expanse of beach spreading out beyond the resort. For just a moment, she longed for the wooded hills of home. How could anyone live without trees and grass and hills? she thought, studying all that flat, grayish-white sand and the painstakingly planted grass leading up to it.

She wondered if there were trees and grass and hills where Reed lived? Or did he live in the city, surrounded by concrete and high rises? And if so, would he want Celia to live there with him eventually? Could she adapt?

She could certainly try.

She continued her search for him. She wasn't at all pleased when she finally spotted him.

He was sitting on a secluded bench beneath two obviously transplanted and rather sickly-looking palm trees at the very edge of the Alexander's property. He wasn't alone. The glamourous redhead was sitting beside him—very closely beside him. Their heads were close together, their gazes locked as they talked in voices much too low for Celia to hear.

She stopped dead in her tracks behind them. She knew neither of them had noticed her. They were much too intent on each other.

She thought of marching up to them and breezily introducing herself to the woman, acting as if Reed should have been expecting her to join him, but something held her back. Maybe it was the way they were talking—they didn't look as though they wanted to be interrupted.

Celia's temper flared. Was *this* Reed's idea of making some important calls? *This* was the reason he'd had to rush away from her this morning? He'd actually expected her to wait alone in her room while he snuggled on a bench with another woman?

She was still watching when the redhead said something that made Reed scowl. And then he shook his head and laughed, looking ruefully amused.

He put an arm around the woman's shoulders then and gave her a hug. One she returned with an enthusiasm that made Celia absolutely furious.

Without waiting to see more, Celia turned on one heel and hurried away. She was half tempted to call Damien and politely ask him to please have Reed beaten up. She suspected that Damien would happily agree.

She didn't call Damien, of course. That would have been childish. Instead, she headed away from the resort, just as fast as she could put the place—and all its accompanying confusion—behind her.

It was early evening when Celia returned to her suite. She'd spent the day keeping busy, utilizing the island trolley system, whimsically dubbed "The Wave," to take her to the tourist places Mindi Kellogg had tried to talk her into seeing before. The University of Texas–Pan American Coastal Studies Laboratories, with its aquariums and extensive shell collection, Sea Turtle, Inc., the Sea Ranch Marina. It wasn't that she'd particularly wanted to visit those places alone, but she had needed the time to think.

Everything had been happening so fast. She needed time to put the past few days into perspective. Had she really fallen in love with a man she hardly knew? Was she really willing to take a huge risk like that with someone who could hurt her worse than she'd ever imagined?

By the end of the day, she had an all-new appreciation for fascinating sea creatures, particularly those of the flippered persuasion, but she hadn't resolved her feelings for Reed. She couldn't say for certain that what she felt for him was love—but she couldn't quite convince herself it wasn't, either.

Needing a chance to freshen up and bolster her courage before facing him again, she slipped unnoticed into her building and tiptoed down the empty hallway, almost as though he could somehow hear her if she wasn't careful. She unlocked her door, stepped into the sitting room, then closed and bolted the door behind her.

And then she turned to find Reed standing in the bedroom doorway, watching her with an expression that could have been carved of hard, relentless stone.

Chapter Twelve

Celia placed a hand to her throat, where her heart seemed to be hanging at the moment. "How did you get in here? You scared me half to death!"

"Where the hell have you been?" Reed demanded, ignoring her question. "I've torn this damned resort apart looking for you."

"I've been out."

"You weren't with Alexander. He's been in his office all day."

She lifted an eyebrow. "You've been watching him, too?"

"Damn it, Celia, I want to know where you've been!"

"Why should you care?" she challenged, facing him defiantly. "It's not as if you've been waiting alone for me!"

"What the hell is that supposed to mean?"

She tilted her chin. She was tired and grubby and hungry, and in no mood to discuss the gorgeous redhead before she'd had a chance to freshen up. "I want to take a shower," she said, trying to speak in a "royalty dismissing the staff" tone. "I'd like you to leave now."

He moved so fast that her heart jumped into her throat again. His hands gripped her forearms with a force that was just short of painful. His dark eyes burned angrily into hers. "Where were you, Celia?"

"I was out," she snapped. "Sight-seeing. Now let go of me."

"Were you alone?"

"No," she answered recklessly. "There was a whole busload of people with me. Are you satisfied?"

"Why did you leave? I told you to wait for me here."

"I know you told me to wait. I chose not to. Who the hell do you think you are, anyway? I—"

Whatever else she might have yelled at him was smothered beneath his angry kiss.

She stiffened, shoving futilely against him. She'd be damned if she'd be manhandled this way! Oddly enough, she wasn't frightened of Reed. Just completely furious.

And then he did something that disarmed her temper as effectively as a bucket of cold water. He wrapped his arms around her, buried his face in her hair and said in a notably unsteady voice, "Oh, God, Celia, I've been so worried about you. Please don't ever scare me like that again."

Utterly astonished, Celia went limp against him. Reed had been worried about her? So worried that his hands shook now as they stroked her back? "Reed? I don't understand. Why were you so worried?"

"I didn't know where you were," he answered, drawing back to search her face, as though looking for injuries. "The last I knew you were headed for your room. And then you disappeared for hours. I heard you'd gone into Alexander's office, but no one knew what happened to you after that."

"Did you ask Damien?" Celia asked, hoping he hadn't gotten Damien worried, as well.

Reed shook his head. "I was just about to go after him. Five more minutes and I would have stormed his office and demanded to know what he'd done with you."

"Reed, I can't believe you're overreacting this way. Why are you so quick to suspect that Damien would do anything to harm me? Why can't you believe that he's really a very nice man?"

Reed grunted.

"He is," Celia insisted, gripping his shirt as though to force him to believe her. "Even when I told him this morning that he and I will never be more than friends, he was very sweet and understanding. He even insisted that I stay on here as his guest for as long as I want. As his friend."

Reed jerked his chin up. "You told him that?"

"Yes. He, er, he asked me if my decision had anything to do with you."

Reed's eyes narrowed. "What did you tell him?"

Her temper kindled again. "I told him it did. That was before I saw you climbing all over that woman this afternoon. Just what the hell is it with you, anyway, Reed? If you're interested in someone else, why should it matter to you who I spent my afternoon with?"

He looked startled. "I wasn't climbing all over anyone!"

"I *saw* you," she repeated. "On the bench with that redhead. You hugged her. And she hugged you back."

He stared at her a moment, then made a sound of utterly male exasperation. "It was just a hug, damn it. We'd been talking about you."

She rolled her eyes. "Of course you were."

His fingers tightened again on her forearms, and for a moment she thought he was going to give in to his obvious urge to shake her. To his credit, he resisted.

"We were talking about you," he repeated much too evenly. "I told her that I had fallen for you. She wished me luck. Then offered condolences."

Celia wasn't quite sure why he'd been talking about his feelings for her with a woman who was supposedly little more than a total stranger to him. And she still didn't understand that all-too-friendly-looking hug. But she couldn't resist asking, "Why did she offer condolences?"

Reed's smile was lopsided. "She said it was obvious that I'm no longer a free man. Said I might as well be wearing a sign saying I was taken. I don't even want to look at another woman. Damn it, Celia, you've got me all but hogtied and branded. I'm yours—if you still want me."

Her knees went weak. She clung to his shirt for balance.

It hadn't been the most romantic speech she'd ever heard. Damien would have phrased it much more smoothly, much more poetically. But he wouldn't have said it with Reed's gruff, painfully frank sincerity.

"Oh, Reed," she whispered, her eyes misting. "Of course I still want you. I've wanted you from the beginning, even when I didn't *want* to want you. Why do you think it hurt me so much to see you with someone else?"

"Celia." He drew her slowly into his arms, his evening-roughened cheek resting gently against her softer one. "I didn't mean to hurt you. Don't you know I'd rip out my own tongue before I'd hurt you?"

She managed a shaky laugh. "There's no need to be quite so graphic about it. I guess I overreacted when I saw you. It's been a very stressful week."

He chuckled, his lips hovering only an inch above hers. "Tell me about it," he murmured, his breath warm on her skin.

He kissed her then, and this kiss wasn't an angry one. His lips were gentle, caressing, his movements slow, tender. Rather than resisting this time, Celia wrapped her arms around his neck and melted into him.

Almost immediately, the kiss grew heated, the flames fueled not by anger now, but by desire. A hunger that was getting harder for both of them to deny.

Celia pressed tightly against him, craving his touch, his warmth. He gripped her hips and pulled her into him, letting her know without doubt that he wanted her. That he ached as badly as she did.

"Reed," she whispered, her fingers buried deep in his thick hair, her lips moving against his. "Make love with me. Now. Please."

He groaned. "I can't. There isn't time."

She didn't know what he meant—and she didn't want to know. She was tired of waiting, tired of being cautious—tired of being afraid. She knew what she wanted now, and she had somehow found the courage to ask for it. "Make love to me, Reed," she whispered, rubbing her lips slowly, savoringly across his mouth.

A hard tremor went through him. He wanted her. She smiled and kissed him again.

"Celia." His voice was hoarse. "I wanted to wait. We need to talk." The words were broken, interspersed with hot, greedy kisses.

She returned kiss for kiss. "I don't want to talk," she murmured, then moved boldly against him.

He gasped, and she smiled in satisfaction, sensing victory. "Make love to me, Reed," she demanded again.

This time he didn't even try to resist. He swept her into his arms, and it was she who gasped as her feet dangled several inches above the floor.

The phone started ringing when he carried her swiftly into the bedroom. Reed grunted a curse and paused in the middle of the room.

She nestled her head into his shoulder. "Let it ring," she murmured, suspecting that it was Damien, asking about dinner.

Reed seemed torn for a moment. Celia settled the matter by reaching up to kiss him, her tongue sliding between his lips.

They let the phone ring. Neither of them even noticed when it stopped.

Reed removed Celia's clothing with unsteady fingers. Her cheeks were hot when she stood naked in front of him, but she lifted her chin proudly. The open admiration in his gaze boosted her ego as nothing ever had before.

"You're so beautiful," he murmured, then shook his head impatiently. "I wish I could think of something more original to say. I'm afraid I'm not very good with flowery words."

She touched his face. "You're doing fine," she assured him, her throat thick with emotion. And then she reached for the buttons of his shirt. It made her feel too vulnerable to be nude while he was fully clothed. And, besides, she wanted very badly to touch him.

His chest was as broad, as tanned and firm as she remembered. She stroked her hands slowly, reverently over his skin, testing the muscles beneath, the light dusting of hair tickling her palm. She'd thought before that he seemed to be in awfully good shape for someone with a desk job. The solidity of the muscles beneath her hands made her repeat that observation. "Do you lift weights?" she asked, touching her lips to his right nipple.

Though he didn't move, she felt a faint quiver of reaction beneath her touch. "Sometimes," he said, sounding as though he were choking.

"It pays off," she murmured dreamily, snuggling against him. His arms closed around her, a tender trap. She made no effort to free herself. She was too happy where she was, held against his hard, warm, throbbing body.

Reed gave a broken groan and lowered her to the bed. He shed his slacks and briefs with more haste than grace and joined her on the huge, soft mattress. Celia welcomed him with open arms and an encouraging smile.

Whether out of consideration for her inexperience, or simply to prolong their pleasure, Reed moved very slowly. So slowly that within minutes, Celia was clutching at him, urging him to hurry. She felt as though she would shatter from a delicious combination of excitement, desire, anticipation and nerves.

He explored every inch of her with his hands, his lips. Her breasts, her throat, her stomach, her legs. Places so intimate that she blushed when he touched her there, then cried out with pleasure when he lingered.

Celia was a quivering mass of flesh long before he'd completed his investigation.

"Reed," she said, her voice a shaken whisper. "Please. I need you."

He moved upward and lay draped across her. He was so hard, so tense, that she knew it was difficult for him to wait. But still he moved slowly, pausing to smooth a strand of hair away from her damp cheek. "I want you so badly," he said, his tone gruff, his eyes glittering with barely repressed need. "Don't let me hurt you."

"You won't hurt me," she said, trusting him then as she'd never trusted any man before. "You could never hurt me, Reed."

He seemed to flinch. "I hope you remember that later," he said obscurely, but he kissed her again before she could ask him to clarify. By the time he released her mouth, she'd forgotten the question.

He made love to her so gently, so tenderly. If there was pain, it was fleeting. And the pleasure that followed more than compensated for any discomfort.

Dazed and sated, Celia lay for a long time against Reed's damp, heaving chest. She moved one leg experimentally, finding that she was sore—but delightfully so. On the whole, she'd never felt better.

So this was love, she thought dreamily.

It seemed strange to her, now, that she hadn't recognized it immediately.

"Are you all right?" Reed asked, tucking her tenderly into his shoulder. "I didn't hurt you?"

"I feel wonderful," she replied, then laughed softly. "I had no idea what I've been missing all these years."

"You wouldn't have felt that way with anyone but me," Reed told her sternly.

She smiled at his tone. "Is that right?"

"That's fact. So don't even think about broadening your horizons to find out. I intend to be the only one to demonstrate anything you think you might have missed."

She propped her chin on her hand and looked at him through her lashes. "You sound very fierce. Very possessive."

His hand tightened in her hair. "You can bet on it. You're mine now."

"I didn't know tax accountants were such a primitive breed," Celia mused teasingly. It seemed safer at the moment to keep the conversation light—though Reed didn't sound at all as if he were joking. The thought gave her an odd little thrill that seemed to be a mixture of nerves and pleasure.

Too fast, she found herself thinking. *It's happening too fast.*

She tried very hard to ignore that annoying voice of warning.

Reed didn't answer her comment about accountants. Instead, he kissed her until she was clinging to him again, teasing forgotten.

How could she want him again so soon? So desperately?

The very intensity of her hunger frightened her a bit. It was almost as though she felt she had to take advantage of every minute she had with him. Almost as though she knew their time together couldn't last.

Impatiently calling herself a compulsive worrier, she pushed those worries aside and gave herself up to enjoyment.

Neither Reed nor Celia said anything for a long time after that. Celia simply didn't have the energy for conversation, and as she lay bonelessly in Reed's arms, she suspected that he felt much the same way. The thought made her smile in secret satisfaction.

When he finally shifted his weight beneath her, she thought he was only getting more comfortable. And then she realized that he was looking at his watch.

She groaned. "Don't start that again."

"I have to go." His voice was a husky growl that sounded so sexy she was tempted to attack him again.

Except that she didn't at all like what he had said.

Startled, she lifted her head. "What do you mean, you have to go? Why?"

"It's getting late."

She ran her fingertips over his whisker-roughened jaw. "Spend the night with me."

"I can't."

"Why?" she persisted, beginning to frown. Why was he suddenly acting so distant? Surely he wasn't having regrets about making love to her. She knew he'd been as well satisfied as she had...hadn't he? "Reed?"

He brushed a strand of hair away from her anxious eyes. "Celia, I have to go," he said gently. "There are some things I have to do."

"Don't try to tell me you have more calls to make. Not at this hour."

"I can't explain right now. I don't have time. I promise I'll tell you everything you want to know—and probably a few things you don't want to know—tomorrow." He slid from beneath her and reached for his clothes.

Propped on one elbow, Celia watched him in growing dismay. "I can't believe you're leaving like this. Reed, why won't you talk to me now? What do you have to do that's so important?"

He looked at her as he stepped into his dark jeans. His eyes were troubled. "I don't want to go," he assured her, and he sounded so sincere she had to believe him. "There's nothing I want more than to sleep with you in my arms tonight. I promise I'll make this up to you, Celia—but I have to go now."

She didn't understand. What would a tax accountant on vacation have to do at this hour? What could be so important? "Reed?" Her voice came out small, vulnerable.

He paused in buttoning his black shirt. "Yes?"

"Are you sorry that we—you know?"

Almost before she knew he had moved, he was sitting on the bed beside her, his arms locked tightly around her, his face buried in her hair. "No," he said roughly. "I'm not sorry. And you'd better not be, either, damn it. You're the best thing that's ever happened to me, Celia Carson. And I'm going to prove it to you."

"Then stay with me tonight," she whispered, suddenly, unaccountably worried—but not knowing why.

"I can't." He kissed her once, then again. Hard. "I'll explain tomorrow, when there's time. I promise."

He paused only a moment in her bedroom doorway, looking back at her as though to memorize the sight of her lying there with her hair tangled, her body covered only by a thin white sheet. And then he groaned. "Tomorrow," he repeated, whether to her or to himself, she wasn't sure.

And then he was gone.

Celia lay for a long time just staring at the empty doorway where Reed had stood. What on earth . . . ?

This was turning out to be one hell of an "adventure," she thought with a sigh. The men she'd been interested in had spent an awful lot of time taking care of business— even the one who was supposedly on vacation!

She flopped onto her back against the pillows.

Okay, so she was no longer a virgin. Funny. She still didn't feel like the wild and wicked woman she'd set out to become when she'd left Percy.

She felt . . .

Claimed.

Hog-tied and branded, Reed had called it.

That pretty well summed up the way she felt.

She sighed and glanced at the clock. It was late, but she was too wired to sleep.

She glanced at the clothing lying in a shameless tangle on the floor beside the bed. The intimate memories flooded her, making her shiver and then feel warm all over. She groaned.

How could Reed have left her like this?

She lay still for a moment, fantasizing about having him still with her. Making love to her again. Sleeping in a damp, tangled heap. Waking to make love again.

It should have been that way, damn it. A woman's first experience shouldn't be wham, bam, thank you, ma'am! Especially when she was so dizzy in love with the guy that she couldn't even think straight.

She couldn't lie there any longer, or she'd start crying. And she had no intention of ending this amazing evening in tears. Shoving herself off the bed, she wrapped herself in a short terry-cloth robe and started straightening the room. She would hate for the maid to see it that way—and maybe doing something would help her relax enough to get to sleep.

She tossed her discarded underthings into the bag with other items to be washed, and neatly hung the oatmeal-colored slacks-and-top set in the closet. A lock of dark hair fell into her eyes, and she blew it back. Which reminded her...

She looked around the room, then frowned when she didn't see the silk scarf she'd tied her hair back with earlier. What had she done with it? Had she been wearing it when Reed had undressed her?

Undressed her. She smiled and half-closed her eyes, remembering...

And then she shook herself back to the present and started searching for the scarf. It was her favorite, a special gift from Granny Fran. She would hate to lose it.

Fifteen minutes later, she had to concede the scarf wasn't in her suite.

Sitting back on her heels after a futile search beneath the bed, she mentally backtracked, trying to picture the last time she remembered wearing it. Had she lost it sightseeing?

No. She could distinctly remember her hair whipping in the wind as she'd toured the aquariums. She'd been too distracted with her worries about Reed to pay much attention then, but obviously the scarf had already been lost.

Her mind flashed a sudden, painfully clear image. Reed and the redhead, sitting so cozily on the bench, Reed's arms around the woman's sexy shoulders. Celia whipping around, storming away. Her hair streaming behind her as she bolted.

She must have lost the scarf then. She'd had it until that point, as far as she remembered.

Was Reed with that woman even now? Was the redhead the reason he'd hurried from Celia's bed?

She shuddered as the unwelcome questions pushed their way to the front of her mind. Was this why she'd been concentrating so hard on the missing scarf? Had she been trying to distract herself from the ugly suspicions that had crept into her mind even as Reed had left her?

There was no reason to think he was with the other woman, of course. No reason at all.

But still Celia worried.

As Damien had pointed out, she really didn't know Reed at all. The only thing she really knew about him was that she'd fallen deeply, desperately in love with him. And that she would be devastated if he'd been using her, for whatever reason there might be.

She took a deep, sharp breath, forcing herself to be calm. Reed wasn't with the other woman, she assured herself. He couldn't have made love to her so tenderly, so perfectly, only to leave her for someone else.

"Hog-tied and branded," he'd called himself. He'd damned well better believe it.

She was snapping a pair of jeans at her waist when it occurred to her that "hog-tied and branded" had seemed an odd way for a tax accountant from Cleveland to describe himself. He'd sounded like a typical Texan when he'd drawled the words.

She impatiently pushed the thought aside. Reed had been in Texas for almost two weeks now, steeping himself in the history and flavor of the area, even spent several hours at the Alamo. Was it any wonder he'd been so heavily influenced by his surroundings?

She pulled a knit top over her head and laced her bare feet into leather sneakers. She slipped her room key into the pocket of her jeans as she left the suite by way of the long, blessedly empty hallway.

Chapter Thirteen

Even as she dressed, she hadn't paused to ask herself why she was doing so, where she intended to go. Once outside, she headed straight for that bench beneath the scraggly palm trees. She wasn't checking on Reed, she assured herself. She just didn't want to lose the scarf Granny Fran had given her.

She couldn't have said why she found herself staying in the shadows as she crossed the compound, avoiding the pools of light cast by the many overhead security lamps. She'd certainly spent a lot of time roaming these grounds in the middle of the night, she thought wryly. Which wasn't at all the sort of adventure she'd had in mind when she'd arrived.

She was just rounding the end of her building, near the storage area, when she heard men's voices. She stopped knowing she was hidden from view of the speakers. It wa only sensible, she told herself, to find out who was there before she blundered into their sight.

One of the voices was low, unintelligible. It sounded familiar, but she couldn't quite identify the speaker. The other man spoke then, more loudly, his voice slurred. This voice she recognized immediately. It was Chuck Novotny, and he sounded angry. And probably more than a little drunk.

She pressed closer to the building, curious about who Chuck was so angry with.

"You said everything was ready," Chuck was saying, his thick voice laced with accusation. "You said all I had to do was show up here, look over the merchandise, put down half the cash and then go home and wait for a delivery. What the hell is the holdup?"

The other man said something in that same low, soothing, unrecognizable voice.

"That's *your* problem!" Chuck responded wrathfully. "I handled my part. I got the money. But this crap you've been showing me is not what I ordered. I could buy weapons like this in any back alley in Little Rock. You promised me heavy-duty artillery, damn it, the stuff from Brownsville. And I ain't paying for anything less."

Celia heard the other man frantically trying to quiet Chuck. She was pressed so hard against the building now that she would probably have a permanent brick imprint on her cheek.

Artillery? Was Chuck buying illegal weapons from someone at this resort? Cody had always claimed Chuck and his buddies were dangerous fanatics, but Celia had never believed him—and everyone else tended to brush off Cody's dark claims as fanciful imaginings fueled by intense dislike.

What if Cody had been right all along?

But why here? Why at this resort? Who was Chuck talking to?

More heated words were exchanged, again in those low undertones that Celia could almost, but not quite identify. Her mind was spinning. How could all this be going on here, right under Damien's nose, without him even suspecting anything? How could Novotny have fooled a shrewd businessman like Damien so easily? Unless . . .

Unless Damien was somehow involved with this.

She swallowed a moan. The men were moving now, mercifully headed in the opposite direction from where Celia crouched, hidden by thick, flowering bushes. She made herself as small as possible, just in case.

She still hadn't identified the man with Chuck, though she could hear him making shushing noises as they departed, having only limited success at keeping Chuck quiet. Celia—or anyone else from Percy—could have told him that Chuck was a bit too fond of liquor to make a dependable conspirator. Chuck had always had plenty of money, one way or another, but brains were something he'd had in less abundance.

She stayed where she was until she was sure they were gone. The compound was relatively quiet, the noises from the lounge and the other resorts muted. The scarf forgotten now, Celia wondered what to do. It was entirely possible that she'd just been a witness to a federal crime—at least to a conspiracy. Shouldn't she tell someone?

Her first thought was to find Reed.

He would probably be in his room, she thought. Making calls or not, he had to listen to her. Though this was no more within his realm of experience than hers, surely he would have some suggestions.

She was just about to emerge from the bush when she heard footsteps on the path ahead of her. She blended back into the greenery, her heart leaping into her throat.

She wasn't certain that she would be in danger if anyone knew she'd overheard Chuck's ramblings, but she was taking no chances. Illegal weapons dealers—if that was truly what she had stumbled upon—weren't known for being kind and tolerant.

She let out a quiet breath of relief when she recognized the man who stepped briefly into a pool of light beneath a security lamp.

Reed. Thank God.

And then she noticed how strangely he was acting. Still dressed in the dark clothing he'd had on earlier, his glasses nowhere in sight, he moved quickly out of the light, his head turning as though to make sure no one had seen him. And then he melted into the shadows toward the back of the building, heading for the storage rooms Celia now suspected were being used to store much more than cleaning supplies.

Reed. Oh, God, no.

Had it been Reed who'd been talking to Chuck only minutes earlier? Had he managed to ditch Chuck and was now on his way back to make sure the storage rooms were secure? Was this the reason he'd left her—to meet furtively with Chuck about a sale of illegal artillery?

No. She refused to believe it. Not Reed. He was a tax accountant from Cleveland, just as he'd told her. A history buff, for Pete's sake. He wasn't a criminal. She simply refused to believe it.

Or was it that she simply couldn't accept it?

She pressed both hands to her pounding temples, remembering so many things that hadn't added up, so many things that hadn't made sense. Yet even with the evidence stacked against him, everything within her rejected that Reed would be involved in anything like this.

She loved him. She had no choice but to trust him.

She took another deep breath and crept out of the bush. She would follow Reed and confront him, she decided boldly. Ask him what the hell was going on, what he was doing out. And if she found out that he was anything other than what he'd told her he was, she'd strangle him. With her bare hands.

Feeling incredibly foolish—not to mention scared to her toes—she scampered from one bush to the next, trying to remain hidden but terribly afraid she might as well be wearing a glow-in-the-dark T-shirt. What did she know about secret surveillance? Stalking wasn't something she'd ever needed on a resumé!

The storage sheds were actually one low, concrete-block building at the back of the resort lined with padlocked metal doors. The landscaping had been designed to make the building blend with the surroundings, and the lighting was muted so as not to draw guests' attention to this less than elegant part of the exclusive resort.

Celia didn't see anyone around, not even Reed. Where had he gone? She'd been certain he'd headed this way.

Just as she was about to risk stepping out into the open, a movement near the end storage room made her jerk back into cover. She watched as Reed slipped out of his own shadows, looked one way and the other, then bent to examine the lock on the solid-looking door.

She slumped against the wall behind her. It was getting harder all the time to believe that Reed had nothing to do with this, though she was still trying.

What *was* he doing?

She was trying to get up the nerve to confront him when Reed was suddenly approached from both sides by two men she recognized immediately—Jim Bennett, Damien's very large bodyguard, and the smaller, olive-skinned man Celia had seen walking on the beach with Mark Chenault. The man Reed had called Perrelli.

Before Reed could react to the men's sudden presence, and before Celia could decide whether to call out a warning, Jim Bennett brought something down hard on the back of Reed's head. As Celia watched, horrified, Reed crumpled in a boneless heap to the ground.

She gasped, then clamped both hands over her mouth to keep herself quiet. She couldn't help Reed if she, too, was caught.

Or was Reed in need of her help?

What if Bennett and Perrelli considered themselves justified in the attack on Reed? What if they'd simply apprehended someone who was trying to break into a building that belonged to the resort which employed Bennett in a security capacity? It made sense, she acknowledged reluctantly. For all she knew, the man with Bennett was a cop. And Reed a criminal.

But then, while Perrelli kept guard, Bennett swiftly unlocked the storage room, lifted Reed, and tossed him inside, taking no particular care to keep from reinjuring the already unconscious man. A moment later, he closed and locked the door again.

The very furtiveness of their movements removed any doubts Celia might have had about their honor. She didn't know what Reed had been doing, how he was mixed up with this, but she knew that Bennett and the other man were up to no good. And she knew without question now that Reed was in danger.

And that she could be, as well, if she wasn't very careful.

* * *

It seemed that Celia waited behind that bush in the darkness for hours, though it couldn't have been more than fifteen minutes before Bennett and Perrelli finally left. They'd spent that time apparently arguing in low voices, hands flying as each had tried to make his point. Celia couldn't have said who won the argument. They left together, their steps hurried.

Going after the guy in charge, perhaps?

Staring at that locked room, Celia tried not to think that Reed could be seriously injured. Or worse. She couldn't help him if she panicked. But what should she do? Who could she turn to?

She ran through a mental list of everyone she knew at the resort. It wasn't very helpful. She had no way of knowing who was involved with Bennett and Novotny, who was innocent. Damien was definitely out. She had to concede, for now, at least, that Damien was probably in on it.

Evan, Maris and Mark were all too loyal to Damien to be of any help to her, even if they weren't involved. Besides, she couldn't stand Mark.

Torres? She liked the manager well enough, but again, he was in Damien's employ.

For some reason, she thought of the waiter she'd befriended, Mike Smith, but the restaurant had been closed for hours, and Smith was probably at home with his wife and kids, wherever that might be. Besides, how could she know he wasn't involved, too?

She was beginning to feel like *everyone* at this resort was a part of some nefarious plot!

She had to go for help, she decided. She would head for the nearest telephone away from the resort and call the San Padre Police. It occurred to her that even the police could be in Damien's pocket, but she brushed that fanciful thought off as being just too paranoid. She was scared—more frightened than she'd ever been in her life, including the aborted attempt at parasailing, but she had to do something. She had to keep her head if she was going to be of any help to Reed.

The thought of Reed, lying alone and injured in that storage room, gave her courage. He had probably stumbled into this mess as blindly as she had, she decided. Maybe he'd been coming back to her room when he'd heard voices, as she had. Maybe he'd thought he was doing his civic duty to investigate. Reed would be the type to think of things like civic duty, she thought anxiously.

Poor Reed. They'd taken him so swiftly, so easily, so utterly unaware. He just wasn't equipped to deal with men like these.

It occurred to her that she was even less equipped to deal with them, but she bravely pushed that worry aside. It was up to her to help Reed.

There simply wasn't anyone else to do it. The resort appeared to be more deserted than usual, even for off-season. Every tiptoed step Celia took seemed to echo like sledgehammer blows in the night. She reminded herself that her fear was exaggerating the silence, though of course there was little activity at two in the morning even at a vacation resort.

The shortest and quickest path to the next resort was down the beach. If she went around her building, ran past the fountains and tennis courts and circled the swimming pool, she'd have a straight shot to the beach, and from there to the next hotel. Once she'd found a safe phone, she would decide what to tell the police.

She ducked her head and barreled out of the bushes.

And straight into the arms of Damien's meaty bodyguard.

* * *

Bennett slapped a huge hand over Celia's mouth before she could scream. "Miss Carson?" he said, looking down at her in disbelief. "What are you doing out here?"

Without releasing her mouth so she could answer, he looked from her to the locked storage room. "Oh, hell. You're with *him,* aren't you?"

Celia tried to ask him to let her go, but the words came out only as a series of muffled grunts. She tried futilely to break away as he dragged her toward the storage room, muttering curses beneath his breath with every step. Bennett didn't even seem to notice her efforts to resist him.

"One sound outta you and I'll have to shut you up the hard way, you got that?" he warned as they reached the storage room.

Eyes wide, Celia nodded. It occurred to her that the words should have sounded trite, almost comical—particularly in the Hollywood "tough guy" growl Bennett had suddenly adopted. But she found nothing humorous in the warning.

She believed him.

Bennett tucked her beneath his left arm like a bundle, an inert object, and used his right hand to unlock the storage room again. And then he shoved Celia inside and closed the door firmly behind her.

Celia pitched forward on her hands and knees, landing painfully on what felt like a rough concrete floor. Her breath left her in a whoosh. At first she thought the room was filled with tiny colored lights, but then her vision cleared and she realized the room was completely dark. There wasn't even a window for illumination.

Her breath caught painfully in her throat. It wasn't that she was afraid of the dark, she assured herself. She just didn't like not being able to see.

She groped around her, locating a stack of wooden crates, and another pile of smaller, cardboard boxes. She jammed her fingers painfully on something hard, and she hissed a curse and pulled them back to her lap.

She was almost afraid to reach out again. What if there were spiders in here? Or mice? But that was stupid. She had much worse to worry about, she reminded herself impatiently. *Real* predators.

And where was Reed?

Hesitantly, she stuck out one hand. Slowly. Cautiously. Her fingertips touched something soft, damp. Sticky. Hair. And flesh.

"Reed?" Frantically, she scooted closer and ran her hands over him, trying to learn by feel alone if he was breathing. He groaned and stirred beneath her touch.

"Thank God," she whispered, near tears at this evidence that he was still alive. "Reed?"

He muttered something incoherent. If only she could see him!

"God, I'm such an idiot!" she said aloud, springing to her feet so quickly she nearly fell right on top of Reed's prone form. Surely there was a light; why hadn't she already looked for it? After bumping painfully into another wooden crate, she located the door and ran her hands over the cool concrete wall next to it. She almost sobbed when she found the switch.

A moment later, the small, square room was flooded with light from a single bare bulb hanging overhead.

The boxes were stacked along every wall, leaving little space to spare in the center of the room. Celia didn't even glance at them as she went back down on her knees beside Reed, who lay on his side, his back to the door. There was a dark, shiny patch at the back of his head, a small puddle of red on the gray floor beneath him. His face was pale and his breathing was shallow. But he *was* breathing, she reminded herself firmly.

She touched his face. "Reed. Please, answer me. Let me know you're all right."

His eyelids fluttered, but didn't open.

"Reed!" She spoke more sharply that time, needing him to look at her. To convince her that he wasn't going to die. "Reed, please. I'll get us out of here somehow, I promise, but first you have to let me know you're all right. Please. Say something."

Again, his eyelids fluttered. This time, to her great relief, they opened. He lay very still, frowning up at her. And then his clouded eyes cleared. "Celia?"

Her held breath came out in a sob. "Yes. Oh, Reed."

He lifted his head, cautiously, looking around him. "What the hell—?"

"Don't move," she told him, quickly pressing a hand to his shoulder. "Bennett hit you on the back of the head. Hard. You should lie still."

Ignoring her restraining hand, Reed pushed himself to one elbow. "Bennett?" he repeated, though he'd just gone about two shades paler.

"Damien's bodyguard." Celia anxiously searched his haggard face. "Reed, you really should—"

She might as well have saved her breath. Reed shoved himself to his feet, hissing a couple of rather shocking epithets beneath his breath as he did so.

Celia hurried to support him as he swayed on his feet. She was afraid he was about to crash back down to the floor, and she worried that she wouldn't be able to catch him if he did.

He brushed her off impatiently. "What are you doing here?" he demanded. "Damn it, Celia, if you're in on this, I'll—"

"Of course I'm not in on this!" she interrupted indignantly. "I was trying to rescue you when Bennett caught me and threw me in here with you. How could you even think I had anything to do with this?"

She was genuinely offended, conveniently forgetting for the moment that she had suspected Reed of everything from fooling around with the mystery redhead to illegal gunrunning.

Reed studied her face for a moment, then relaxed and nodded. The movement made him wince and put a hand to the back of his head. It came away smeared with red.

He looked at his gory palm for a moment without expression, then turned back to Celia. "You were following me?"

"Not at the beginning," she assured him. "I lost a scarf my grandmother gave me and I was going out to look for it. Then I heard Novotny and some other man talking about artillery—and then I saw you—and then Bennett hit you—and then when I tried to run for help, Bennett caught me and threw me in here with you."

He seemed to follow the broken story with only a minor effort. He grunted, and she took that to mean that he understood at least most of her explanation.

"Are you all right?" he asked.

She hid her abraded hands behind her back. "I'm fine. But what about you? You're bleeding, and you're so pale. Shouldn't you sit down? What if you have a concussion?"

"It wouldn't be the first time," he muttered, moving toward the door. He looked at the latch, then tested it. It was still securely locked from the outside. "Damn."

"Do you think these boxes have guns in them?" Celia asked him in an exaggerated whisper. "Are they the artillery Chuck was talking about?"

He flicked a glance around the tiny room. "Yeah."

It seemed to her that Bennett had made a big mistake locking them in a room full of weapons. "Maybe we could use one of the guns to get out of here. We could fire it in the air and someone might hear. Better yet, we could shoot the lock off the door," she exclaimed on a sudden inspiration.

Reed rolled his eyes. "You've been watching too many action movies," he said. "These aren't harmless little pellet guns, Celia. You don't fire an AK-47 in an eight-by-eight concrete room."

"An AK-47?" Celia repeated, looking warily at the boxes. "Is that as bad as it sounds?"

"Not as bad as what Novotny had hoped to find in here. But bad enough. Be quiet."

She opened her mouth to protest the summary command, then closed it with a snap when she heard the noise that had caught his attention. Someone was standing outside, talking. Bennett and Perrelli?

Celia tensed, turning to Reed. What would they do now? Shouldn't they at least try to defend themselves? Why didn't Reed look more nervous? And how did he seem to know what was going on even though she still hadn't told him everything she'd heard?

"Shouldn't we get one of the guns or something?" she whispered, moving as far as possible away from the voices. As though that slight distance would protect her.

Reed ignored her. He straightened his shoulders, pushed his hair off his forehead and moved to one side of the door. "Scream," he said.

She frowned, utterly baffled by the order. "What?"

"Scream," he repeated, giving her a sharp look. "Now!"

He spoke that with such forceful command that Celia found herself obeying without further hesitation.

She screamed.

* * *

Celia's scream was still echoing in the tiny room when the door burst open and Bennett rushed through. "Would you shut up?" he demanded, glaring at her. "You—"

She watched in utter disbelief as Reed, wounded and half Bennett's size, proceeded to knock the man senseless, using nothing but one swinging foot and the back of one downward-slicing hand.

Bennett fell with a heavy thud. He didn't move again.

Celia stared at the inert body, then back up at Reed. "How did—?"

Perrelli came in swinging. Reed ducked, turned, kicked out and followed with the now familiar slash of his hand.

Perrelli landed on top of Bennett. Not quite out, he groaned. Reed silenced him with a vicious thump on the head. Perrelli collapsed like a deflated balloon.

Celia felt her jaw drop. Just how would a mild-mannered tax accountant know hand-to-hand combat?

Before she had a chance to ask, Reed grabbed her arm. He pushed her toward the open doorway, a little gentler with her than Bennett had been earlier. "Out," he said.

When she didn't move as quickly as he wanted, he placed a hand in the center of her back and shoved. She stumbled, but remained on her feet.

Reed hardly spared her a glance. He closed and locked the storage room, then jerked a chin toward his right. "Move it."

He sounded very much like a man who was accustomed to having his orders obeyed without question. Celia didn't like it. Not only that, she was beginning to have serious doubts again about his professed career.

No tax accountant she'd ever met had behaved quite like this man.

A long line of flowering bushes—Celia didn't know what they were called—lay between the storage buildings and the back of the darkened restaurant. Reed headed for the bushes at a run, dragging Celia with him.

There was a muffled shout from behind them, then a funny popping sound. With another hissed curse, Reed almost threw Celia into the bushes, then dove in behind her. He landed on top of her with enough force to drive most of the remaining breath out of her lungs.

It suddenly occurred to Celia that they were being shot at. The very possibility was almost too bizarre to accept.

Things like this just didn't happen to her!

Spitting palm fronds out of her mouth, Celia clawed her way to her feet, then turned to run again, only to stumble into someone else's arms.

This time, she thought furiously, she wasn't going to be taken so easily. She struck out. With some satisfaction, she heard her opponent grunt when her fist connected with a firm jaw. The arms that had held Celia fell, releasing her.

"Damn it!" It was a woman's voice, husky, but most definitely feminine.

Startled to realize that she'd hit a woman, Celia hesitated, then prepared to strike out again. Whoever this woman was, Celia had no intention of meekly surrendering. She wasn't going back into that storage room again!

Reed caught Celia's wrist from behind. "Chill out, tiger, this is the cavalry," he murmured, sounding almost amused. "My partner, Kyle. Kyle, someone's behind us. He's armed, and he's using a silencer."

"I know. It's Novotny. Don't worry, Mike's taking care of him."

Her arm still caught in mid-swing, Celia squinted, trying to see the woman through the shadows. *Reed's partner?* She caught a glimpse of a long, slender body clad in dark clothing, hair twisted behind her head. Colors weren't visible in the darkness, but Celia glumly suspected the woman's hair was red. Bright, glorious red.

Cautiously avoiding Celia, the woman touched a hand to Reed's blood-streaked head. "You okay, Reed?" she asked, with such obvious concern that Celia's teeth clenched in sheer, raging jealousy. She almost swung again. Reed held her firmly.

"Yeah." Reed released Celia's wrist as he spoke, but kept his hands on her shoulders.

Maybe, she thought seethingly, he knew that if he released her, she'd go for the woman's throat.

"What happened to Bennett and Perrelli?" Kyle asked, still ignoring Celia.

"Locked in the storage room."

"Yeah, okay. At least we've got enough evidence on them already to hold them, even if we still don't have enough on Alexander. If only we'd caught them together, making the exchange. This isn't the way this was supposed to go down."

"I know." Reed spoke stiffly. "I screwed up."

Kyle shrugged in the shadows, and spoke dismissively. "So, join the club. It was your turn this time."

Only half hearing the conversation, Celia was trying desperately to assimilate everything she'd heard thus far. This woman was Reed's partner—in what? And who was the Mike who'd supposedly taken care of Novotny? She pictured the affable waiter from the restaurant. Surely not...

But then, nothing that had happened during the past hour or so made any sense to her just then.

"Where's Alexander?" Reed asked, his hands still resting lightly on Celia's shoulders as he questioned Kyle.

"Last I checked, he was in his suite. I haven't seen Chenault for a while, though."

Celia twisted her head to look up at Reed. "Is Damien involved in smuggling stolen military weapons?" she asked quietly. "The stuff from Brownsville," she added in a murmur, remembering something Chuck had said.

Reed and Kyle both stiffened. "How do you know about the merchandise from Brownsville?" Reed asked, his fingers tightening on her shoulders.

Celia shrugged, though she didn't manage to dislodge his hands. "Something I overheard."

Speaking more urgently now, Reed asked, "Was it Alexander you overheard talking?"

"I don't know. It was dark—not long before Bennett caught you at the storage room. I heard Chuck talking to someone about the stuff from Brownsville, but the other man spoke so softly I couldn't identify the voice. It took me a bit to figure out what they were talking about. I couldn't believe it at first, even though Cody always said—"

"You didn't hear Alexander's name mentioned?" Reed broke in to ask.

"No."

"Damn." Reed looked at the other woman. "Unless one of the others talks, we still don't know for sure."

"Damn it, Reed, who *are* you?" Celia asked, the question exploding from her in frustration.

He patted her arm, absently. Dismissively. She almost bit him.

"Let's go check on Alexander," he said, still speaking to Kyle. "Mike and Leahy can take care of the others for now."

Leahy? Celia didn't even want to know.

Reed caught Celia's wrist and tugged, letting her know that he wanted her to accompany them. She thought of resisting, but she didn't really want to be left behind at this point.

"Reed," she whispered urgently, staying close to his side. "I insist that you tell me what's going on. Who are you? What are you really doing here? Why are we going to check on Damien?"

"Be quiet, Celia. We don't know who else is involved in this."

His curt order infuriated her. Though he still had her wrist shackled in his hand, she took a swing at him with her free hand. "Damn it, Reed, I rescued you from those guys when they knocked you out and locked you in that room! The least you could do is answer my questions."

Reed stumbled. "You did *what?*"

Kyle snickered, obviously having overheard every word. "She rescued you," she repeated helpfully. "When those guys knocked you out and locked you in a room."

"They caught me off guard," Reed said defensively. "I was, er, thinking of something else for a minute. It's never happened before, damn it, and no one knows that better than you!"

"Good thing your PYT was around to rescue you, wasn't it?" Kyle asked a bit too sweetly.

PYT? Celia didn't think she even wanted to ask. Nor did Reed give her time. "She didn't rescue me," he said. "She got herself thrown in there with me."

Celia started to make an indignant protest. After all, if it hadn't been for her scream, Reed would probably still be lying in there bleeding.

Again, Reed interrupted before she could speak. "Just shut up and come on. Both of you." His tone didn't encourage any further teasing.

He turned and stalked away, leaving the women to follow or not, as they chose. Celia followed resentfully. When this was over, she told herself firmly, she and Reed were going to have a very long talk.

And she fully intended to tell him to shut up and listen to what she had to say!

Chapter Fourteen

Damien's windows were open, the lights on. From a hidden vantage point outside, they could see him in the sitting room, reading a book, sipping a drink, looking completely unaware that anything was going on outside his comfortable surroundings. Celia wondered why he was still awake if he wasn't expecting something to happen tonight.

She studied the handsome face of the man who'd been her friend for almost a year now. She remembered the pleasant evenings, the shared laughter, the gentle kisses and playful hugs.

She had always defended Damien against those who'd maligned him. Had she really been so wrong about him?

"Damn it," Reed growled. "I wish we could be sure whether he's involved in this or not."

Celia looked at him with a quick surge of hope. "You aren't sure?"

"All we have to this point are rumors," Kyle admitted. "Circumstantial evidence. Deliveries at locations where Alexander and his entourage have been. Business meetings scheduled in close proximity to survivalist groups who are in the market for weapons—such as in your area of central Arkansas. We *know* some of his people are involved, but if he is, he's kept a damned low profile."

"You mean, Damien may be completely unaware that there's gunrunning going on in his organization?" Celia asked, just for clarification.

"He has to be involved," Reed told her coolly. "Do you really think his staff could carry on something like this right beneath his nose?"

Celia thought about it a moment. "Yes," she answered simply.

Reed snorted. "Yeah. Sure."

"No, Reed, I'm serious. It's entirely possible. Damien trusts his staff completely—especially Mark Chenault. He fully believes in delegating responsibility to leave him free to handle the big stuff. I've heard him say it dozens of times. He doesn't question every move his staff makes, wouldn't monitor their every activity unless he had reason to suspect something. And maybe he hasn't had a reason before now."

"Let's just watch him for a few minutes," Kyle suggested. "Maybe he'll do something incriminating."

"Like what?" Reed asked sarcastically. "Use an Uzi for a bookmark?"

"Why don't you just ask him if he's involved?" Celia asked reasonably.

Even in the dim lighting that reached their hiding place, she could see that the looks Reed and Kyle gave her were the same they might have given a naive, and rather simple child. And they infuriated her.

Without responding to Celia's suggestion, Reed turned back to Kyle. Moments later, they were arguing about what to do next, the quarrel conducted in curt whispers.

Hands on her hips, Celia watched them. She didn't know what it was these two did, exactly, or who paid their salaries—though she was beginning to suspect *she* did—but at the moment, she wasn't overly impressed.

She looked back at Damien's window. While she watched him, he smiled at something he read, turned the page, scratched his chin and kept reading.

"This is ridiculous," she muttered, knowing that no one was listening to her. "Damien's no more a gunrunner than I am." Why would he be? She knew for a fact that he wasn't particularly interested in political or social causes. He had more money than God, already. He was too unrepentantly self-indulgent to risk spending time in prison, which he would probably detest with every atom of his pampered being.

He was adventurous, but he took his chances in sports—mountain-climbing, skydiving, racing motorcycles. He worked very hard to make his resorts successful, taking pride in their popularity. He wouldn't throw it away just for kicks, which had to be the only reason a man of his resources would get involved in something like this.

She wavered there in the darkness for a moment, feeling rather alone and a bit scared. What if she was wrong?

Her answer came from that same courageous corner of her mind that had made her believe in Reed.

She wasn't wrong about Damien.

Straightening her shoulders, she headed for his door, leaving Reed and Kyle still plotting behind her.

She heard Reed hiss her name just as she reached the glass-paned French door that led from Damien's suite to the beach walk. It was too late for Reed to stop her from tapping on the door. "Damien?" she called softly. "It's Celia."

Reed had been racing toward her, but he ducked back when the door suddenly opened. Celia could hear his muttered curses drifting on the air, and knew she was in for a heated lecture later.

She would worry about that when it became necessary.

"Celia?" Damien couldn't seem to believe that she was outside his suite in the wee hours of the morning. "What the hell? Is something wrong? Are you all right?"

He was already pulling her inside, his expression so worried, his tone so sincere that Celia knew again she had to be right about him.

"I'm fine," she assured him. She left the door ajar behind her and kept Damien close, her voice clear enough to carry outside, but no louder than usual. "I have to talk to you."

"What's wrong?" he asked again, his blue eyes searching her face. "Is it that Hollander guy? Has he done something to upset you? If he has, just tell me. I swear I'll make him sorry he ever—"

Though Celia had let him ramble for a moment—she figured Reed deserved to hear that—she stopped him then by placing a hand on his arm. "It's not that, Damien. It's something else. Something I overheard. And I'm afraid it's going to upset you."

Knowing Reed and Kyle would be straining to listen, she told Damien everything. The conversation she'd overheard between Chuck and an unknown man, Bennett and Perrelli's attack on Reed, her own capture and subsequent escape.

By the end of her explanation, Damien was looking at her as though she were demented. "Gunrunning?" he said "Jim? And Chuck? Celia—"

"You don't believe me."

He threw up his hands. "How can you expect me to believe this? Sweetheart, it's very late. Are you sure you weren't dreaming?"

"No, I wasn't dreaming. Jim Bennett grabbed me and threw me in a storage room! Look at my hands." She held her hands out for his inspection. Her filthy palms were deeply scraped, and smeared with blood—her own and Reed's. She'd been trying to ignore the painful stinging. She knew her knees were bruised and scraped, as well, from her contact with the concrete storage room floor.

Damien caught his breath. He took her wrists gently in his hands, examining the painful-looking wounds. "We have to clean these," he said. "They look terrible. How did you hurt them?"

Celia exhaled gustily. "You aren't listening. Jim Bennett threw me in a storage room—a storage room full of guns. I hurt my hands when I landed on the concrete floor. Now Bennett and Perrelli are locked in there, and Chuck's probably tied up somewhere, but there may be others roaming around that we don't know about. Mark—or Evan—even Enrique, any of them could be involved."

"Celia, you have to understand how incredible this all sounds. These are my friends you're talking about, my employees. You really expect me to believe they've been involved in something like this without my knowledge?"

"I know how it sounds. But it's the truth," Celia said quietly, laying a battered hand on his arm. She looked up into his eyes without smiling, willing him to believe her. "It's the truth," she repeated.

He started to shake his head, studied her expression, then seemed to slump. "You really mean this, don't you?"

"I'm sorry, Damien. I know it hurts you."

He sighed and covered her hand with his own. "What do you want me to do?"

Celia was just about to suggest that they call Reed in when she heard a noise behind them. She and Damien turned at the same time.

Mark Chenault was standing in the doorway to Damien's living room. And he was holding a gun.

"Mark?" Damien looked stunned. "What are you doing?"

"I've gotten myself in a bind, boss," Mark replied, sounding oddly breezy and matter-of-fact, considering the circumstances. "I find myself in need of your assistance."

"Since when do you ask for my help at gunpoint? What the hell is going on here, Mark?"

Chenault motioned with the gun toward Celia. "You can blame your two-timing little girlfriend, here. And her new boyfriend. You really shouldn't have invited her here this week, Damien. I tried to tell you it wasn't a good time."

"You said you thought we were too busy to be entertaining," Damien snapped. "You didn't say anything about selling guns."

Chenault flicked Celia a cool glance. "So she's been talking to you. And you believe her?"

Damien looked from Mark's face to the dark, deadly weapon in his hand. "Looks like I'm going to have to believe her."

Aware that Reed and Kyle were outside, Celia tried to stay calm. Reed would do something, she told herself, no longer in doubt that he would know how to handle this. She remembered the ease with which he had overtaken Bennett and Perrelli. Whatever it was he did for a living, he was no mild-mannered tax accountant.

"What is it you want, Mark?" Damien asked, and there was so much pain in his voice that Celia automatically laid a sympathetic hand on his arm. She knew this must be hurting him. Damien placed a very high value on loyalty and friendship.

"I want your helicopter here in less than half an hour. I want your plane and your pilot on standby to take me to Central America. And I want enough cash to support me in style once I get there. You can arrange all that for me, Damien." Mark flashed a smile that made Celia shiver. "It's so nice to have money and power available for one's every whim, isn't it?"

He looked at Celia then. "You really were very stupid to choose a bumbling cop over our wealthy friend here, Celia. Damien would have given you anything you wanted, for as long as his interest in you lasted—which, I'm afraid, wouldn't have been long. What's your cop friend got to offer, hmm? A federal employee's salary? Doesn't run to Mercedes and luxury vacations, I'm afraid—especially if he's one of that rare breed known as an honest cop."

"He is," Celia said. She didn't even know for certain that Reed *was* a cop—or a federal agent, or any of the other possibilities that had crossed her mind during the past half hour—but if he was, she was sure he was an honest one. "I don't care how much money he has."

"Then you're an idiot," Chenault said contemptuously. "Money is the only thing that matters in this world. With it, you're everyone's best friend. You can't do anything bad enough that you can't buy forgiveness, can you, Damien? Without money, you're just someone's 'valued assistant.'"

The scorn in his final words made Damien flinch beneath Celia's hand. "You were more than that to me, Mark," Damien protested. "You were my friend."

"Yeah, right. You were the one who had the big money, the pictures in the paper, the invitations to the White House and the bedrooms of the most beautiful women in the world. Money is power, and I wanted my share. I wanted to be the head of my own organization."

"And you were using my business as cover." Damien sounded thoroughly appalled.

Mark shrugged. "Only when it was convenient. And the location you'd scouted out in central Arkansas was very convenient. Those radical survivalists love that area—and they were willing to pay very well to buy the weapons they thought they needed to defend their turf. All I had to do was plug in to a few connections in stolen military weapons, set up a few meetings on the side when you made your boring real-estate deals and cash in the profits. But you had to screw everything up. You had to bring *her* into it. Damn it, Damien, she isn't half the woman you usually go after. She's passable, but hardly world class."

"Shut up, Mark." For the first time since she'd known him, Damien sounded dangerous to Celia. There was raw fury overlying the pain in his eyes now.

Mark snorted. "Still fancy yourself in love with her, Damien? Even when she's screwing someone else? God, how did you ever get where you were without my help?"

"I was doing just fine before I hired you," Damien replied coldly. "And I'll still be doing just fine when you're behind bars."

Mark's eyes narrowed. Celia tightened her fingers on Damien's arm, warningly.

Mark looked at Celia. The indulgent affability had left his voice completely now. He sounded hard. Mean. "Where's your boyfriend? Your *other* boyfriend? The cop?"

She met his eyes without flinching. "I don't know. He ran off and left me behind."

"I don't believe you. He's somewhere nearby, isn't he?"

Celia had to make an effort not to glance toward the slightly opened door. "I don't know," she repeated.

Mark motioned again with the gun. "Come here."

Damien quickly covered Celia's hand with his own. "Stay where you are, Celia."

Mark coolly aimed the weapon at Damien's forehead. He flicked Celia only a glance. "I said come here."

"What are you going to do?" Celia asked, hesitating. She didn't want Damien hurt, and she had no question that Mark would pull the trigger. But she didn't want to blindly step into danger, either. She just knew Reed and Kyle were making their plans. If only she could stall long enough to give them a chance to rescue her.

"I'm just providing myself with a little insurance, as they say in the gangster movies," Mark said with a twisted smile.

"Do I need to point out that it rarely works in the gangster movies?" Damien asked quietly, still holding Celia's hand.

Mark shrugged. "It's not like I've got any other choice," he said bitterly. "Get over here, Celia. Damien, you get on the phone. Start making the arrangements. And maybe you'd better let everyone know that I'm not fooling around here. If one thing goes wrong, she's dead. And so are you."

Celia and Damien didn't move. They looked at each other, neither certain what to do.

Reed? Where are you? What are you doing? Celia hoped her mental message somehow made its way to him.

An ominous clicking sound came from the gun. Celia had watched enough of those gangster films they'd mentioned to recognize the sound. Mark was prepared to shoot Damien, and then proceed from there.

"*Now*, Celia," Mark said.

Celia pulled her hand from Damien's and took a step toward Mark.

Damien reached out automatically to stop her. She shrugged off his hand. "Be careful, Damien," she whispered, her eyes locked with Mark's.

"Good advice, Damien," Mark mocked. "Be very careful."

The moment Celia stepped within reach, he grabbed her, his fingers digging brutally into her wrist as he pulled her in front of him. She stumbled, and he jerked her upright, bending her arm behind her as he did so. She couldn't help gasping at the sharp pain in her twisted arm.

Damien automatically moved toward them. Mark stopped him by holding the barrel of the gun to Celia's forehead.

"Do you really want to risk this, Damien?" he asked, and there was a new undercurrent of desperation in his voice.

Celia knew it was important to keep him calm. Panic was much too dangerous when his unsteady finger was curled around the trigger. "I'm okay, Damien," she said breathlessly, trying to ignore the throbbing in the arm Mark still held behind her.

"Make the calls," Mark said, motioning sharply toward the phone. "Get the helicopter here. Hope you're not as afraid of helicopters as you are of parachutes, Celia," he added derisively. "You'll be going with me for the first part of the trip, of course."

Even though she knew Reed would intercede before that became necessary—she simply *had* to believe it—Celia felt a cold knot of fear settle deep inside her.

The telephone was on a small walnut writing desk at the far side of the room. Damien approached it slowly. He laid his hand on the instrument without picking it up. "Mark," he said, his expression beseeching. "You have to know this is foolish. Give yourself up now, before something tragic happens."

"As far as I'm concerned, something tragic has already happened. I've failed." Mark spoke with bitter self-recrimination.

Damien started to say something else, but a muffled sound from outside made Mark jerk in that direction, swinging Celia with him. The movement twisted her arm even higher behind her. She cried out and instinctively bent to ease the pressure, pulling downward on Mark's hand.

"Damn it, stand up!" he snapped, and the panic was more evident now. "Make the call, Damien."

Celia tried to cooperate, but her awkward position, combined with the shooting pain from her arm, made her clumsy. She stumbled again.

His control slipping rapidly, Mark hit her with the back of his gun hand, almost snapping her neck backward. "Stand *up!*" he bellowed.

Still reeling from the blow, Celia tried to regain her balance, but her vision was clouded, her ears ringing. She could feel her knees buckling. She slumped against Mark's arm, pulling him off balance with her.

"Damn it!" He pulled back his other hand to hit her again.

Damien threw himself forward. He hit them with his full weight just as Celia opened her mouth to warn him away.

The three of them went down in a tangle of flailing limbs. Celia heard the door burst open, heard Reed shouting something, but she couldn't quite make out the words.

And then she heard the shot.

Someone landed solidly, heavily on top of her. And then there seemed to be people everywhere, shouting, running, grappling.

Celia opened her eyes. She couldn't even remember when she'd closed them. And she saw who lay across her, his eyes closed, his skin deathly pale.

"Damien?" She pushed at him, frantically trying to get him to respond. "Damien!"

Large, strong hands helped her free herself. "Celia." Reed's voice sounded strange, hoarse as he ran his hands over her. "Are you all right? Have you been hit?"

"No," she said, shaking her head quickly, ignoring the various aches and pains throughout her body. Her attention now was all for Damien, who lay crumpled beside her, his left shoulder covered with blood. She stared at that spreading stain in horror. "Oh, Reed, he's been shot. Please. Help him."

Reed dropped his hand from her arm. Unencumbered, she reached out to her wounded friend. "Damien? Damien, can you hear me? Oh, please, say something."

She couldn't bear it if Damien died because of her.

Reed was on his feet now. "Get an ambulance," he shouted to someone. *"Now!"*

Some distant part of Celia's mind noted the innate command in his voice, and the way everyone else in the room seemed to snap to attention in response to it.

"It's going to be all right, Damien," she whispered, her hand on his clammy, pale cheek. "Reed's taking care of everything now."

She didn't know if Damien could hear her, but the words gave her courage.

The emergency medical technicians arrived with admirable speed. Celia was pulled out of the way as they bent over Damien, who was partially awake and groaning now. The front of her shirt was stained with his blood, and there was a trickle of something warm and sticky from a lump on the side of her head. But they were alive, she reminded herself. Mark had been taken away, and she and Damien would be all right.

She said a quick prayer of thanks, adding a plea that Damien would recover quickly. She wouldn't even allow herself to consider the possibility that he might not recover at all.

The EMTs briskly, efficiently lifted Damien onto a gurney. They were moving toward the door when he spoke. "Celia?"

She rushed to his side and took his hand. "I'm here, Damien."

"You're all right?" His voice was weak, his lips stiff and rather blue, but his eyes looked clear, coherent, giving her hope that his injuries weren't immediately life-threatening.

"I'm fine," she reassured him. "And you will be, too. Let them take care of you now, Damien."

His eyelids drooped. "Tell that cop—"

She bent closer, straining to hear. "What?"

"Tell him—take better care of you after this."

She kissed his cold cheek. "I can take care of myself, Alexander," she murmured. "You do the same, you hear?"

"We have to go, ma'am," one of the medical technicians said.

Celia stepped out of the way.

"I want to ride with him," Maris Cathcart insisted, her eyes locked on her employer's face. She had arrived a few minutes earlier, hastily dressed in a misbuttoned shirt and slacks. Evan had been right behind her, wearing nothing but a pair of jeans. Celia had gotten the impression that Damien's two secretaries had been together when they'd been summoned. Maybe that would amuse her later, when she remembered how to smile.

"You're in charge, Evan," Damien murmured just as he and Maris were hustled out of the room.

The secretary straightened his bare shoulders and lifted his chin, assuming an immediate air of command. "Someone tell me what the hell has happened in here," he said, sounding so much like his beloved employer that Celia was wearily amused.

She left others to bring Evan up to date. She turned to find Reed.

He was sitting on Damien's soft leather couch, his shoulders slumped, his eyes closed. A gun lay loosely in his right hand, apparently forgotten.

A battered, weary warrior, Celia found herself thinking. No one would mistake him now for a mild-mannered tax accountant.

Kyle was bent over him, her sleek red head close to his as she examined the back of his head where Bennett had hit him. Celia's stomach clenched. They looked so comfortable together, she thought, her teeth digging into her lower lip. So close.

And then Reed looked up. His eyes met hers. He pushed Kyle's hand aside and shoved himself to his feet.

"You're bleeding," he said, touching gentle fingers to the oozing lump at the side of her head.

"I'm okay. It's just a bump where Mark hit me."

A muscle jumped in Reed's jaw. "I should have killed him," he said, the dramatic words spoken in an oddly calm, matter-of-fact tone.

"You almost did," Kyle reminded him, then glanced at Celia. "I unwrapped his fingers from the guy's throat and sent him to make sure you were all right. I've never seen my partner quite so emotional making an arrest."

Reed groaned. "Tell me someone read the guy his rights," he said, as though the thought had just occurred to him.

"Except for your performance, everything went strictly by the book," Kyle assured him with a note of suppressed amusement. "He won't get off on technicalities."

Reed appeared relieved.

Kyle looked from Reed's wounded head to Celia's injured face. "You two look terrible. Come on, we'll find someone to check you out."

"I want to make sure Damien's okay," Celia insisted. "Can you drive us to the hospital where he's been taken?"

"Yeah. Let me make a few quick calls first."

For the first time, Celia realized the three of them were alone in Damien's living room. She didn't know where Evan had ushered the others. The sudden silence was startling in comparison to the earlier chaos.

Celia looked down at her filthy, bloodstained clothing. "I want to change," she said, thinking of the clean clothing right across the hallway. "I'll just be a minute."

Reed was massaging the back of his neck. "You can clean up later," he said.

She plucked distastefully at her shirt. "I want to change now."

"Go with her, Reed. Make sure she doesn't keel over or anything. This will take me about five minutes," Kyle said, phone in hand.

Reed didn't seem to care for being on the receiving end of orders for a change. But he nodded stiffly and turned to Celia. "All right. Let's go."

She wasn't feeling particularly subservient at the moment, either, but she knew it would be a waste of breath to protest his curt tone. She turned without another word and headed for her suite. Reed followed close at her heels.

Chapter Fifteen

The lights were still on in Celia's bedroom. The bedclothes were still tangled and twisted. She swallowed hard, remembering that she and Reed had shared that bed only hours before. She didn't know what time it was now—an hour or so before dawn, probably—but everything had changed during this eventful night.

It was hard to believe so much had happened in so short a time. That her perceptions of him had been altered so dramatically since he'd left her bed.

Suddenly shy, she avoided looking at him as she quickly opened a drawer and pulled out a clean T-shirt. "There's an ice maker in the bar in the other room," she said. "Why don't you put an ice pack on your head while I change? I promise to hurry."

"I don't want an ice pack."

She bit her lip, nodded and moved toward the bathroom to change.

Reed stopped her with a hand on her arm. "Stay in here where I can see you. You're still too pale. I don't want you passing out in there."

Despite what had passed between them earlier, it bothered her to think of undressing in front of him now. In some ways, he wasn't the same man she'd made love with before. "I'm not going to pass out," she assured him, still without looking at him. "I just want to wash up a bit."

"Celia." His voice sounded strained, as if his patience had worn much too thin. "Change the damned shirt and let's go. I want someone to look at your head. You could have a concussion."

So could he, she thought in quick remorse. Reed must be feeling terrible. This wasn't the time for inappropriate modesty on her part.

She tugged the soiled T-shirt over her head. She couldn't bite back a faint groan when the neckline rubbed against the raw lump on her forehead, and her scraped palms stung in protest of the activity. She ached all over.

Reed's hand fell quickly on her shoulder, her thin bra strap the only thing separating his palm from her bare skin. "Are you all right?"

"Yes." She concentrated on finding the hem of the clean T-shirt.

"Celia." He exerted enough pressure on her shoulder to turn her toward him. "Why aren't you looking at me? Is your vision blurred? Are you seeing double?"

He tilted her face upward, anxiously searching her face, studying her eyes with clinical thoroughness.

To Celia's chagrin, she felt her eyes brim with hot tears.

Reed reacted immediately. He tugged the shirt out of her hand, tossed it aside and pulled her into his arms. "It's okay, Celia," he murmured, one hand supporting the back of her head. "It's all over now."

She clung to him, burying her face in his shoulder. His shirt was crumpled, dirty, dampened with sweat and drops of blood. She didn't care. She soaked up his warmth, his strength. And prayed that when he'd said it was all over now, he wasn't talking about them.

He stroked her bare back, soothingly, slowly, murmuring something she couldn't quite catch. After a moment, she lifted her head and looked at him. "I'm sorry," she said. "I didn't mean to fall apart."

"You have every right to do so," he said, still holding her close. "It's been a hell of a night."

He could say that again. She'd lost her virginity, stumbled onto an illicit arms deal, witnessed an attack on Reed, gotten herself captured and thrown into a room full of guns, escaped, discovered that Reed wasn't at all what he'd pretended to be, been held at gunpoint, watched her friend get shot...

"Yes," she said. "I guess you could say it's been an eventful night."

Reed smiled crookedly and rested his forehead against hers. "Poor Celia. You found more adventure than you bargained for when you left Percy, didn't you?"

She'd found adventure, all right. And so much more. "Reed?" she asked in a very small voice.

He tenderly smoothed a strand of hair away from her injured forehead. "What?"

"Was it all an act?" She motioned toward the bed. "Everything?"

He stiffened. His eyes flashed. If she hadn't already known he was a dangerous man by that time, she would have realized it then.

His voice was a low growl. "Are you asking if I made love to you as part of my job?"

She tilted her chin and answered bravely. "Yes. I guess that is what I'm asking."

"Damn it, Celia, don't you know I could have *lost* my job because of you? Hell, I still might, as badly as I screwed up this assignment."

She searched his face, looking for any reason not to take him at his word. "You lied to me," she said. "About your job, your reason for being here."

"Honey, I lied to you about damned near everything," he groaned. "But I didn't lie to you about this," he added just before he covered her mouth with his own.

Celia couldn't respond immediately. She still had that odd, disconcerting feeling that the man holding her now wasn't the same man she'd fallen so hard for during the past week.

As though sensing her confusion, Reed lifted his head and looked down at her. Their eyes locked. His held a plea that Celia couldn't misinterpret.

Suddenly reassured, she rose onto her tiptoes and pressed her mouth to his.

His arms closed around her so tightly she could hardly breathe. She didn't care. This was Reed. Whatever his job, whoever he was, she loved him.

That was the only thing that hadn't changed during this long, terrifying night.

Someone pounded on the outer door. "Reed? Come on, let's go."

In response to Kyle's summons, Reed lifted his head. "We'll talk later," he promised. "And I'll tell you everything you want to know."

Celia nodded and stepped away from him, moving dreamily toward the door.

Reed detained her with a hand on her shoulder. "Aren't you forgetting something?" he asked with quiet humor. Her clean T-shirt dangled from his hand.

Celia blushed and reached for it. She tugged it hastily over her head.

Reed was smiling at her when she emerged from the neckline of the bright red shirt.

For the first time in hours, she was able to smile back.

When they reached the hospital, Celia insisted on checking on Damien before she allowed anyone to look at her head. Reed protested at first, a deep frown creasing his forehead, that familiar look of jealousy squaring his jaw.

"Reed," Celia said, resting her hand on his arm. "He's my friend. And he was hurt trying to protect me. I have to know he's all right."

Reed hesitated, then exhaled and nodded. "I understand."

She smiled. "I knew you would."

Damien was lying in a hospital bed, heroically pale and bandaged, being hovered over by his fiercely loyal secretary, Maris, and Enrique Torres and his flustered wife, both looking as though they'd dressed hastily. Mindi Kellogg, who was looking less cheerleaderish than usual, stood in a corner of the room and wrung her hands. Probably, Celia thought somewhat cattily, trying to think of some way to involve Damien's visitors in cheerfully organized hospital games. Gurney races? Bandage rolling?

A nurse bustled around the room, trying to keep some kind of control over the visitors. She didn't look pleased to see three more walk in. She probably wasn't used to so much activity at this hour in the morning, Celia thought. Celia could certainly sympathize.

With a determined smile, she approached the bed while Reed and Kyle lingered by the door. "Look at you," she said, shaking a finger at Damien. "I thought I'd find you on the verge of death and instead, you're lying here like a sultan, basking in all this attention."

Damien gave her a charmingly crooked grin. "Can I help it if I'm just naturally hero material?"

She groaned. "Oh, Lord, now you really have a line to use on the ladies, don't you? Not to mention a picturesque scar to show off to them."

His eyebrow lifted. "Think it'll work?"

"It probably will," she admitted.

He glanced toward the doorway, then back at her, his smile still in place, but a bit strained now. "I don't suppose there's any need for me to waste the line on you."

"No," she answered seriously. "You don't need to use lines on me, Damien. I already know you're a hero. You were hurt trying to protect me. I don't know how to thank you for that."

For the first time since she'd known him, Damien flushed. "Aww," he muttered. "It was nothing. Are you okay, Celia? That's a mean-looking lump on your head."

"It's just a scratch," she assured him, patting his hand. "What about you? Are you in much pain?"

He shook his head, though the faint lines around his mouth belied the denial. "No sweat," he assured her. "The bullet just grazed my shoulder. Some soft tissue damage, but nothing permanent. The doctors assure me I'll be back in top form within a few weeks."

"I'm glad." She leaned down to give him a careful hug. "You scared me half to death!" she chided him, suddenly fierce. "Don't ever do anything like that again, you hear me?"

"I hope it won't be necessary," he answered. "When I think of what was going on within my own organization, right under my nose—damn it, it just makes me feel like an idiot."

"Because you trusted your friends?" She shook her head. "Don't feel that way, Damien. You couldn't help it that some of your employees didn't deserve your faith in them."

She nodded toward Maris and Enrique and Mindi, who stood so loyally nearby, and thought of Evan, who was valiantly trying to carry on back at the resort. "You should consider yourself fortunate that you have so many good friends who would never dream of betraying you that way."

"Like you?" he asked, taking her hand.

"Like me," she agreed gently. "You're my very good friend, Damien. I hope you always will be."

He sighed, but squeezed her hand before releasing her. He glanced back toward the doorway. "Your policeman friend is beginning to look very fierce. I'm starting to get worried. One bullet's enough for one night, don't you think?"

"Reed's not going to shoot you, Damien," Celia promised with a shaky smile, but she moved a step away from him, anyway. "You need some rest—and so do I. I'll see you tomorrow, okay?"

"Yeah. Have someone look at that head, you hear? And tell them to add it to my tab. This has been one hell of a vacation I've provided you, hasn't it, sweetheart?"

She chuckled. "Well, it has been full of surprises."

He looked toward the door again, then asked, "Do you think my picturesque scar will have any influence on the tall redhead?"

"I don't know. Why don't you try finding out?"

"Maybe I'll do that. After I've had some rest, of course." He suddenly looked very worn and tired. Celia's heart went out to him, but she only smiled and bade him good-night.

There was really nothing else left for her to say.

Celia wasn't sure what woke her much later that same day. Bright sunlight was streaming through her bedroom window when she opened her eyes, so bright she squinted in reaction. It had to be late afternoon; she'd been sleeping for hours.

She stirred against the pillow, wincing when she remembered the bandaged lump on her forehead. She raised a tentative hand to it.

"Does it hurt?" The deep voice made her gasp and sit up in surprise.

Reed sat in a chair near the bed, looking as though he'd been there for a while. He had showered and changed into a clean shirt and jeans since she'd last seen him, when he and Kyle had brought her back to her suite and left her there, drained from exhaustion and delayed reaction. There hadn't been any other opportunities for them to be alone, and Reed hadn't offered to come in when he'd brought her back. They'd both been too tired to talk then—or do anything else, for that matter.

"How long have you been sitting there?" she asked him, her voice husky from sleep.

He shrugged. "Not long."

Which didn't answer her question, of course. "Haven't you gotten any sleep?"

He nodded. "Enough."

She studied him anxiously. He did look somewhat more rested. There was more color in his face, and his eyes were clearer—especially since he was no longer wearing his glasses. Had he ever really needed them?

"How's your head?" she asked.

He shrugged again. "Okay. How's yours?"

"Okay." The laconic repetition was deliberate. She pushed the bedclothes aside, leaving her clad only in a soft, oversized nightshirt. "Excuse me a minute."

He nodded. She passed his chair on the way to the bathroom. She felt him watching her, but he remained still. She closed the door between them.

She took her time in the bathroom. She washed her bruised face, brushed her teeth and her hair, rubbed antibiotic cream into her scraped palms and knees. She knew she was stalling, but still she didn't hurry.

She needed this time to find the nerve she seemed to have misplaced sometime during the night.

Reed was still sitting in the chair when she finally rejoined him. He didn't look as if he'd moved so much as a muscle.

She sat on the end of the bed, facing him. "You're not really a tax accountant, are you, Reed?" It was a stupid question, really, but the first one that occurred to her.

Reed didn't smile. "No. I'm not a tax accountant. I'm a federal agent."

"And you're not from Cleveland, either." It wasn't a question.

"Taos," he said. "New Mexico. Cleveland seemed more in character."

"Are your parents still living? Are you really an only child?"

"Yes. And no. I have two younger brothers, one of them still in college at my parents' expense. My parents couldn't afford to give me a vacation like this if they wanted to."

She moistened her lips. It seemed to get worse with every revelation. "Was your birthday really last week?"

"No. Next month. I'll really be thirty-three then, though."

The last, rather hopefully offered tidbit didn't cheer her much. "Are you married?" she asked, her fingers twisting in dread.

He looked startled. "No. Of course not."

She didn't see that there was any "of course" to it. "Is your name really Reed Hollander?"

"Yes."

For some reason, that meant a great deal to her. At least the name she'd called out in ecstasy had been his real one.

She had only one more question, and it was the hardest of all to ask. She wasn't at all sure she could find the courage to do so. But she was just as certain she couldn't go another minute without knowing the answer. "Do you love me?"

"Yes." Reed answered without hesitation.

Her eyes flooded in relief. "Then—that's all that really matters, isn't it?" she asked, a bit brokenly.

A moment later, the chair was empty, and Reed was beside Celia on the bed, his arms locked tightly around her. "I'm sorry," he said, his clean-shaven cheek against hers. "I'm sorry I lied to you. I'm sorry I didn't trust you from the start. I'm sorry I made such a mess of everything and almost got you killed. I'm sorry I hurt you."

Tears were beginning to overflow her eyes. "Oh, Reed."

"But—" he said, as though she hadn't spoken at all "—I'm not sorry I met you. I'm not sorry I fell in love with you. I will never regret that, no matter what happens in the future. Do you believe me?"

"Yes," she whispered, touching trembling fingers to his hard, tanned cheek. "I believe you. I love you, Reed."

"Oh, God, Celia." He kissed her, roughly, deeply. And then he kissed her more gently, lingeringly.

Almost dizzy with love and happiness, Celia wrapped her arms around his neck and pulled him down to the bed with her.

It was a long time later before either of them spoke again. "I have so much to learn about you," Celia murmured, stroking her hand down his bare, still heaving chest.

Reed covered her hand with his own and held it over his pounding heart. "You already know everything that's important to me. I love you."

She smiled and kissed his jaw. "I love you, too. It's strange, isn't it? We've known each other such a short time. We should be little more than strangers to each other. And yet I feel as though in some way I've always known you."

He smiled and touched her lower lip. "Are you going to turn sappy and sentimental now?"

"Probably. Do you mind?"

"No. Go right ahead."

She laughed softly at his indulgent tone. "You're still trying to make up to me for lying to me, aren't you? Something tells me you're going to be very agreeable today."

"Anything you want," he promised recklessly. "To-day—and always."

She swallowed, wondering if he'd meant that the way it sounded. "Always?" she repeated carefully.

"For the rest of my life," he said, his tone even and utterly sincere.

"Wow," she breathed.

He laughed. "I'm taking that as a yes," he warned her.

She drew a shaken breath, then nodded. "That's a yes."

He kissed her tenderly. "You really have gotten brave lately, haven't you?"

She smiled and rested her cheek against his chest. "I might even take up parasailing. I suppose you've done it before, despite what you led me to believe before."

"Uh, yeah. I've, er, tried quite a few things I haven't mentioned."

"I'll just bet you have," Celia muttered, the earlier image of the mild-mannered, rather shy and cautious tax accountant almost a joke now. How could she have ever fallen for it in the first place?

"You did come here looking for adventure, didn't you?" he asked teasingly.

"True. Of course, this isn't exactly what I had in mind."

Reed scowled suddenly. "I know what you had in mind," he muttered. "And exactly *who* you had in mind. But we'll let that go for now."

"Big of you, considering I haven't asked one question about the gorgeous redhead you introduced as your partner," she retorted pointedly.

"Kyle?" He seemed surprised that she'd even mention the other woman.

"Kyle."

"She's a friend. A good friend."

"And so is Damien," Celia said sweetly. "Okay?"

He shook his head at the realization that he'd just been neatly manipulated, but he agreed. "Okay."

"Besides," Celia said a moment later, her teasing mood returning, "I still don't feel exactly adventurous. I've managed to get myself—er—hog-tied and branded by the first man I ever went to bed with. That's pretty average and traditional, wouldn't you say?"

Reed rolled onto his side, looming over her, a look of pure devilment in his clever hazel eyes. "I wouldn't exactly call ours an average, traditional courtship, would you, love?"

Love. The simple endearment made her shiver. "No," she murmured dreamily. "It hasn't been average and traditional."

His lips moved against hers. "I think we have quite a few adventures still in store for us."

She pulled him closer, her pulse already racing in anticipation. "Oddly enough—I feel the same way," she murmured, just before Reed covered her mouth with his.

Epilogue

Frances Carson's doorbell chimed at the same time her telephone began to ring early Saturday evening. She rushed to the door and threw it open. "Come on in, Lila. I have to answer the phone."

She dashed into the kitchen just as her friend came into the living room. They were on their way to a choir special at their church, and Frances didn't want to be late, but she could never leave the telephone ringing unanswered. "Hello?"

Several minutes later, Frances rejoined her friend in the other room, the telephone call over.

Lila was still standing, her purse and gloves in her hands, her posture impatient. "We really must be going, Frances, or we'll never get a decent seat. You know how I hate to be late."

Her fussing broke off suddenly as she searched her longtime friend's face. "Frances, what is it? Is something wrong? You look..."

"Stunned?" Frances supplied with a little laugh. "Flabbergasted?"

"Well—yes," Lila admitted, relaxing a bit as she realized that Frances wasn't terribly upset. "Who was that on the phone?"

"That was Celia. Lila, you'll never believe this—but she's gotten married!"

"Married?" Lila repeated with a gasp. "Celia's gotten married?"

Frances nodded her head in shared astonishment. "Yes. It's so hard to take in.... I suppose the phone will be ringing off the hook shortly when the others in the family find out."

"Let me get this straight. Your youngest granddaughter has actually married that man who's always in the gossip magazines? That jet-setting Damien Alexander everyone's been so worried about is actually going to settle down and start a family?"

Frances laughed again. "She didn't marry Damien Alexander. She's married a man named Reed Hollander—a man she's known less than two weeks. And she sounded deliriously happy about it. She promised me I'm going to love him."

Lila's knees seemed to fold beneath her. She sat heavily on Frances's sofa. "Oh, my. What an impulsive, reckless thing for her to have done."

"Yes." Frances looked at Celia's photograph and smiled mistily. "It's exactly what Celia was hoping to find."

"I hope she hasn't made a terrible mistake," Lila, always the worrier, fretted.

"So do I. But something tells me she hasn't," Frances, the eternal optimist, replied.

Now, she thought, turning her attention to another photograph on her old piano. If only her dear, stuffy grandson Adam would find someone who could make him do something so romantic and daring....

*   *   *   *   *

Silhouette®

SPECIAL EDITION™

COMING NEXT MONTH

#973 THE BRIDE PRICE—Ginna Gray
That Special Woman!
Wyatt Sommersby couldn't help but be attracted to the passionate Maggie Muldoon. When her free-spirited nature resisted Wyatt's tempting proposal of marriage, it left Wyatt wondering—what would be the price of this bride?

#974 NOBODY'S CHILD—Pat Warren
Man, Woman and Child
Feeling like nobody's child compelled Lisa Parker to search out her true parents. It brought her face-to-face with J. D. Kincaid, a man whose emotional past mirrored her own, and whose tough exterior hid a tender heart....

#975 SCARLET WOMAN—Barbara Faith
Years ago, Clint Van Arsdale watched as his brother eloped with Holly Moran, a girl from the wrong side of the tracks. Now Holly was a widow—yet despite the pain of a shared past, Clint could no longer escape their undeniable attraction.

#976 WHAT SHE DID ON HER SUMMER VACATION—Tracy Sinclair
Melanie Warren's vacation jaunt unexpectedly landed her in an English country manor. When the very proper and very sexy David Crandall invited her to become nanny to his adorable twins, she just couldn't turn him down....

#977 THE LAST CHANCE RANCH—Ruth Wind
Life's hard knocks forced Tanya Bishop to leave her son in the care of strong and sensible Ramon Quezada. Returning home to reclaim her lost child, she didn't count on falling under Ramon's seductive spell.

#978 A FAMILY OF HER OWN—Ellen Tanner Marsh
Jussy Waring's lonely heart longed for that special kind of family she'd only heard about. When Sam Baker came into her and her young niece's life, would she dare hope that her dream could finally come true?

MILLION DOLLAR SWEEPSTAKES (III)

No purchase necessary. To enter, follow the directions published. Method of entry may vary. For eligibility, entries must be received no later than March 31, 1996. No liability is assumed for printing errors, lost, late or misdirected entries. Odds of winning are determined by the number of eligible entries distributed and received. Prizewinners will be determined no later than June 30, 1996.

Sweepstakes open to residents of the U.S. (except Puerto Rico), Canada, Europe and Taiwan who are 18 years of age or older. All applicable laws and regulations apply. Sweepstakes offer void wherever prohibited by law. Values of all prizes are in U.S. currency. This sweepstakes is presented by Torstar Corp., its subsidiaries and affiliates, in conjunction with book, merchandise and/or product offerings. For a copy of the Official Rules send a self-addressed, stamped envelope (WA residents need not affix return postage) to: MILLION DOLLAR SWEEPSTAKES (III) Rules, P.O. Box 4573, Blair, NE 68009, USA.

EXTRA BONUS PRIZE DRAWING

No purchase necessary. The Extra Bonus Prize will be awarded in a random drawing to be conducted no later than 5/30/96 from among all entries received. To qualify, entries must be received by 3/31/96 and comply with published directions. Drawing open to residents of the U.S. (except Puerto Rico), Canada, Europe and Taiwan who are 18 years of age or older. All applicable laws and regulations apply; offer void wherever prohibited by law. Odds of winning are dependent upon number of eligibile entries received. Prize is valued in U.S. currency. The offer is presented by Torstar Corp., its subsidiaries and affiliates in conjunction with book, merchandise and/or product offering. For a copy of the Official Rules governing this sweepstakes, send a self-addressed, stamped envelope (WA residents need not affix return postage) to: Extra Bonus Prize Drawing Rules, P.O. Box 4590, Blair, NE 68009, USA.

SWP-S795

As a
Privileged Woman,
you'll be entitled to all
these Free Benefits.
And Free Gifts, too.

To thank you for buying our books, we've designed an exclusive FREE program called *PAGES & PRIVILEGES™*. You can enroll with just one Proof of Purchase, and get the kind of luxuries that, until now, you could only read about.

Big Hotel Discounts

A privileged woman stays in the finest hotels. And so can you—at up to 60% off! Imagine standing in a hotel check-in line and watching as the guest in front of you pays $150 for the same room that's only costing you $60. Your *Pages & Privileges* discounts are good at Sheraton, Marriott, Best Western, Hyatt and thousands of other fine hotels all over the U.S., Canada and Europe.

Free Discount Travel Service

A privileged woman is always jetting to romantic places. When you fly, just make one phone call for the lowest published airfare at time of booking—or double the difference back! PLUS— you'll get a $25 voucher to use the first time you book a flight AND 5% cash back on every ticket you buy thereafter through the travel service!

SSE-PP3A

𝒯REE GIFTS!

A privileged woman is always getting wonderful gifts.
Luxuriate in rich fragrances that will stir your senses (and his). This gift-boxed assortment of fine perfumes includes three popular scents, each in a beautiful designer bottle. <u>Truly Lace</u>...This luxurious fragrance unveils your sensuous side. <u>L'Effleur</u>...discover the romance of the Victorian era with this soft floral. <u>Muguet des bois</u>...a single note floral of singular beauty.

YOURS FREE!

$50 VALUE

𝒯REE INSIDER TIPS LETTER

A privileged woman is always informed. And you'll be, too, with our free letter full of fascinating information and sneak previews of upcoming books.

𝑀ORE GREAT GIFTS & BENEFITS TO COME

A privileged woman always has a lot to look forward to. And so will you. You get all these wonderful FREE gifts and benefits now with only one purchase...and there are no additional purchases required. However, each additional retail purchase of Harlequin and Silhouette books brings you a step closer to even more great FREE benefits like half-price movie tickets... and even more FREE gifts.

L'Effleur...This basketful of romance lets you discover L'Effleur from head to toe, heart to home.

Truly Lace... A basket spun with the sensuous luxuries of Truly Lace, including Dusting Powder in a reusable satin and lace covered box.

Complete the Enrollment Form in the front of this book and mail it with this Proof of Purchase.

PROOF OF PURCHASE

Pages & Privileges

Offer expires October 31, 1996

SSE-PP3